W9-CBC-973

"YOUR FATHER WAS A WIZARD WITH EVERYTHING."

The warrior chuckled, a thin laugh that rattled in his throat like small, dry bones. "Only one thing I'm sure of, young emperor-to-be, and that's that you'd better decide who you are. If you're going to be just one of the fellows, then you'd best not expect us to follow you blindly into combat. If you want to be above us, keep yourself apart."

"And if I don't?" Jason asked.

"Well, then you'd better hope that your father is alive. In either case, you'd best not spend the night asking a simple soldier what we'll find at the end of the trail. Go to sleep, Jason. . . ."

Fabulous Fantasy and Sensational Science Fiction
BY JOEL ROSENBERG

☐ **THE SLEEPING DRAGON.** Book One in the *Guardians of the Flame* Series. Playing wizards and warriors was good, safe fun until college buddies Karl, Andrea and their gang find themselves transported to an alternate world and into the bodies of their characters. Now, their only "game" is to find the door to the world they left behind ... a place guarded by the most deadly enemy of them all—the Sleeping Dragon.
(162137—$3.95)

☐ **THE SWORD AND THE CHAIN.** Book Two of the *Guardians of the Flame* Series. Karl and his gang pledge to bring this incredible world the only treasure it lacked—freedom. But in this realm where a wrong step could transform friend into foe, could Karl and his band survive long enough to fulfill their pledge?
(159829—$3.95)

☐ **THE SILVER CROWN.** Book Three of the *Guardians of the Flame* Series. In an effort to provide a haven for slaves, Karl and his comrades establish a stronghold called Home. But, caught between the slaver's forces armed with a new magical weapon and elves attempting to steal the treasured secret of gunpowder, they fear the walls of Home may not be standing for long....
(159837—$3.95)

☐ **THE HEIR APPARENT: Book Four of the *Guardians of the Flame* Series.** Karl had gained an Empire—now what price must he pay to assure its future? He and his friends had freed many from the bonds of slavery, but now they were bound by the furious vendetta of Ahrmin of the evil Slavers Guild....
(162129—$3.95)

☐ **THE WARRIOR LIVES: Book Five of the *Guardians of the Flame* Series.** When Karl is declared dead it is up to his son, Jason, to take on the responsibilities of leadership. But soon rumors surface of unauthorized raids ... and a cryptic message is left on the corpses of the enemy— "The Warrior Lives!" Could it be? Jason must learn the truth.
(450019—$4.50)

Prices slightly higher in Canada.

Buy them at your local bookstore or use this convenient coupon for ordering.

NEW AMERICAN LIBRARY
P.O. Box 999, Bergenfield, New Jersey 07621

Please send me the books I have checked above. I am enclosing $_____ (please add $1.00 to this order to cover postage and handling). Send check or money order—no cash or C.O.D.'s. Prices and numbers are subject to change without notice.

Name_____

Address_____

City _____ State _____ Zip Code _____
Allow 4-6 weeks for delivery.
This offer is subject to withdrawal without notice.

THE WARRIOR LIVES

A Guardians of the Flame Novel

JOEL ROSENBERG

A ROC BOOK

ROC
Published by the Penguin Group
Penguin Books USA Inc., 375 Hudson Street,
New York, New York 10014, U.S.A.
Penguin Books Ltd, 27 Wrights Lane,
London W8 5TZ, England
Penguin Books Australia Ltd, Ringwood,
Victoria, Australia
Penguin Books Canada Ltd, 2801 John Street,
Markham, Ontario, Canada L3R 1B4
Penguin Books (N.Z.) Ltd, 182–190 Wairau Road,
Auckland 10, New Zealand

Penguin Books Ltd, Registered Offices:
Harmondsworth, Middlesex, England

The Warrior Lives previously appeared in an NAL Books edition.

First Roc Printing, April, 1990
10 9 8 7 6 5 4 3 2 1

Copyright © 1988 by Joel Rosenberg
All rights reserved. For information address Penguin Books USA Inc.

 Roc is a trademark of Penguin Books USA Inc.

Printed in the United States of America

Without limiting the rights under copyright reserved above, no part of this publication
may be reproduced, stored in or introduced into a retrieval system, or transmitted,
in any form, or by any means (electronic, mechanical, photocopying, recording, or
otherwise), without the prior written permission of both the copyright owner and the
above publisher of this book.

BOOKS ARE AVAILABLE AT QUANTITY DISCOUNTS WHEN USED TO PROMOTE PRODUCTS OR
SERVICES. FOR INFORMATION PLEASE WRITE TO PREMIUM MARKETING DIVISION, PENGUIN
BOOKS USA INC., 375 HUDSON STREET, NEW YORK, NEW YORK 10014.

for Sprague and Catherine,
role models

Acknowledgments

I'd like to thank the people who helped: Will Shetterly and Emma Bull, who found me the place to finish this book; Pamela Dean and Nate Bucklin, for the last-minute proofreading; the rest of the Minneapolis SF crowd, for reasons both trivial and profound; Mark J. McGarry, who made it better, again; Felix Tang and John Jaser and the other good folks at Logix Microcomputer; Scott Raun, who quibbled a bit; Harry Leonard, who quibbled a lot; my editor, John Silbersack; my wife, Felicia; and always, particularly, my agent, Eleanor Wood.

PRELUDE

Laheran

Every man is like the company he is wont to keep.
—Euripides

"You have to find him," said Slavers' Guildmaster Yryn.
"You have to stop him."

Yryn looked old, and stoop-shouldered. His neck
seemed to have trouble holding up his massive head, and
his eyes were more of a dull gray than the sharp, piercing
slate-gray that Laheran remembered from his apprentice-
ship in the guild.

As they walked through the garden, Yryn fondled the
piece of sun-bleached leather, his nail-bitten fingers strok-
ing it as if it were a magical talisman, which it wasn't.

There was little enough in the world to be sure of,
Laheran thought, but the leather wasn't magical. It had
been carefully examined by a competent wizard, a master
in Pandathaway's Wizards' Guild, and while the wizards
couldn't always be relied on—they were notorious cowards,
for one thing—they could be trusted to know if something was magical.

1

The inner courtyard of Slavers' Guildhall was a quiet place, one for reflection. Marble benches surrounded a lawn that was always ankle-height, the garden guarded by cornered hedges, the precision of it all maintained each night by scissor-wielding slaves working under smoky torchlight.

Except for the flowers. A gardener, fealty-bound to the guild, had the responsibility for their care. Flowers were different, Laheran thought, as he bent to sniff the rich fragrance of a blood-red rose. They required loving attention, not just fearful care.

Laheran liked the garden. It was the one quiet place in the city, the only place he could get completely away from the noise and the bustle and the smells of Pandathaway.

"You have to stop Karl Cullinane," the guildmaster said, as though Laheran hadn't heard him.

"You said that." Laheran held up an admonishing finger, hoping that Yryn would slap him down for his insolence, silently begging the guildmaster to assert his authority.

But the older man just nodded.

Laheran could have cried. The guildmaster was losing his grip on himself. Could his grip on the guild be far behind?

It was a bad time to be leaving Pandathaway. Perhaps Laheran oughtn't have any delusions about having a chance at the guildmastership—there had never been a guildmaster in his twenties, and damned few in their thirties—but as the youngest full master in the guild, it wasn't at all impossible that he could have some impact on the outcome of the contention.

If there was to be a contention. Perhaps what the guild needed now was stability, even if that meant that somebody would have to be the power behind the throne.

Laheran held out his hand to accept the piece of leather. It was about two handbreaths across, not of terribly high quality, probably cut from a leather food sack of some sort.

There was writing on the rough surface; Laheran recognized it as dried blood. He couldn't make out most of the writing, although he suspected it was in that Englits that Karl Cullinane and his friends were turning into a common trade language throughout the Eren regions and beyond.

But below the scratchings that he couldn't decipher, there were the words he could:

The warrior lives, they said. Beneath were three crude drawings: a sword, an ax, and a knife—a threat that Cullinane would kill them with whatever was handy.

It was the third such piece of leather Laheran had seen. The first he himself had brought back from Melawei; it had been pinned to the corpse of a brother slaver, a man who had been split with an ax from his brow almost to his waist.

The second had been discovered in Ehvenor, tied to the hilt of a sword that had been struck through three bodies; the killers had either discovered the slavers in a dark alley or drawn them into it, leaving them behind dead, dead, and dead.

This third one had been found in Lundeyll, in a rented room at an inn there, again pinned to the corpse of a slaver, this time by a knife that projected from the dead man's open mouth like a bloodied metal tongue. Nimyn was his name; Laheran knew him slightly. He was a journeyman on a routine trading mission, traveling down the coast toward Ehvenor with a string of a dozen well-tamed male slaves, most of whom were born into servitude. There were two other slavers with Nimyn, but they were left alone.

The guildmaster finally put it as a question. "Will you find him? Stop him?"

"Yes," Laheran said, stooping to pick a rose, twisting

the stem loose from the bush with deft fingers that managed to avoid the thorns. He fixed it to the collar of his
cloak with a long silver pin.

He wished he had a mirror with him; he was pleased
with the way he looked. He knew what he would have
seen: a tall, slim, elegant young man in blue and gray,
his hair the color of autumn flax, his short, neatly-trimmed
beard only a few shades darker. A light, crimson cloak—
more of a cape, really—fastened with a braided silver
rope, hung elegantly from his right shoulder, the cut
of his tunic and mid-calf breeches more elegant, more
careful than was usual among guildsmen.

He rested his palm for a moment on the hilt of his
sword, striking a pose. He knew he looked somewhat
younger than his twenty-five years, and knew that his age
and his foppishness tempted others to either underrate or
overrate him. That suited him.

"I believe that I will," he said finally. "What resources
do I have?"

"Come with me," the guildmaster said.

The two of them passed into the dark cool of the marble
halls.

The walls were spotless and the floors only barely
dirtied by the day's traffic, but there was a strange smell
in the halls—beyond the usual stink of human sweat, of
pain and fear—that never could be scrubbed out of the
tiles. Whip a slave to death—although with the economics
of slavery these days, that was the luxury of a bygone
era—and he would leave his smell not only on the rough
stone walls where you chained him, but throughout the
rest of the hall.

But there was something else. As the two slavers passed
by an open door, the scribes working at their desks in the
room looked up, a quick flash of panic passing across
their faces.

This was Slavers' Guildhall; there should have been no trace of fear on the face of a guildsman.

But there was: the place also stank of slaver's fear.

It somehow smelled different than the fear of a slave.

They all feared that Karl Cullinane would come for them, and not just outside, somewhere in the field. That would have been different. That was frightening, but acceptable. You had to learn to look over your shoulder when you were away. Raiding or trading, you had to sleep lightly, listening for the quiet patter of unshod feet on deck, the muffled whisper of a sword leaving its scabbard, the snick of a cocked hammer.

No, it wasn't only an assault in the field they feared now, but one in the guildhall itself.

Laheran followed Yryn upstairs into the master's meeting room, where ten men sat around the wide oak table.

None of them were master slavers, but they were all reliable journeymen, most of them well scarred: tough and blooded, men who made their business as raiders and tamers, not just as sellers.

The guildmaster introduced him around the table; Laheran exchanged guild grips with each man in turn. And each man in turn gripped Laheran's hand just a bit too hard, as though grabbing for reassurance, not simply confirming Laheran's guild membership, or returning his courtesy.

"I can have a hundred more men for you in two tendays," the guildmaster said.

Laheran shook his head. "No. The guild has tried that before. A small group this time, with a small, fast ship. We'll go quietly from Pandathaway, not loudly announcing who we are. We take his trail, find him, and kill him." There was no great rush. If it was possible to catch Cullinane—and it had to be possible to catch Cullinane—then Cullinane was headed north.

Possibly by way of Pandathaway and the guildhall?

No, that was unlikely. There were too many defenses, both physical and magical, at Slavers' Guildhall. Cullinane wouldn't be able to get in here.

But, conceivably, he would stop off in Pandathaway and kill a slaver or two, hunt them down outside the guildhall. And that could work to Laheran's advantage: the larger the monster, the larger the reward for killing it.

Laheran eyed them all levelly. "We will find Karl Cullinane, and we will kill him."

The warrior lives, indeed. Perhaps Laheran was younger than all previous guildmasters, but perhaps that wouldn't matter if Laheran killed Karl Cullinane.

He smiled at Guildmaster Yryn.

"Leave it all in my hands," he said.

PART ONE

HOLTUN-BIEME

CHAPTER 1

Breakfast in Biemestren

It ain't over till it's over—and maybe not then, either.
—Walter Slovotsky

Wearing only a faded pair of Home denim jeans, Jason Cullinane bent over the washbowl beneath the mirror, scrubbing gingerly at his face. The early morning water was even icier than it should have been.

As he dried his face on a fresh-smelling towel—royalty hath its privileges, it occurred to him for not the first time—he felt at his chin. It was a bit stubbly, although he had shaved the day before. He tossed the towel aside and reached for the bone handle of the straight razor sitting on the sideboard, but as he eyed himself in the mottled mirror he decided that the faint stubbling made him look older. He let his fingers drop to his side.

A distant laugh sounded in his head.

Take on a few responsibilities and your beard starts growing, eh?

He didn't smile.

Your father would have laughed at that.

"Perhaps he would have." But he wasn't his father. He looked into the mirror. Through the mottled glass—Empire glassmaking wasn't even up to Home standards, and Home standards weren't high to begin with—under a shock of dark brown hair, two dark brown eyes looked back at him. Just the other day, U'len had told him that he was looking more and more like the Emperor. In particular, there was something about his eyes, she said.

I can't see it, he thought. They were just brown. He shook his head as he stared at himself in the mirror. He couldn't see it at all. He wasn't the giant that Karl Cullinane had been; Jason's jaw didn't even seem to have the firm resolve that his father's had had; there wasn't that I-can-handle-anything-that-comes-along look.

He shrugged. Maybe he didn't look so different, but everything else did. Things seemed so changed since his return to Biemestren. His room on the third floor of the residence tower felt smaller. Hell, even the castle seemed to have shrunk in his absence, although he couldn't quite figure out how or where.

His fingers reached up to his neck, the familiar feel of the leather thong and the small crystal amulet comforting. It wasn't that it prevented him from being magically located; he didn't have to hide in Biemestren, and if trouble came looking for Jason here, it would have the House Guard to deal with. The comfort came from its familiarity. The leather and crystal hadn't changed.

They're waiting for you. Hurry down.

Give me a second.

He took a fresh soft cotton tunic from where Elarrah had laid it out on top of his bureau late the night before and pulled it over his head, then padded barefoot across the rug to where he'd left his boots by the door. He considered the rising scratch marks in the age-darkened oak of the door jamb, from the cluster of six or so that were about chest-high, to the one that was on the same level as his eye, and the two close together a bit above.

He turned about and worked his heels closer to the wall, then set his hand on top of his head, resting his fingers against the doorjamb, before turning about to see that there indeed was a difference; his fingers were a good half-inch above the previous high mark.

He reached down to his belt, drew his knife and marked the spot.

Jason at seventeen, although just barely. He drew himself up straighter.

Let's try for at least eighteen. You had better move it: breakfast is being held for you, and you've got a workout with Tennetty in an hour.

"A workout? Today?" He sat down and pulled his boots on. He was leaving for Home and Endell in a few days; if he wasn't good enough with pistol and swords by now, he surely wasn't going to be a lot better by then.

Nonsense. You grow a little each day, Jason; you'd better learn a little each day.

True enough. He was nowhere as good with a sword as his father had been—

—and that wasn't good enough, at least once. Remember. You've got to outthink problems; you can't count on outfighting them. Even if you were as good as Karl was, which you aren't.

Again, true enough.

He went downstairs.

Breakfast in the castle had been an informal, catch-as-catch-can thing in the old days, despite Mother's claim that breakfast was the most important meal of the day, and U'len's insistence that he sit and eat a full meal instead of bolting down a sketchy breakfast. U'len tended to take what Mother said, as Father used to put it, like it came out of a burning bush.

Whatever the hell that meant. Another question he'd never be able to ask his father.

But it wasn't the old days. Too much had changed since Jason's return to Biemestren with the news that Karl Cullinane was dead. Mother and Bren Adahan had tried to minimize things with ceremony, trying to hide in some sort of formal arrangement of their lives the fact that the core of it all was gone.

Dead.

The dining hall fell silent as Jason entered. He gave a brief bow to the two dozen people in the room, then quickly walked to the head of the table, seating himself in *his* chair as though he belonged there.

"Please, be seated, all," he said. Mother still wasn't down, but they could be comfortable while waiting.

Doria Perlstein was already sitting; she didn't take to court manners. From her chair halfway down the table, she smiled a good morning.

He returned her smile. Strange, though. He knew she was as old as Father and Mother, but when she'd shed her Hand persona, she'd also shed all of what the years had done to her body, but not quite all that they had done to her face: her eyes weren't those of a twentyish girl. They seemed much older.

"Morning, Jason," Tennetty said as she took her seat at his right. Turning her chair to let her single eye sweep the room, the skinny woman scanned the assemblage with reflexive suspicion before deciding there wasn't anybody to kill, not quite yet; she relaxed into her chair.

With a "Good morning," a smile and the clack of heels striking the floor, Jason's sister Aeia stalked across the room and dropped lightly into her own chair by the foot of the table, rubbing at her sleepy eyes, then gathering her long hair behind her head and tying it into an improvised ponytail. She was dressed in a pair of tight leather trousers and a loose, ruffled blouse that was almost impossibly white.

"Going riding this morning?" he asked.

She nodded as she reached for a roll, then dipped it in a honey tub and took a huge bite. "I'm going to get all the riding in I can here." Back Home, what with teaching at the local school, Aeia had little time for riding, something she had grown to like.

Tell her she'd better watch the eating, Jason thought. *I think she's starting to put on weight.*

No, you don't.

Ellegon must have relayed the exchange; she chuckled and turned to Bren Adahan, who had taken his usual seat by the foot of the table, next to her. "My little brother seems to think I'm getting old and fat. You willing to disagree with the Heir?"

Bren Adahan nodded slowly. "On this matter, I am."

"Fair enough, Bren—but sit over here. We've got some stuff to talk about before the council." Jason beckoned to him, and waved at a seat next to his own.

The Holtish baron's thin mouth twitched in irritation, but then Bren Adahan studiously blanked his face for a moment before displaying an easy smile that looked genuine enough. He nodded briskly, then leaned over to whisper a few words to Jason's adopted sister before taking the seat Jason had indicated. He stroked idly at a small cut at the point of his square jaw. Adahan had cut off his beard a tenday before, and had taken to shaving twice a day.

Jason tried to conceal the fact that he didn't like Adahan. Maybe it was that Bren Adahan was more than ten years older than Jason, and carried his extra age as though it conferred both wisdom and respect.

Not fair. He doesn't get enough time with Aeia as it is.

I have to talk to him about some things. We might as

well get it all settled during breakfast, Jason thought back, knowing that he was lying to himself. That was all true, but it wasn't the reason. Jason didn't like the way Bren looked at his sister, like he wanted to—

*He *does* want to. Humans are like that. It's all perfectly natural, as Elarrah could have told you two nights ago. Your sister is more than ten years older than you are, and knows what she's doing. And she is going to let him, eventually, on her terms. So leave well enough alone.*

Jason reddened. *Elarrah?* The fact that the upstairs maid was sneaking into his bedroom at night was supposed to be secret. He didn't want it noised about.

Relax; I'm reasonably discreet. But it's silly to leave her alone just because I'm around. I have been reading your mind, such as it is, since before you were born. The next time you want some privacy, just ask me to tune you out. Like your father used to.

I don't want to talk about it.

There was a distant chuckle. He couldn't tell whether he heard it in his ears or his mind.

Bren Adahan reached out and touched Jason's arm. "Are you all right, Jason?"

"No." He shook his head to clear it. "I mean, yes. I'm fine; I was just talking to Ellegon."

Bren Adahan nodded, and looked down the table at the two empty chairs near the foot. One was Danagar's, who was freshly returned from his travels through Nyphien, trying to find out who was behind the Kernat slaughter. While Danagar had only negatives to report, his trip had been much longer and far more exacting than Karl Cullinane had planned for him; he looked to be shy about twenty pounds.

At Thomen Furnael's urging, Jason had installed Danagar in a room in the residence tower, with orders that he sleep late—

And fatten himself up.

Although there was something strange about Thomen of late. Jason was tempted to ask Ellegon to peep him, but. . . .

But that's not right. Your father used to tell me not to peep family and friends, and I'm beginning to understand how right his instincts were, at least on that. Either brace Thomen and insist he discuss what's wrong with him, or wait until he brings it up.

Jason nodded. That could be put off for a while; for now, they had a problem in the other conspicuously empty chair: Mother's.

Bren caught his stare. "It's getting late. You really should send for her."

Jason shook his head. "No. We'll start without her." He raised his voice. "U'len, you can start serving breakfast."

Half waddling, the fat woman brought the first tray out herself, setting it down between Jason and Bren Adahan before lifting a huge stack of oatcakes onto Jason's plate, following that with a fist-sized cube of ham.

He held back a smile. "I can't eat that much," he said.

She waved a finger at him. "Eat it you will, either for breakfast or as your dinner. You're leaving tomorrow, and I'm not going to have you going out and getting yourself killed with only the remembrance of road food on your mind. When you get your stupid head blown off, it's not going to be because you were too hungry to think straight. It's *not* going to be my fault," she said. She picked up the honey tub and poured the thick honey on his oatcakes as if she were pouring water on a fire.

"Just go away and leave me alone," he grumbled.

"Shut up and eat."

He loved the peevish old woman—she'd been watching out for him for as long as he could remember—not that either of them would ever admit it out loud. U'len wouldn't like that.

"I leave when you start eating," she said, crossing her arms over her massive bosom. "So eat."

He picked up his fork and set to work.

Everybody else followed his example; the room was filled with the familiar clatter of plates and tableware, and the sounds of low voices talking between mouthfuls.

I'm starting to get a bit concerned about Mother. Relay, please: everybody's down for breakfast except you.

I don't want to. It's not fun being in her mind. . . . Oh, very well. The mental voice fell silent.

What is it?

I don't want to tell you.

"What *is* it?"

Tennetty kicked back from the table and had a flint-lock pistol halfway out of her holster before Doria laid a gentle hand on her free arm, stopping her.

Everybody was looking at him.

Jason shrugged a *pro forma* apology. "Sorry. I was talking to Ellegon." *Please.* Deep inside, he knew what the dragon was going to say.

She's not in her room. She's in her workshop, bent over her bench, crying. Again. She won't answer me.

He started to push himself away from the table, but noticed that, once again, all the eyes were on him.

There was a long silence until Bren Adahan turned to him. "Please forgive me; I should have mentioned that I spoke to your mother late last evening; she said that she was going to be involved in some sort of work last night, and would probably sleep through breakfast, or get up early and go to her workshop."

He says, "That's the lie you should have told. Now attend to your responsibilities. We have an agreement on that score, Jason Cullinane."

"So we do," he whispered.

So keep it.

"In that case," Jason Cullinane said, "everybody please be seated, and let us finish our meal."

Unembarrassed, Tennetty seated her pistol firmly in its holster and herself in her chair, then picked up a bacon roll and began to eat as though nothing had happened.

Jason was grateful. He had to try to hold things together, but sometimes he wasn't sure that he could, even for the little things: they ate in silence, the hall empty of Karl Cullinane's booming voice.

CHAPTER 2

Andrea Cullinane

Walk wide o' the Widow at Windsor,
  For half of creation she owns:
We have bought 'er the same with the sword an' the flame,
  An' we've salted it down with our bones.
    (Poor beggars—it's blue with our bones!)
Hands off o' the sons o' the Widow,
  Hands off o' the goods in 'er shop,
For the Kings must come down an' the Emperors frown
  When the Widow at Windsor says "Stop!"
    (Poor beggars!—we're sent to say Stop!)
                                    —Rudyard Kipling

One of the differences between Karl and me—and it's a
major one—is that I'm far too considerate to ever leave
my wife a widow. Guess I'll just have to live forever.
                                    —Walter Slovotsky

Squinting in the bright morning sunlight, Jason Cullinane
walked past the salutes of the two guards and out into the
day. It was a pretty day, the sky above was—
  Huh?

He turned. "Kethol? Durine?" What were they doing on guard duty?

Bringing his flintlock carbine back up to port, red-headed Kethol split his weatherbeaten face in a grin. "Good morning, sir."

Tossing his head to clear a shock of hair from his eyes, massive Durine nodded a good morning, bringing one huge paw up to scratch at where his rough grown beard really didn't end, and his bull neck really didn't begin. The man was built like a bear.

"Morning, sir," Durine echoed.

"What are the two of you doing on front door duty?"

Kethol shrugged. "Got into a bit of trouble last night with the general." A tall, rawboned man, he gripped his rifle with knuckles like walnuts.

"Doing what?"

"It was mainly my fault, sir." It was Durine's turn to shrug. "I had too much beer last night. Got into a little barracks fight."

Jason looked them over more carefully. There was a nasty bruise over Kethol's left eye, and the knuckles on Durine's left hand were almost raw.

"Over what?"

Durine shrugged again.

"One of the whores in town," Kethol said. "Pirojil's taken a fancy to her. Loryal's been bothering him about it."

"Loryal?"

"One of the new troops, from Tyrnael. Him and his three brothers joined up just before the Emperor and us took off for Ehvenor. When Piro punched Loryal, two of the brothers jumped him, then Loryal and another brother jumped *me* when I tried to come between them and settle things down." He broke into a toothy smile. " 'Course, I was calling them poxy sons of a motherless cur while I was trying to calm them down. All Durine did was pull two of them off, while Piro and I settled things, two-on-two."

"Injuries?"

"Just a few." Durine shrugged, again. "Pirojil lost two teeth, and the Spider says some of Piro's ribs are cracked. He took a nasty bite in the ear; Loryal beat him kind of bad. Kethol's dance-partner is lucky the cleric got to him pretty quick, or he'd be singing lead tenor. My two got their heads cracked, just a little. All resting in the infirmary. The Spider put Piro's teeth back together, but left the rest. They all start their punishment tours when they're up and about."

Jason nodded. Valeran had given him long lectures about barracks discipline. What Garavar had done was sound economics, and even sounder discipline: use the minimum magic necessary to heal the combatants beyond danger or permanent damage, but let them ache for a while—the more, the better.

But to every rule there were exceptions. Durine, Kethol and Pirojil had been his father's companions on his last ride to Ehvenor. "I'll see Garavar—"

*As you *were*, Jason.* Ellegon's voice was firm. *Even when you're wearing the crown, you'd better have a better reason than that for overruling Garavar.*

He tried to cover the interruption with a cough, and wasn't at all sure he was successful. *But—*

But nothing. Now let's go see your mother.

"I'll see you later, then," Jason said, knowing that he hadn't covered his gaffe well.

Actually, you didn't cover it at all. They know you were going to meddle in Garavar's domain. But they probably won't say anything about it.

Jason left the path for the grass. It was shaping up to be a pretty day. A light, gentle wind blew in from the west, accompanied by only the fluffiest of clouds in the blue sky overhead.

The grass was up to his calves, trimmed that morning by sweeping scythes into a rippled sea of lush green. Jason breathed in the rich smell of the new-mown grass, enjoying it.

That was the thing about peace, *he* used to say; it gave people time and inclination to care about something as trifling as the height of grass on a lawn. There were limits to even an Emperor's powers; it was simple to forbid everybody except the caretakers to walk on the grass, but during wartime it was hard to find somebody to care for it.

He walked around to the side of the main residence tower, stepping from the softness of the lawn to the stones of the parade ground.

A huge, vaguely triangular head lifted from the warmth of the stones and stared at him.

"Morning, Ellegon," Jason said as he walked over to the massive beast. Father used to say that Ellegon was the size of a Greyhound bus, which Jason had never quite understood. Now, a bus was a kind of cart, but wasn't a greyhound a kind of dog, a small mastiff or something?

Ellegon was huge; Jason couldn't imagine a dog a twentieth that size.

Good morning, Jason, the dragon answered. With a deep grunt, he got first his forelegs and then his rear legs underneath himself, then raised himself to his feet, his massive, leathery wings curling and uncurling almost spasmodically, while smoke and steam issued from nostrils the size of dinner plates.

The dragon's mouth sagged open to reveal rows and rows of teeth the length of a forearm . . . and an incredible miasma of dragon halitosis, painfully bad breath that reeked of decaying flesh and rotting fish. Ellegon wasn't fastidious about what he ate.

Jason gagged. "Turn your head away, *please.*"

Sorry. Scales creaking in the morning air, Ellegon turned his massive head away, clearing the air with a quick shot of flame.

It never really made sense to Jason, the way that others had to restrain a fear of Ellegon. It was like, well, like being afraid of Tennetty's swords. The universe was divided into two kinds of people, and only one kind was endangered by either.

They're not just afraid of being eaten. Humans don't like me because I know too much.

Way too much. It was one thing for Ellegon to save Jason from making a fool of himself in front of Kethol and Durine; it was another for the dragon to probe into . . . private matters.

I won't mention it again, the dragon said, although Jason could have sworn he heard a distant mental mumble: *Just like his father. Spends too much time thinking with what's between his legs rather than what's between his ears.*

"And you eat too much, too.—Let's go see her."

It was only a few hundred meters across the parade ground to the northwest corner—too short for Ellegon to bother with flying.

Jason walked quickly, the dragon lumbering along behind.

Normal humans like to steer well clear of working wizards; it's only prudent. Andrea Cullinane's workshop was far away from anything else within the walls of the castle. If it hadn't been for security considerations, everybody involved would have been more comfortable with putting it outside the inner curtain wall, or perhaps in Biemestren township itself.

But security considerations had been involved; Mother's Biemestren workshop had, as far back as Jason could remember, been in a low stone building in the northwest corner of the inner ward.

Jason knocked on the door. There was no answer. "Mother, it's me. Jason."

Nothing.

She's in there. Do you want me to try?

No. I'd better do this myself.

His hand trembled at the door latch.

One of the things he'd been taught early was not to interrupt Mother when she was working. It was one of the few lessons that involved switching; Mother hated hitting him almost as much as he hated it. She said that "don't disturb the wizard" was the This Side equivalent of "don't touch the driver," whatever that meant.

That was the trouble with dealing with the Other Siders, like his parents, and Walter Slovotsky, and Doria Perlstein—they kept talking in terms that nobody could understand. It wasn't just all this stuff about cars and planes and microwaves (and what *was* a microwave, anyway? Was it how an Other Side dwarf said goodbye?) it was that their frame of reference was, so often, so completely different from normal people's.

But while he couldn't understand the referent, the lesson had long since been driven home, and learned below the level of conscious decision. He *knew* that she wasn't really working anything dangerous: Ellegon would have warned him.

You got that right.

Still, his hand shook. Damning his traitor fingers for trembling, Jason lifted the latch and swung the heavy oak door slowly inward, slipped inside, and closed the door behind him.

"Mother?"

He sniffed involuntarily. The inside of the stone building was dark and dank, the thick air heavy with smells strange and familiar. There was a distant odor he couldn't quite place, although he could make out the rich, musky fragrance of marrhymh and the sharp tang of burning peppercorns. Mainly the smell reminded him of stale sweat.

The only light in the room oozed out of a crack at the junction of wall and ceiling; all that it revealed was the narrow entryway where Jason stood, and the dark hall beyond. Rows of black gauze curtains obscured everything beyond that.

"Mother?"

He pushed through a layer of curtains, and another, and then another. The curtains were dry to his fingers, but they seemed to cling wetly to his face; shuddering, he pushed inward.

"Mother?"

He could barely make out the light of a lamp through the last set of curtains. He pushed through to see the form of his mother, huddled over her workbench, making jerking, almost random jottings with her quill pen, while an oil lamp flickered above her. To her right, a crystal globe lay supported in the coils of a brass snake, its head impaled on the north pole, staring languidly at the world. At her left was a rough clay statue of a man standing with his arms crossed over his chest. Where his left hand lay on his arm there were only two full fingers; the other three were stumps.

The statue was still visibly wet; beyond it lay a clump of clay and a half dozen small knives, short sticks bearing wire loops, and other clayworking tools he couldn't readily identify.

"Mother," he said, "put it away."

She didn't answer, but continued to scribble.

"Mother," he said. "Put it away."

Nothing.

"I'm going to count to ten, and then take it away from you."

She shook her head, flinging stringy black hair back and forth. "No. I got closer last time. Maybe I can—"

The crystal glowed brighter.

"See!"

"That doesn't mean anything, not unless you can see *him*. Which you can't, because he's dead."

"You didn't see the body." The crystal grew yet brighter, and brighter still—

The light died, leaving the interior of the room lit only by the flicker of the oil lamp.

"No!" She pounded a fist on the table, then turned to face him.

He forced himself to repress a shudder. Her eyes were red, the lids swollen with tears and lack of sleep, and deep hollows had taken up residence in her cheeks.

"Mom. . . ." He took her hands in his, momentarily shocked at how feebly she pulled away. "Please. We—all of us—saw the explosion. Walter and Ahira stayed behind. He couldn't have survived the blast, but if he had survived the two of them would have brought him here by now."

Walter Slovotsky and the dwarf were still an open question. There wasn't any sign, not any word from them. While it would have been a bit soon for them to get themselves back to Holtun-Bieme, they should have reached Ehvenor by now, even if they were traveling by Mel dugout; or gotten over the mountains, if they were trying the overland route.

Where were they? That was the live issue. Father was dead.

"I'm still going to try. Until I can locate the body or until I see him."

But he was blown to bits, he thought. He couldn't say it, not to his mother, not to his father's widow. "Your spell isn't going to recognize . . . what's left of him. Put it down, Mother, then go change your clothes and wash up. We have council tonight, and you're going to have to. . . ." He let the words trail off.

You're going to have to look alive. That was what he meant, but he couldn't bring himself to say it. Sometimes you have to live on the silences.

"Mother . . . you know he's dead. There's one proof, beyond what we all saw."

"Yes?" Her voice, usually a warm contralto, squeaked and cracked at the edges.

"Father loved you. If he was still alive, there's nothing that'd keep him away from you."

Her lower lip trembled. "He didn't even send a last message back to me."

"He didn't need to; he told Tennetty that." Jason's eyes filled with tears. "What could he have had us tell you? That he loved you? Mother, didn't you *know* that?"

She turned away, and her shoulders shook silently.

Please. Jason is right. We have to carry on, Andrea. All of us.

Slowly, her crying stopped and her breathing slowed. She took in a deep, ragged breath, then turned slowly, wiping her face on her sleeve. "Just let me try a bit more. Please?"

"No. There are things to be done, and you've got to make yourself . . ."

For a moment, her old smile peeked through. "Presentable? Less like an old hag?" She shrugged. "Easy enough."

She pushed him back a few inches, and held her hands out in front of her, muttering words that could only be heard and then forgotten.

She changed.

The hollows in her tear-dampened cheeks dried and filled out, the flesh growing firmer in front of his eyes. Her stringy hair seemed to shed its oil, and gained body as she straightened herself, her chest lifting, her body straightening, and just for a moment she was clear of eye and firm of step, the way she had always been.

"I *thought* that was what you've been doing." Doria Perlstein's calm voice cut through the dark; she pushed the curtains aside and stood next to Jason. "Send the seeming away."

For once, Doria didn't look younger than Mother did. She held herself like a much older woman—unbent by the years, but perhaps more weighted down with knowledge.

"Send it away, Andrea." Doria swallowed. "Or I will."

When Doria had shed her clerical persona, she'd lost the ability to gain more spells; all she had left—all she ever would have—were the few in her head. Exactly what they were and how many there were was a secret, but each was irreplaceable.

"Why does it matter?" Andrea's voice was rich and melodic, something out of Jason's childhood. "This will serve, as well as anything else, and better than most."

"Nonsense. It doesn't make you healthy. It just makes you *look* healthy, whether you are or not. That's all. It's like putting nitrites on salad—remember nitrites?"

"I don't miss nitrites. I used to be horribly allergic to them."

Doria returned her smile. "Even if you weren't, it was a bad idea to use them on food. They don't preserve the quality of it, just the color." She took Andrea's arm. "Send it away, now. You can take on a seeming, if you have to, to make yourself look worse; never cover up what's really happening to you. Jason, take her other arm."

He did, and it felt firm and supple in his hand, until his mother murmured a harsh word that melted in the air . . .

. . . and the arm seemed to shrink.

"You've been fooling yourself, and the rest of us."

Doria *tsk*ed once. "You're just wasting away. We're going to build you up, okay?"

Andrea's grin was weak. "You know a lot about that?" Her voice creaked.

Doria's grin was strong. "I used to be a home ec major, remember? Training for my MRS, Walter used to say, when he wasn't accusing me of taking mommy lessons. Well, you need a mommy now. There is nothing really wrong with you—nothing that a lot of food, exercise, and rest can't help. You keep out of here, understood?"

"No." Andrea flared. "I've got to try, at least. I've got to locate him, if he's still alive, if he—"

Doria sighed, "He's dead, Andrea. Please try to accept it. Let's go get you some breakfast. Then we're going to see if I can walk you off your feet. Then some sleep, and then more food and exercise." Her smile returned. "Until you really do look as good as the seeming made you look."

"You're forgetting." Jason shook his head. "We've got a council tonight."

Doria glared at him. "You and Thomen are going to have to run it, then. Your mother has a date with a feather bed. Understood?"

I have two messages. One from your mother: "I'll make it down for the council; don't worry." She means it. The other's from Doria; she says: "Like hell she will. Act like you give a damn about somebody besides yourself." But she really only means it a little.

And what do you say?

I'm with Doria on this one. If you and Thomen can't handle things tonight, it's about time we found out, isn't it?

CHAPTER 3

Before the Council of Barons

Our swords shall play the orator for us.
—Christopher Marlowe

I've always figured that talking beats fighting. And talking is only about my third favorite thing.
—Walter Slovotsky

Jason Cullinane sat alone in the great hall of Castle Biemestren, looking at the place as if he had never seen it before.

In a sense, he hadn't. Not from this perspective. He'd had to sit in Father's place at table—but there hadn't been any formal dinners since Jason's return.

He walked over to the long oak table and sat in his own place, his old place, to the left of Father's seat, then ran his fingers across the dark surface that had been much battered from years of use, and abuse. He rubbed his thumb across a slight depression, all that remained of a little notch. He'd carved the notch

29

in the table himself, during one long, boring formal dinner, until Father noticed what Jason was doing. Father, his huge hands gentle as always, had taken the knife from Jason's hands and sighed in deep disappointment. Other fathers hit their sons, but Karl Cullinane had always said that was wrong.

A man whose profession is violence must never use violence on his own, he'd said.

Karl Cullinane had just sighed, and looked disappointed, and maybe older than he should have, and then dismissed everybody else from the hall. The two of them had gone down to the carpenter's shop to fetch a file, a sandcloth, brushes and varnish. He and Jason had smoothed out the notch, and then varnished over it, then cleaned and replaced the tools. All the while, Karl Cullinane had looked worn around the edges, a bit defeated.

Jason would have preferred it if Father had hit him.

Mikyn's father had hit Mikyn a lot.

At that, he shook his head. That was something still left undone. He'd have to face Mikyn and the rest of Daherrin's team. He could take that. Jason Cullinane might have run like a coward, but he'd hunted down and killed Ahrmin, just as his father had killed Ahrmin's father.

There was a lot left undone—like this damned Baronial Council.

I don't know how to run one of these things. I have to learn, I guess. But it wasn't right that he should have to learn on the job.

That is dreadful. It's so incredibly unfair. I find it hard to think of a greater injustice in the history of the universe.

Fire flared outside the far window; Jason walked over to it, pulled the shutters back and threw one hip over the sill. Below, Ellegon stood in the courtyard, his wings furling and unfurling; above, the night winked down, distant faerie lights pulsing in odd chords of color.

Jason forced a chuckle. "You wouldn't happen to be suggesting that I'm feeling a little sorry for myself, would you?"

Suggesting, no. Asserting, declaring, announcing, maintaining, stating, affirming and averring, yes. The dragon dipped its mouth to take a man-sized bite out of what was left of an ox.

"I guess that's what we keep you around for. It isn't because we've got a lot of cattle we need eaten."

There was a vague draconic chuckle, but then Ellegon's mental voice sobered. *I'll be back shortly; I'd best do my evening patrol before this council starts.*

He'd been alone for only a few moments when he heard a sound behind him.

He turned to see Thomen Furnael walking across the blood-red carpet toward him, his eyes missing nothing. He was about Jason's height, but his extra five years had filled him out: his chest and shoulder muscles were corded from frequent workouts. A trim black beard was full on his face, although it, like his short-cropped black hair, was speckled with silver. Furnael men turned gray young.

As usual, Thomen Furnael was dressed elegantly, befitting his status as baron and regent. His scarlet tunic was cut loose across the shoulders and tight at the waist. Trimmed with black leather along the seams and hem, it was laced up the front with a snaking of silver chain. A short black cape hung elegantly over his left shoulder, half-concealing his left arm. His black trousers were buttoned up the front with nacrestones; his square-toed boots were of finely tooled black leather.

Incongruously, it was a broad, plain weapons belt that held his tunic tightly around his hips, a cord-handled smallsword sheathed on the left side, rigged to stay within easy cross-belly reach of his right hand; an unadorned flintlock pistol stuck butt-first out of a plain holster on his right side.

"Jason, what are you doing here?"

"Just waiting. Figured I'd get here first."

Thomen shook his head. "No, you get here *last*. You make everybody sit around waiting for you, until it's time to make your entrance. Then you make them stand up while you walk in slowly and take your seat." He chuckled. "Helps to remind them who's in charge."

"And who *is* in charge?"

"You are. Or will be, if you keep reminding them of that." He pointed down, at one of the woven grass runners that protected the rug. "Ignore those, too—let everybody else stay off the rug."

Jason had never known Thomen's father, but Father had always spoken highly of him, and of Rahff, and once had declared that the three Furnael men he'd known were a counterargument to Tom Paine's claim that the trouble with hereditary aristocracy was that virtue wasn't hereditary.

"You're sure?" Jason said.

"Now, don't go Cullinane on me. Trust me. Or, if you don't, get yourself another regent, send me back to my courtroom—better, to my barony." His tone was light, but there was a serious undercurrent. Thomen's mouth twisted. "No, I don't really mean that. Right now, there's nobody else really competent to take over. Everybody's got his private agenda, except maybe Bren and Garavar, and old Gar figures that the best way to handle any threat is with volleyed fire. Bren wouldn't be bad, but the rest of the Biemish barons wouldn't stand for a Holtish regent."

"You would?"

Thomen nodded. "If it was Bren, yes. He admired your father almost as much as I did—as I do." He beckoned to Jason. "Come on. Let's get out of here before they start wandering in. We've a bit of time to kill; what do you feel like doing?"

"I want to talk about whatever it is that's been bothering you for the past few days."

What could it be? Mother had been distant ever since Jason returned from Melawei, and the return of Danagar was cause for relief, not concern. But the duties of regent seemed to be weighing unusually hard on Thomen's shoulders.

"Well, there is a problem." Thomen Furnael bit his lip. "Can I think about it a while longer? It's . . . a bit complicated, and I want to work out how to handle it."

Jason shrugged. "Fair enough. Tomorrow?"

"Sooner, maybe. It'll come up at the council."

"Shouldn't we talk about it before?"

"Not really." Thomen shook his head. "Now: what do you want to do until then?"

Jason smiled. Maybe he couldn't figure out the politics as well as Thomen could, but there was one thing he could do better, usually. "Two-swords. Best three points of five?"

Thomen Furnael nodded. "Might be a good idea to work off a bit of that energy that you always have too much of."

"Father used to say that when you're speaking English, you're not supposed to end a sentence with a preposition."

"Walter Slovotsky always used to say something like, 'Okay, let's work off a bit of that energy that you always have too much of, asshole.' "

They got the engineer on duty to open the armory, and while Thomen stripped off his tunic and boots and pulled out the practice swords and masks, Jason took a taper and went around the room, lighting lamp after lamp after lamp, until the low-ceilinged stone room was passably illuminated by the flickering yellow light. Hopping first on one foot and then the other, he pulled off his boots, tossed them aside, then accepted a steel mesh mask and two weapons from Thomen. The mask was basically a mesh bucket suspended from the headband inside. The first weapon was a very stiff foil, its tip protected by a welded-on cap twice the size of Jason's thumbnail; the second was a short wooden stick, about the length of his forearm, a substitute for the dagger that was the secondary weapon when fighting two-swords style.

Setting his weapons down so that he could hang his tunic on a peg on the wall, Jason worked his shoulders, trying to loosen them. He set the mask on his head, then picked up the weapons and tried a few practice lunges, still feeling the strain in his thighs from his earlier workout with Tennetty. But that was something old Valeran had taught Jason: the lessons that counted most were the ones that you got when you pushed yourself hard.

Thomen slipped on his mask, then quickly saluted and took up a fighting stance, his foil held out in his right hand, his practice dagger carried low in his left, by his side. "Start off with foil touches on saber targets, then switch to saber rules?"

"Sure. Saber rules always with the dagger, though."

"Of course."

Jason took a slow breath, let it out slowly, then repeated the process twice. It helped to settle the mind.

He was ready. Saluting, Jason took up the same stance that Thomen had been holding, then moved in slowly, first holding his place, stepping back as Thomen whistled the tip of his foil through the air and lunged in a classic high-line attack.

Jason brought his foil quickly across from left to right, steel ringing on steel as he brushed Thomen's foil aside; while the baron tried to retreat, Jason riposted, lightly touching Thomen on the chest.

"My point," Jason said. "One to nothing. Bad habit, Thomen; break out of it before it breaks you."

"What do you mean?" Thomen said, parrying, then retreating when Jason tried a lunging, low-line attack. The foils clashed, and when they broke Thomen scored a solid touch on Jason's right arm.

"One-one," Jason said. "And you know full well what I mean: you always make the first attack real simple, and let your opponent get in the first point while you're seeing how quickly he can move."

"You don't like that, eh?"

"Valeran would have bladed you for it. It's—"

Jason lunged, but Thomen riposted easily, stopping Jason's cut-over as Jason pulled back.

"—a game technique. You don't want to get pinked in a real fight just to see if the other man's any good."

"But this is just a game." Thomen smiled. "I don't have to fight for real; I'm a member of the effete ruling class, remember? All I have to do is look pretty sitting on a judge's bench or a baron's throne. Or I can—"

They engaged again; this time Jason tried a quick cutover, and it was Thomen's turn to parry and riposte. Jason brought his left hand up to parry that, but Thomen disengaged, retreated two steps, then lunged again.

Jason could barely keep up as the foils whistled through the air.

Parry high, bind, riposte, then stop-thrust, never forgetting that the left hand carried a knife, too.

Thomen's high-line marching attack met Jason's lunge. Each tried for a parry, but their momentum was too great. As they came together, Jason kicked out at Thomen's knee—but it wasn't there. He was off balance for only a moment, but that was long enough for Thomen to score two quick touches on his chest.

"Only counts as one. Two-one. Saber rules?" Thomen asked.

"Sure." Jason beat Thomen's blade aside, hard, and flipped his sword at Thomen's head, but Thomen retreated a step, catching the foible of Jason's weapon with his forte, loosening Jason's grip as he beat Jason's sword completely aside and leaving him exposed from face to ankles, without enough time to bring up his dagger.

Thomen slashed once, a stinging blow that would have opened Jason from left shoulder to the waist, then stepped back and saluted. "Three to one. Mine."

Jason returned his salute. "Another best of three?"

Thomen shook his head as he walked to the washbasin in the corner. "No. By the time we sluice ourselves off and dress, they should all be waiting upstairs."

He was trying to hold it in, but Thomen Furnael was indecently pleased with himself. Jason could practically read his mind: Maybe the father had once kicked Thomen in the balls, but damned if he couldn't out-fence the son.

Jason would have felt pleased with himself, too, if only he'd deliberately let Thomen win.

Damn it, Thomen was *good*.

CHAPTER 4

The Council of Barons

The fundamental purpose of the Baronial Council is to force the Biemish barons to put themselves under my sword; whether they walk out with or without their heads is up to me, and depends on their behavior.

The Holts are a different case. They haven't been called in for Council, yet, not because they don't "deserve" it or some such nonsense, but because they're already under Imperial control. Hell, the Holtish barons' military governors can hang them first, and explain it to me later.

As we start to return Holtun to civilian rule, though, the Holtish barons will have to attend council, too. It'll just about double the council size. Which will at least quadruple the amount of time spent in meetings.

I wish I knew British history better. Is this the way Parliament started?

—Karl Cullinane

Guy I used to know once said, "That government isn't best which governs least—it's the best government that needs to govern least." I'd swipe it as one of Slovotsky's Laws, but it's just a bit too serious, and maybe a smidgen too true.

—Walter Slovotsky

Jason stood outside the great hall, waiting, until he decided he'd had enough of waiting.

At the door he stopped next to the ceremonial guard—a short, loud-voiced corporal named Nartham—wondering how he was going to be announced, realizing that he'd forgotten to arrange it. Nartham had presented Thomen with a loud "Thomen, Baron Furnael, the regent"—Thomen was here as both regent and noble, not as a judge—but what was right for Jason?

He rapped the butt of his halberd on stone three times to get everyone's attention. "Ladies and gentlemen, the Heir."

Jason walked across the carpet, trying to make it look slow and graceful, feeling more awkward than he'd ever felt before. Thomen had primed him for the council, but it just didn't feel right.

He paused for a moment at the foot of the table. Mother's chair. Standing next to it, Doria gave him a slight nod, then put her hands together and tilted her head, miming sleep.

Good. Aeia's eyes twinkled as she stood by her chair, her back just a bit too ramrod-straight, as though to say, *I used to change your diapers, Jason: I'm not about to take you seriously as a ruler.*

"Good evening," he said, keeping his voice level, as he took his seat—*his* seat!—at the head of the table. "Be seated, all. We have a full agenda."

The Biemish barons, each with a single adviser, seated themselves along the left side of the table, while Holtish barons, each save one with the military governor of his barony, took seats on the right.

Vilmar, Baron Nerahan, was conspicuously alone, as though to remind everyone present that his was the single Holtish barony released from direct Imperial government. The trim, compact man settled stiffly into his chair, then smoothed the pleated front of his immaculate white tunic before folding his hands genteelly in his lap and turning a vaguely interested but generally blank expression on the world, the eyes under the heavy brows missing nothing.

Still standing was Tennetty, who moved back and leaned against the near wall. Clad as usual in a mannish leather tunic and worn leggings, she hitched at her combo belt as though to remind everyone present that she was carrying a blooded saber, a Nehera-made bowie and two loaded pistols, instead of a formal smallsword.

Thomen leaned over and whispered in his ear. "I asked the dragon to be around in time for this, but he isn't back, yet. We'd best handle the simple items first. But you'll have to start with the matter of your mother." Thomen beckoned to the court secretary, a burly engineer who looked incongruous sitting at the writing desk next to the long table of the great hall. The red-bearded man looked like he'd be much happier taking a shift in the gunworks.

Thomen gave a slight nod.

"Very well," Jason said, rising. Thomen had been explicit: he must start on his feet. Tower over them, dominate the meeting, make it clear that he was in charge. Even if he wasn't. Particularly if he wasn't.

"Welcome, all, to the council. There's much to discuss tonight, so I'll skip any long speech about how much we all miss my late father, and let us get down to work. First item: the absence of my mother. She's been working far too hard lately, and has been ordered to rest herself for the next few days, until I leave."

There was a quiet rush of muttering at that.

Thomen spoke up. "We know that you'll all wish to pay your respects in person to the empress, so I've arranged for your quartering for the next few days."

Bren Adahan shook his head. "Maybe the rest can stay, but Ranella and I ought to get back to Adahan, by way of Furnael and Little Pittsburgh. Production's slip-

ping, and we've got to find out what's behind it—from
the reports, it sounds like there's supply problems in
Adahan, but—"

An emperor, even an emperor-to-be, has to be obeyed.
"Ranella can handle it. You'll do as you're told," Jason
said.

The room was suddenly cold. Bren Adahan had spoken casually; he hadn't been ready for Jason to bite his
head off.

"Your pardon, sire," Bren Adahan said. "You are
quite correct; I shall do precisely as I am told. It was a
figure of speech; I meant to inform you and the regent
that there are urgent matters requiring attention in both
my barony and in barony Furnael, and to suggest that
Governor Ranella and I ought to handle them." He
inclined his head perhaps a mite too deeply, then straightened, his expression stony.

Thomen momentarily rolled his eyes heavenward, while
the others around the table stirred.

Flame flared in the windows.

Good evening, all, Ellegon said, announcing himself
as he thumped to the ground in the courtyard outside.
Leathery wings flapped in the breeze as the dragon settled himself in.

And good evening to you, Ellegon said, his mental
voice taking on the timbre that told Jason the dragon
was talking to him alone, *shit-for-brains. Looks like
I got here too late.*

What are you talking about? And what kept you?

*Nothing important. I just picked up a small party
traveling later than seemed sensible, so I had to duck
behind the next hill and wait until they pulled around the
bend close enough that I could read them. They were
clean.*

The dragon's caution made sense. Ever since Ellegon
had been shot during the Holtun-Bieme War, Ellegon

had been careful of approaching humans. Much better for Ellegon to have some cover between himself and some unknowns than to try to fly low enough to deeply read them, and risk being taken by an assassin's dragon-bane-tipped crossbow bolt.

Everybody was looking at Jason, waiting.

"Well," he said, "where were we?"

You're about to apologize to Bren Adahan. That's where we are. Now, Jason.

But—

Don't argue, just repeat after me: My apologies, Baron Adahan . . .

"My apologies, Baron Adahan—"

. . . you'll have to excuse me . . .

". . . you'll have to excuse me . . ."

. . . but as you all know, I'm new to this ruling business, and I'm afraid it's set my temper a bit on edge—and you'd damn well better smile ingratiatingly here, asshole.

"I'm . . . really new to this ruling business, and I think it must have set my temper on edge."

He tried to smile ingratiatingly, but wasn't sure if it came off. Jason Cullinane couldn't ever remember trying to smile ingratiatingly before. He was one of the people others smiled ingratiatingly *at*.

It had worked, he decided, when Bren Adahan sat back in his chair, clearly mollified.

No, it didn't. What worked is that I just relayed privately, on your behalf: 'Sorry I'm such a jerk; I'll apologize later—would you and Aeia meet me for a drink after the council?'

"The next item," Thomen said, "is the matter of the Heir's planned absence."

"If I may?" Ariken, the white-haired baron from Krathael, leaned forward, and continued at Thomen's consenting nod. "You have brought up an . . . important matter. This . . . leaving of yours we have been hearing about . . ." he said, in voice creaking with age. "I . . . respectfully, yes, always respectfully . . . counsel against it, and ask why you seem to find it necessary to leave at such a . . . difficult time. Until you've assumed the crown— and your full duties—it would seem, almost, perhaps irresponsible to leave the Empire, even for a short . . . period of time." He sat back hard in his chair, panting, his lined face ashen. "And it . . . does me good to see you, from time to time."

Isn't there anything that can be done for him?

Have you a cure for old age? There was nothing that could be done, either for the baron or the situation. Barony Krathael had been overrun by the Holts during the Holtun-Bieme war; the baron was fiercely devoted to Karl Cullinane, his rescuer, and to his heir. As long as he could run the barony adequately, it would both be and seem an act of rank ingratitude to force him to abdicate in favor of his son.

Arrifezh, the rapier-slim baron from Arondael, shook his head. "If he is going to spend time away, best to do so now. At least. . . ."

"At least he isn't abandoning the Empire like his father did? Is that your charge, Baron Arondael?" Baron Nerahan put in. He was a cruel-looking man, his two shifty brown eyes staring out at the world from under heavy brows. His sharp nose and bristly mustache always reminded Jason of a rat's whiskers. During the Holtun-Bieme war, he had been directly responsible for incredible cruelties.

But since then, as your father used to say, he's been a Boy Scout. And while he's still trying to rout Arondael, he's trying to do it as your follower, so you'd best treat him kindly.

"Is that your charge?" Nerahan repeated. "Do you claim that the Emperor abandoned us?"

"It's *my* charge, if no one else has the nerve. *Yes!*" Tyrnael slammed his hand down on the table, dismissing Tennetty with a snort when she let her hand drop to the butt of a pistol. His chin set stubbornly, Listar Tyrnael tossed his head, clearing his unruly black hair from his eyes. "He abandoned us. His responsibilities were here, with us. He was the Emperor."

"Baron," Thomen said, his voice cutting through the murmurs. He pursed his lips, then drummed his fingers on the timeworn surface of the table. "It was his decision, not yours, and not mine. He paid in full for his decision, and did his best to see that we don't have to. Let it be."

Tyrnael wasn't inclined to let matters rest there. "There's a lesson in this, and I—"

"Baron, please." Bren Adahan spoke up. "He's right. For the sake of the realm, let it be."

At Nerahan's nod, Arondael's brow wrinkled.

"And," Thomen Furnael went on, "as to the Heir traveling to Home now, I do have a bit of news that might affect your views on that. But there are some matters to discuss first."

Tyrnael, still visibly bothered, subsided.

Kevalun, the military governor of Irulahan, sat forward at that. Perhaps he'd caught something in Thomen's manner. "News, Baron?" he asked, perhaps a touch urgently. It would have been easy to think of young-looking Kevalun as almost a contemporary, Jason reminded himself, but the general was into his fifties. In fact, Kevalun had a son in his thirties, and a daughter of about sixteen—a rather attractive daughter of about sixteen.

Just keep it in your pants and listen up.

"News, General. In good time, we'll get to it. Before we discuss the Home issues, and the matter of the Heir's trip," Thomen went on, "we have several items to go over on the agenda. Let's get to it."

The first item was the progress of the removal of Imperial troops from barony Nerahan, and the return of the barony to civilian rule. Predictably, the transfer of power was proceeding too slowly to suit the Nerahans and the Holts, and was both proceeding too quickly and was too abrupt to suit most of the Biemish.

After that, matters turned to appropriations: Ranella and Bren Adahan argued forcefully for increased development in the Little Pittsburgh steel facilities, while Thomen formally recused himself, on grounds of conflict of interest: the plant, although near the Adahan border, was in Furnael.

The consensus, surprisingly enough, was to spend the required money.

Not really surprising. Thomen's had bowies, made from samples of the new batch of steel, sent to each of the barons. It's good stuff, almost the quality of Home wootz. The promise of an endless supply of it, cheap, is worth some investment.

That led to the question of the railroad. While the barons had been almost unanimous in their approval of increased spending on the steel plant, they were—with the sole exceptions of Thomen and Bren Adahan—completely united in their opposition to any excessive spending on what Terumel, Baron Derahan, referred to as "this dubious Engineer magic."

Ranella looked over at Jason. She was a thick, plain woman, whose hands were always nicked and stained from some set of experiments that hadn't gone quite as planned.

She wants your support on this. Thomen thinks she's right, but he says that the barons aren't going to go for it.

Jason stood. "I'm very much in favor of a railroad," he

said. "Just as the roads hold Holtun and Bieme together and link the two, a railroad can do more."

"Yes, yes, yes," Arbert, Baron Irulahan said, dismissing the obvious with a wave. "But this will involve huge revenues—tens of thousands of marks, just to start. When do we see the return on such an investment?"

General Garavar had sat silent so far; at this he stirred. "Immediately, if we build it correctly." He beckoned to his aide, who produced a map. "I've been giving this long and careful thought," he said as he spread the chart out on the table. It was a simple map of Holtun and Bieme and the surrounding countries. "Ranella wants to put the first line here, to link Biemestren and Little Pit-sa-burg," he went on, stumbling over the still-awkward English words. "There's much sense in that, surely; Biemestren is the capital. But I say we run it here, from Biemestren into barony Tyrnael, terminating here, at Kernat village."

Kernat village. The room fell silent. The matter of the Kernat village slaughter was not at all closed, despite Danagar's failure to fix the blame. Was it an attempt by the Slavers' Guild to provoke another war in the Middle Lands? Or was it a probe by Prince Pugeer of Nyphien, an attempt to see just how hard he could push the Empire before it pushed back?

"And the payoff?" Tyrnael raised an eyebrow.

"It's now a four day ride from Biemestren to Kernat village—perhaps three days, if I push the men. They'll arrive tired, their horses tired, their fighting ability limited until they've had at least a good day's rest. If we had a railroad it would be a one-day trip, and the men and horses would arrive rested, ready to fight.

"Put the railroad here, and I can put the entire Home Guard, plus cannons, into Tyrnael, ready to strike into Nyphien or repel a strike, within a day." He paused to let that sink in. "Put spurs out, spanning the country, and not only can we trade with ourselves easier, faster, not only can we move steel and grain from one end of the Empire to the other, but we can move soldiers more quickly."

"It's still an . . . awful lot of money," Baron Krathael said. "There's land to be cleared, some of it in my barony. How will I be compensated for that?"

The conversation degenerated into a discussion of right-of-way. There had long been precedent for the throne, both in Holtun and in Bieme, declaring a right-of-way for the purpose of building military roads. The owner of the land was always to be compensated, but there was no clear precedent as to how much would be paid.

Karl Cullinane probably would have said something like, *Precedent be damned—we'll figure out a reasonable way to handle it and then implement it.*

Ranella looked over at Jason. "If I may? A compromise: could I build just a demonstration line, run it from the castle out, say, half a day's ride? The local farmers could use it for bringing goods to market in Biemestren, and we could test its ability to move troops."

Jason knew that he should say something, but what could he say? Garavar and Ranella had made all the sound arguments; all that was left to Jason was pounding on the table, and that would have been silly.

Thomen took the initiative. "With the consent of the Heir, Engineer Ranella is authorized to build a demonstration railroad."

Nod, please.

Jason nodded. "I consent, of course."

Thomen looked down at the paper in front of him. "Next matter: Baron Nerahan has applied to have his soldiers trained with, and armed with, rifles. Baron Nerahan."

Nerahan rose, and made an impassioned plea. Jason would have been impressed with his depth of feeling—if Ellegon hadn't told him that Nerahan had expected to have his request denied the first time around, and was merely laying the groundwork for a future, successful request. That surprised Jason—that somebody might plead so hard for something he didn't expect to get was a bit bewildering.

Arondael, unsurprisingly, led the Biemish assault against Nerahan's request; the other barons' opposition was more *pro forma* than anything else. With one exception.

Thomen Furnael stood. "I'm speaking not as judge or regent now, but just as a member of this council." He paced the room as he spoke. "There are dangerous forces at work in the world. I'm not just speaking of the Nyphien problem, although we're going to have to face that soon enough, one way or another. I'm not just speaking of the rumors I've been hearing of late about strange things coming out of Faerie, either."

Strange things? I hadn't heard anything.

Thomen has better sources of news than you do. Well, that's not true: he has the same sources of news, but he listens somewhat more carefully to them. He works a lot harder than some people I could name.

Jason brushed the dig aside. *So, what's the news?*

Not much, not really. But there have been some bizarre killings around Ehvenor. The information isn't reliable, but there's talk of finding only the front halves of a string of six horses, the rear halves having been cleanly bitten off, and of finding dead humans, and of parts of dead humans, and of beasts that fly away like dragons, or other large creatures that run away, creatures that can't be seen when you look directly at them. The dragon gave a mental shrug. *How much weight should be given to all of this is a good question. Rumors are completely false some of the time and largely false most often.*

Thomen was still speaking. "—and part of that plan is to return as much of Holtun as possible to baronial rule as soon as possible. I understand that many of us aren't minded to trust Baron Nerahan, but I invite you all to consider the effect of not trusting him, not trusting any Holtish barons."

Baron Tyrnael nodded. "Given that, I'd prefer that we start this with Adahan, not Nerahan." Bren Adahan smiled tightly. "Baron Adahan has demonstrated his loyalty to the crown, and his . . . associations with the family are well known."

Aeia smiled tightly. "And what associations might those be, Baron?" Her voice was deceptively light, but Jason knew she was seething inside.

Family trait: you Cullinanes don't like having your, err, affairs discussed in public.

Tyrnael smiled. "You two are always seen together, Lady. If you spurn his company, that would not be so. And if Baron Adahan has *not* asked you to marry him, then will I recommend to the Heir and regent that they take his barony away from him permanently, and give it to someone who is not a fool."

"I'm not a fool," Bren Adahan said with a grin.

"My point precisely."

That pacified Aeia, although not Bren Adahan. "I'd rather . . . not resume day-to-day control over Adahan, not yet. For one thing, military government gives us a good reason to keep enough Imperial troops garrisoned near Little Pittsburgh to protect it, if necessary. For another, I've much to learn from the Engineer, and can't study with him while I'm in Adahan. 'For sage advice, go where the sage is'—I intend to resume my studies at Home." He looked to Aeia for just a moment, then looked away.

She nodded. "Think of what an engineer-baron is going to mean to Holtun, in the long run."

A muscle twitched in Tyrnael's jaw. "I am."

"Very well," Thomen said with a nod that dismissed

Tyrnael's comment as a concession. "Which brings up the next matter, and it's something that you may find as distressing as I do." He produced a piece of paper. "We've received, via a Home trader, a letter from Lou Riccetti. The Engineer is talking about selling guns and powder to Therranj."

CHAPTER 5

The Silver Crown

Wealth I ask not, hope nor love,
Nor a friend to know me;
All I ask, the heaven above
And the road below me.

—Robert Louis Stevenson

I'm a simple man. All I want is enough sleep for two
normal men, enough whiskey for three, and enough women
for four.

—Walter Slovotsky

"Much of the letter is personal," Thomen said into the silence. "But of the rest, part of it reads:

Lady Dhara is here from Therranj, again wanting to
discuss, as she puts it, "the status of the Valley of Varnath."
I'm not sure that's really important to them, not anymore,
although she offered me a package deal under which we're
granted title to and sovereignty over Home, plus a rather
substantial amount of metals (including gold, silver, and

mercury!) *and gems—she brought a small chest full of industrial-grade diamonds with her, as a gift. Nice stuff.*

In any case, reports are that things are heating up between Therranj and Melrhood.

Our part of the package, though, would be some guns and powder, plus—preferably—the secret of making gunpowder.

Given Ranella's new wash, that might not be a bad idea, if the price is right. Eventually, how to do you-know-what is going to be worked out; but how to do the other kind of you-know-what is a lot trickier, particularly when you come to the problem that the Brits ran into when they switched over too soon.

Ranella frowned as Thomen read, opening her mouth as though to interrupt, then sitting back when Bren Adahan touched her arm and shook his head.

In any case, can you spare a couple of tendays and take the Dragon Express out so we can discuss this? I've put the elves off for now, but they don't like it much, and I don't like that they don't like it. I prefer to get along with my neighbors.

I also need Ellegon out here. We've got a security problem: there's five new probationers out here who he hasn't mindprobed yet, and either he's going to have to do that before long, or we're going to have to work out something with Thellaren. Besides the fact that the Spiders can't probe as deeply as Ellegon does, Thellaren just isn't thorough, and I don't completely trust him.

Also, you and I have got to discuss communication security matters. It's been happening a bit slowly, but the other day an apprentice pointed out to me how English is quickly becoming the lingua franca for trade between species where Home is involved, and the practice is spreading. . . .

*   *   *

Thomen set the paper down and looked over at Ranella. "Can you explain this to us? What is this 'wash'? And this 'you-know-what'?"

"No," she said. "It involves a trade secret. I may not reveal it, except on orders of the Engineer himself."

Thomen nodded at that. "I understand. Still, this is the sort of thing that's known to both the empress and Doria Perlstein. Would you have us ask them?"

Ranella shrugged. "Go ahead."

Tennetty hitched at her pistol as she looked at Jason, as though asking who she ought to shoot.

Jason shrugged, then made a patting, be-still gesture, so that she wouldn't decide that his shrug was permission to shoot whoever she felt like.

He tried to puzzle it out. It had something to do with the secret of making gunpowder, and perhaps another kind of gunpowder—slaver powder, perhaps?—but only the Other Siders and a very few, very senior engineers knew how to make any kind of gunpowder at all. Surely, many juniors had some idea of portions of the process, but the whole of it was a trade secret. Even Jason knew that part of it involved the dirt from the uninhabited portions of the engineers' caverns—beyond the region that Lou Riccetti called the Batcave, for some reason or other.

Ariken Krathael cleared his throat. "Governor, are you telling us that you put your . . . obligations to this mayor of Home ahead of those to the throne of Bieme—of Holtun-Bieme?"

At that, a series of cross-arguments broke out, some barons raising their voices in criticism of Ranella, Bren Adahan almost shouting his own support.

Better get involved in this, or Ranella's going to be in trouble.

But what do I say ?

Try pointing out that this is an additional reason for you to go to Home, as well as Endell.

So it was. "Excuse me," Jason said, rising.

The voices quieted, but they didn't quite die down.

Bang!

Tennetty lowered a smoking pistol, cocking her head critically at the hole in the overhead beam.

"A bit off the mark, alas. Guess I'm getting old." She drew another pistol and cocked it, not quite pointing it at anyone. "I think the Heir is asking for your attention?"

There was a thunder of footsteps on the stairs, and four guards rushed into the room, two with pistols drawn, a third with a naked saber, a fourth carrying a pike.

Tennetty grinned. "Nice response time, folks. End of test; return to your duties."

Thomen nodded, dismissing them with a wave and a glower.

Over at the door, the guard muffled a grin behind his hand. Aeia didn't bother hiding hers.

"I'm not sure I approve of firing warning shots indoors," Terumel Derahan said.

The smell of gunsmoke hung heavily in the air, a reek of char and sulfur.

Tennetty holstered the empty pistol and drew another, cocking it. "Neither do I. Now, when Karl hacked your father's head off, *that* was a warning. To his descendants. Heed it."

Ellegon—

I tried to shut her up, but she's not having any. Tennetty's not completely tame, you know.

I worked that out.

Tennetty was still talking. "See that dark spot on the rug? It's—"

Jason stood, swallowing heavily, and tried to summon up a command voice. "Tennetty, shut up. Right now."

"—what's left of your father, and—"

"Shut up."

Her eyes met his for a long moment.

There was a taste of bile in the back of his mouth. Wasn't she going to back down?

Out of the corner of his eye, Jason could see Bren Adahan and Aeia slowly moving their chairs back, but he didn't dare drop his gaze. "Put the gun away, Tennetty," he said. "Right now."

Fire flared in the courtyard outside; the dragon roared. *Put it away.*

Jason didn't turn to look. He kept his eyes on Tennetty's. *"Now."*

Swearing under her breath, she uncocked the pistol and holstered it. "You do his voice very well," Tennetty said. "But he wouldn't have used it like that on me, not when I was backing him. So maybe one day we'll see just how well you walk in his footsteps. Maybe real soon, one way or another."

With that, she turned on her heel and stalked from the room.

Jason found that his knees really didn't want to support him; he sat down heavily. "My apologies, everyone. Tennetty was devoted to my father, and she misses him. And my particular apologies to you, Baron Derahan. While it was your father who issued the challenge, my father should have given him a chance to reconsider."

Derahan didn't look mollified.

Why should he? You've now implied that his father was a fool for challenging yours. He was, mind, but that doesn't make it politic to say so. Now sit back and let Thomen change the subject.

"In any case," Thomen was already saying, "this does suggest that the Heir ought to travel to Home, in the company of Ellegon and perhaps a few others. Clearly, it would be wrong for the Engineer to give out the secret of gunpowder to the elves, no matter what the pay to Home. With the Emperor dead . . ."

". . . I'm the best ambassador you've got," Jason said.

Smile, and repeat after me . . .

Jason smiled.

"Unless you think there's another who outranks me?"

"Unless you think there's another who outranks me?"

"I've got an idea." Bren Adahan chuckled. "Whoever thinks they outrank Jason gets to tell Tennetty."

"You've made a good point." Nerahan pursed his lips judiciously. "Gunpowder is the advantage that Home and the Empire share; it's valuable to both, but only as long as it is secret. Perhaps the Heir can persuade Lou Riccetti of that."

"Yes, yes, yes," Baron Hivael put in. "But why this other trip? This one to Endell?"

Jason opened his mouth to answer, *Because Walter Slovotsky told me to.*

But, actually, that wasn't true. Walter had told them to have Ellegon bring Kirah and the children to Holtun-Bieme as soon as possible. He hadn't said that Jason ought to go along.

But it was Jason's job to do it; it wasn't something he felt right about assigning to somebody else. Part of it would be to tell Kirah and Slovotsky's daughters that their father and Ahira were still missing. He just couldn't delegate that.

"Because I promised I would," he said. That was truthful, even if it wasn't the whole truth. He'd promised himself another trip away, before he settled down as prince of Bieme and emperor of Holtun-Bieme.

Jason rose. At the near end of the room stood the slightly raised podium, where the richly carved throne of the prince of Bieme stood. Next to the throne was a locked strongbox. Taking a large brass key from his belt, he knelt and unlocked the box, pulling from it a simple circlet of silver, the beauty of the mirror-polished metal more enhanced than overshadowed by the rubies, diamonds and emeralds that studded it.

"Warriors swear on swords. I've sworn on this," he said, adding privately, *as of now*, "that I'll take this trip, before I even consider assuming the crown and my full responsibilities. Who here would make me a liar?"

Surprisingly, at least to Jason, the murmurs ceased. Thomen gave him an admiring nod.

As the meeting tapered off, Jason turned to Thomen. *Relay, please: Well, how'd I do?*

Thomen frowned.

He says, "Pretty poorly, actually. The admiring nod was for my audience, not for you. But perhaps you didn't do too badly, for a beginner."

Jason put the crown away in its cloth bag, and then looked out in the courtyard.

And I suppose I'm going to be graced with your opinion, whether I want it or not.

Good guess. Below, the dragon was settling in for the night, neck stretched out so he could rest his chin on the ground, his legs tucked catlike underneath his body. *Me? I think Thomen was half right. The first half.*

Well, at least it was settled that Jason was going. Now, all there was to do was decide on a team. Best to talk that over with Tennetty; her judgment about these sorts of things was better than his. Even if she was ticked at him.

INTERLUDE

Laheran and the Dead Men

Be not angry that you cannot make others as you wish them to be, since you cannot make yourself as you wish to be.

—Thomas à Kempis

The wind came across the Cirric, blowing across the guildhall and the kennels, which, oddly enough, didn't smell of anything. That was strange; slave kennels always smelled of shit and piss and fear, and sometimes death.

There were a dozen people standing on the hot stones of the courtyard of the Erifeyll guildhall, and most of them smelled of fear.

Fear wasn't the only thing that the two ragged men and the girl stank of; there were no baths to be had in Erif's dungeon. The fools—didn't know how to handle merchandise. There was no way for them to run, and nowhere to run if they did.

Not only were all three chained at the wrists, throat and ankles, but a half dozen of Lord Erif's armsmen stood by, armed cap à pied.

Erifeyll, just two days away from glorious Pandathaway.

"The entry was through the rear," a guard said. "Somebody pulled the bars right out of the wall," he added. "But at least they didn't get away."

Laheran ignored him. The idiot seemed to think that because some of the slaves were recaptured, this wasn't a horrible defeat. The details didn't matter. This was *Erifeyll*. Did that mean that Pandathaway was next? Probably not. That was too obvious. So, probably Pandathaway was next, because they'd think that the guild would think not. So probably not, so probably, so—

Laheran sighed. One thing he had learned as an apprentice was that when you didn't know how to solve a whole problem, it made sense to solve what you could while you were thinking. He turned to the slaves.

The girl whimpered and squirmed as Laheran examined her collar. Not guild work. There was a reason that most guild collars were dipped in gold, despite the cost. Gold didn't rust.

The iron of these collars was rusty, and like sandpaper. The rust had worn her neck raw underneath; at Laheran's nod, two of his men gripped her with practiced hands so that he could inspect her more closely. His probing finger came away with blood and a greenish pus.

"Idiots," he said. And: "Key."

The guard sergeant thought about protesting for a moment, then shrugged and pulled a key out of his pouch. Laheran quickly unlocked the collar and dropped it to the dirt.

The wound was festering badly.

Amateurs. As though the only way to treat slaves was with beatings and chains. The girl was twelve, perhaps thirteen. Her round eyes and sharp chin proclaimed her of Shattered Islander stock, clearly, possibly Klimosian or Bursosi. She could be almost presentable, quite attractive in a year or two, and might well respond better to kindness than the whip if she wasn't to be brutalized into scarred ugliness and sullen tractability.

Practiced fingers felt at her forehead—she was running a fever—then dropped to feel at the rest of her. Hmm . . . perhaps sooner than a few years.

He turned to Kelimon. "Take the three of them to the ship. A bit of healing draughts on the neck should be enough, but examine them all thoroughly; she may need more." Laheran turned to the guard sergeant. "They are all property of the Slavers' Guild; all were caught as fugitives."

But the majority of the dozen or so slaves in the kennels—Laheran would have to check the records in order to be sure just how many—had escaped, taking with them what horses and what money the guild had had here.

Still, there was nothing more that these three could tell him. They'd only seen the dwarf, who had hustled them outside through the rear window of the slave cage.

The guard shook his head. "I think Lord Kuryil—he's the keeper of the dungeon—expressed an interest in her."

"Then he should have had the sense to see that her health was attended to," Laheran said from between taut lips. "She is not for sale here. Take them away, Kelimon, take all three of them away. We'll drop them off at guildhall in Pandathaway."

Normally, Laheran would have taken the guard's comment as an opening for a negotiation. But if Kuryil was deliberately degrading the girl's condition in order to lower her price, he ought to be taught a lesson. Besides, Laheran was irritated with all of them. He was honest enough to admit to himself that that was the real reason he was rebuffing Kuryil—not to educate the lord, or even because he suspected that a bath, some healing, and a few tendays of gentle but firm handling might increase the girl's value.

The gray-robed wizard and his apprentice stood to one side, twin masks of indifference on their bearded faces. The apprentice looked like a painting of the wizard as a young man; Laheran could see where the squint-lines were beginning to form, tracks of a buzzard around the eyes.

"Shall I open it now?" the wizard asked. "Or shall we all stand out in the hot sun all day?"

Laheran stood in front of the door. As before, there were those awkward Englits scrawlings and the signatures were symbols—a sword, a knife and an ax—but the final words were in Erendra.

The warrior lives, they said.

And: *Don't open this door. A surprise for slavers waits inside. Preserve it for them.*

Laheran looked at the wizard and at the guards. "You take orders from Karl Cullinane, do you?" he asked, more rhetorically than otherwise.

One of the guards bit back a response.

"Well?" Laheran snapped. "Out with it."

"It cost Lord Erif a goodly amount of money to have it preserved for you, Master Laheran," the guard said. "He did it for you, as a gesture of cooperation with your guild, not because he takes orders from Karl Cullinane, or anyone else."

Laheran nodded. "There's truth in that. My apologies." He set his palm against the splintered wood of the door, but it didn't move. He pushed harder, and harder, but still there was no motion, not even the slight give of a bolted door.

He walked to a shuttered window, worked his fingers in between the overhang of the shutter and the wall, and pulled.

Again, nothing happened; the spell of preservation had kept the building sealed, just as the murderers had left it.

He sighed. Enough; it had to be done sometime.

"Release the spell," Laheran said.

The wizard stepped up to the door and lightly touched it with a split-nailed finger, quietly but carefully pronouncing three syllables that could only be heard and forgotten, not remaining on the tongue or the mind.

The shutter released and swung violently open, barely missing Laheran's nose. The slam of it against the wall sent hands reaching for swords.

He drew his own sword and, standing carefully to one side of the window, stuck it inside and waved it around.

Nothing happened.

One of the guards stepped forward. "I don't understand why all the delay," he said as he took a step forward and pushed on the door.

Laheran moved quickly, catching the guard across the waist in a leaping tackle, just as the door swung wide.

Thwup.

A feathered bolt bit into the guard's shoulder; the heavy man dropped his weapons and screamed.

Laheran rolled easily to his feet, brushing himself off. "Best take your man to the Spider," he said to the other guards, as one knelt over the pale form of the idiot who had opened the door. "There's nothing to interest you here."

Laheran stepped inside. It was as he'd thought: one of the dead men was Daviran. He'd apprenticed with Daviran years ago; Davi was one of Laheran's few friends.

And now clever Davi sat in a chair, his face pale in death, his throat slit from ear to ear.

There was nothing alive inside the kennel. He could see one body spread out on the floor, and there was another dead man sitting in a chair, and yet another tied upside-down to the top crosspiece of the slave cage, but a live man hadn't fired the bolt; a crossbow had been nailed to an open closet door opposite the entry, and an improvised rope and pulley arrangement set up to make it fire through the opening door.

Laheran knelt to examine the body under the table. The right hand was crushed, splinters of bones peeking through the bloody flesh, as if someone had run the hand through a wine press.

That hadn't killed him, though; his chest was crushed, the breastbone smashed inward, probably killing the man instantly.

That smelled of the dwarf, Ahira, and Davi's slit throat spoke of Walter Slovotsky.

And the poor, dead bastard tied upside-down to the cage was pure Karl Cullinane. Laheran let his hand rest on the short length of spear that projected from the dead slaver's chest.

He could just see the monster tying the guildsman upside-down, and then taking his time hefting a spear, only to throw it almost through the slaver.

The three of them would die, and that was all there was to it.

Laheran drew his knife and considered the edge. Was it really possible to cut a man ten thousand times without killing him? Ahrmin had been right: Cullinane was too much of a threat to be allowed to live. He had to die. And his friends with him.

Laheran looked once again at the parchment note on the door.

The warrior lives, you think? Not for long, Karl Cullinane. Not for long, you murdering animal.

Laheran tore the parchment down from the door and slashed it to ribbons.

CHAPTER 6

Tennetty

The business of the samurai consists in reflecting on his own station in life, in discharging loyal service to his master if he has one, in deepening his fidelity in associations with friends, and, with due consideration of his own position, in devoting himself to duty above all.

—Yamaga Soko

The difference between being a trusted friend and a devoted vassal is non-trivial. Me, I'd rather be the first; vassals tend to go to the well too often.

—Walter Slovotsky

"Come in," she said.

Her room, a small cubicle down in the dungeon level of the tower, was lit only by a flickering lamp set in a stone niche at eye-level. It was cold down below the ground, and it smelled of ancient mold, but that didn't seem to affect Tennetty as she sat tailor-fashion on her rumpled bed, considering the edge of a bowie, her face cast into shadow, hiding the patch over her missing eye.

"So," she said. "You let them talk you out of it?"

"What are you saying? That I don't want to go?"

She snickered. "You have a keen eye for the obvious." From somewhere in the darkness she produced a whetstone, spat on it, and began to hone the edge of the knife with slow, even strokes.

Jason didn't like that kind of accusation, and he didn't know how to deal with it. "I thought I proved something in Melawei," he said, not realizing how foolish the boast sounded until the words were out.

She eyed him evenly. "You proved that you could use a rifle, once. You did it when it counted, I'll give you that. But you didn't prove that you're a substitute for him, boy. You sit in *his* chair, and you expect all of them to look up to you like you're *him*. . . ." She spat on the stone and continued to stroke it down the edge. "Well, you're not. Not by me."

"Tennetty, I—"

With no warm-up, no hint that she was about to move, she lunged at him, springing from the bed.

"Guards!" he shouted, as he caught her knife-arm, trying for a kick to her kneecap.

She got her leg behind his and swept his feet out from under him, landing heavily on his chest, one arm trapped underneath him.

The tip of the knife flickered in the lamplight, descending—

—and halted an inch from his eye.

"Your *father* would have beaten me, Jason. You're just not as fast as he was, not as brave, not the ruler he was, not—"

A rifle-butt slammed against her head with an audible *thunk*. From the edge of his vision, a huge hand reached out and fastened itself around her wrist; another, somewhat smaller hand gripped her by the hair and lifted her up, not at all slowing at her muffled groan of pain. She struck out with a free hand but it was blocked, the sound like a fist slapping a side of beef.

"Take her, Durine," Kethol said, releasing his grip on her hair, stooping to help Jason up.

She tried to lash out with a savage groin-kick, but Durine, moving more gracefully, more quickly than any man his size had a right to, had already turned to catch the kick on his hip.

Like a mastiff with a rat he grabbed her, then shook her hand until the knife dropped from it. Durine yanked her toward him with one hand, punching her in the pit of the stomach with the other.

Retching, she staggered, and would have collapsed if Durine hadn't economically spun her about and thrown her to the ground, then knelt beside her, gripping both her hands in one massive paw, drawing a beltknife with the other.

He looked up at Jason, who was standing half-supported by Kethol. "Do you want to do it, sir, or should I?" Massive shoulders shrugged under his leather jerkin. "Makes not much of a difference to me."

Jason struggled to sit up. "Would you all—"

Tennetty snarled, a sound more animal than human. "Just testing him, I was just testing him," she said, the words coming out as a threat, not a plea.

"Let her up, Durine," Jason said. He straightened, a salty taste in his mouth; he reached to the bleeding corner of his lip. He couldn't remember how, but it must have been cut in the fight.

Durine looked at Kethol, who shrugged, as though to say, *It's up to him.* Reluctantly, the big man let go of her hands and rose, not sheathing his dagger. "I'd not go for that knife, Tennetty," he said, his voice casual, perhaps a touch embarrassed, as if he'd caught himself repeating a transparent platitude like, *Remember to dress warm when it's cold.* "It'd be sort of a foolish idea."

She nodded and worked her way over to the edge of her bed, pulling herself up to it, rubbing her hand against the side of her head. In the flickering lamplight she looked old, and about used-up. "I hear you."

"I think you've done enough testing of him." Kethol picked up her pistol belt from where it hung near the bed and slung it over his shoulder. "Well, young sir, what do we do about this?"

"I just came to ask her about the party, the one I'm taking to Home, and then to Endell." Jason tried to dismiss it with a wave. "We got into a disagreement about how ready I am, and she tried to prove a point."

Kethol's mouth twisted into a smile. The expression didn't look right. "With respect, sir: this is why you called for help? You were perhaps proving that you've mastered that form of self-defense?" He turned to Durine. "What do you think?"

Durine shook his head. "I don't like it. We haul her in front of the general, at least."

Kethol snorted. "After he told us that he doesn't want to see our ugly faces for the next two tendays? Maybe Captain Garthe instead?"

"Over an assault on the Heir?"

"I'll decide what's done about it!" Jason snapped.

Durine thought it over for a moment, then nodded. "Yes, sir. We can discuss it with the general while you're gone, I guess. Long as you're not taking her with you. You give a dog one bite, not two."

Tennetty shook her head. "Wrong. I'm going with him. I'm as good as there is at what I do."

"Threatening royalty?" Kethol shrugged. "Who's going to keep an eye on you?"

She shook her head, then clearly regretted it. "If we're going to carry any cargo at all, we've got to keep the group down—remember, we've got to bring Slovotsky's woman and kids back from Endell. Bren Adahan and Aeia are bound for Home, and that means we can take maybe three more. Jason, me, and three more. I was thinking of Garthe, Teven, and maybe Danagar, if he can travel, but—" A spasm of pain creased her face and closed her single eye, leaving it watering.

"A corporal and two of the general's sons? Captain Garthe would be fine, but I've got a better idea," Kethol said, looking at Jason. "What would you say to me, Durine and Pirojil for the other three? I'd mean you'd have to talk the general into letting us off our punishment, and getting Piro healed up."

Which wouldn't bother Jason at all.

"Me instead of Pirojil," Tennetty said. "You either take me or kill me. Karl told me to watch out for you, Jason." Moving with exaggerated slowness, she rose from the bed and walked over to him. Durine glanced quickly at Jason, but Kethol's eyes never left Tennetty as she unstrapped her pistol and slowly, carefully, pulled it from the holster, handing it butt first to Jason.

"Cock it," she said.

Durine raised an eyebrow. Kethol shrugged, then nodded.

Jason cocked the weapon, holding it as he'd been taught, the barrel pointed toward the ceiling.

"Lower it now, point it at me." Again moving slowly, she reached out and pulled his arm down, until the muzzle was resting just underneath her chin, cold steel against her flesh.

"Either trust me or shoot me, now," she said, as though she didn't care one way or another.

"It's your decision, sir," Durine said. "Your father used to have a high opinion of Tennetty, but I don't know as you'd want to give her another bite. You give a dog one bite, not two."

"You already said that," Jason said.

"So I did. Well?"

Jason jerked his head toward the door. "Leave us alone for a moment or two," he said, not lowering the pistol. Was she really betting that she could beat the hangfire?

"We'll be just outside the door." Durine said. He and Kethol scooped up their rifles and left.

"What would you advise my father, Tennetty?" he asked.

She didn't hesitate. "I'd tell him to shoot. You can't trust somebody like me, not after I've come this close to killing you."

"Even though I know you won't do it again?"

"You *don't* know. You can't know. *I* don't know. Your father wouldn't give me another chance."

Jason nodded. "Maybe you're right." He pulled back the hammer, lowered the weapon and uncocked it, then handed it to her. "Then again, as you were so kind to point out, I'm not my father." He turned away from her and walked out of the room, his back feeling quite naked and completely vulnerable.

CHAPTER 7

Goodbyes

I've never liked cats' ways of taking their leave—the ungrateful little creatures just go without saying anything.

Not my way. Saying goodbye is something we humans do pretty well.

—Walter Slovotsky

Aeia escorted him into the bedroom. "Take it easy on Mother," she whispered. "She's not doing too well."

Doria was already there, her legs curled under her as she sat in an oversized chair by the window, a lapdesk and pen across her lap. As Aeia and Jason walked in from the outer room, she set the lapdesk on an end table and walked to them.

Andrea Cullinane was asleep in the bed, her face seemingly a little younger, a trifle less worn around the edges than it had been when Jason had seen her in the workshop. For a moment her breathing speeded up and her eyelids fluttered, but just as Jason thought she was going to wake up she turned over on her side and buried her face deeply in her pillow.

"She'll be fine, I think, but she's been overdoing it with the magic for a long time now," Doria whispered, her lips pursed in professional disapproval. "Just think of her as a recovering junkie and you'll have a good picture." She guided them out toward the hall, far enough away that the whispers wouldn't carry to the bed, but close enough so that the three of them could still see Andrea's sleeping form.

" 'Junkie'?" Jason asked.

Doria's brow furrowed. "Drunk, then. Think of her as a drunk trying to give up drinking. The trouble is, she can't give it up; but she has to cut it down to the point where it's not going to hurt her."

Aeia shook her head. "But she's going to be okay?"

Doria didn't answer for a moment. "Remember that I'm not what I was, but—"

"But you've still got a feel for the way of things," Aeia said firmly. "That's what Andrea says," she added, when Doria seemed about to protest.

"Perhaps," Doria said. "But. . . ." She shrugged it away. "In any case, I don't want her to have any more shocks, not right now. When she's well, she's a lot stronger in body and soul than most people are, but—"

"How do you know that? This 'feel' of yours?" Jason was skeptical. Doria had lost her persona as a Hand healer when she'd defied the matriarch in Melawei. He was grateful to her—hell, she'd defied the matriarch by using her spells to save Jason's life—but that didn't blind him to what she'd given up.

Doria's face went stony. "Because after the two of us were gang-raped," she said calmly, levelly, almost mechanically, "she recovered from what sent me into catatonia. She was able to deal with it and, not too much later, to resume a normal sex life with your father. That takes a kind of strength of character that I doubt *you* have, boy," she said, her whisper momentarily vehement. She fought for control of herself, and found it. "But she's not at her best right now, which is why both of you are to play this up as an easy little vacation before you settle down to marriage and work or whatever—"

"Doria?" Andrea's sleepy voice interrupted itself for a yawn. "What is—oh, Jason, Aeia," she said, sitting up in bed and smiling. She held out her hands to them.

Awake, she looked dreadful. Her eyes were puffy and red, and there were crusts at the corners of her mouth and eyes. Jason took one of her hands in his. Hers were dry and hot, the skin loose as an old woman's. But Mother couldn't be getting old, could she?

She smiled at them. "The two of you will watch out for each other, now. And be careful."

Or maybe she could.

He shrugged. "Nothing to it. Just a quick jaunt on dragonback, and a pickup in Endell. Nothing to it," he repeated.

Why did the words sound insincere in his ears? That was about the size of it, in fact: it was just going to be a handful of days away from Biemestrèn, that was all.

Andrea didn't seem to hear him. "I haven't seen Janie for years and years. My, she must be as big as you are. And I only know about little Doria Andrea from Walter's and Kirah's letters." She smiled at Doria. "Although I did notice that you got top billing."

"Then again," Doria said, "naming her 'Andrea Doria' would have been a—"

"No, don't say it!"

"—it would have been a disaster."

The two Other Side women giggled like a couple of girls. He didn't understand it; he spread his hands to confess ignorance when Aeia looked at him curiously, then shrugged as though to say that she didn't understand it either.

But their laughter was infectious, and Jason and Aeia soon found themselves laughing, too.

Laughter made the goodbyes easier.

Doria caught up with them in the hall. "She's not in the best shape. She's been substituting seeming for real health for too long, and that's an awful trap. So I want her to rest, and not worry. . . . And I also want both of you to get back when you're supposed to. Understood?"

Aeia hugged her. "Understood, Aunt Doria."

Jason nodded. "I'll miss you, too."

She bit her lip and smiled. "There is that, too, boychick. Take care."

PART TWO

HOME

CHAPTER 8

Outside of Enkiar

Miscellaneous is always the largest category.
        —Slovotsky's Laws

The night was clear and bright above, dark and threatening below. Off to port and perhaps a mile below, the murk of the Enkiar streets was relieved only by a precious few lanterns, and by the glowing coals of three garbage fires at the town's western perimeter.

The stars flickered brightly, while distant faerie lights pulsed in a lethargic adagio of scarlet and cerulean. Again, Jason tried to look straight ahead, past the straining neck of the dragon, as the rush of air beat tears from his eyes. He wiped at the dampness at his temples and let himself ease back into the straps.

A massive hand gripped his shoulder. "It shouldn't be too much more," Durine said, his voice pitched to barely carry over the wind and the flapping of wings. "Any time now." He gave Jason's shoulder a reassuring squeeze.

Behind Durine, half-hidden behind tied-down canvas sacks, the others were strapped in their saddles, Kethol, still wide-eyed, looked down with more than a little apprehension, Tennetty watching everything with active indifference. Aeia took flying as a matter of course—she'd ridden on dragonback since before Jason was born—while Bren Adahan kept his expression under strict control.

They weren't at the first of the usual campsites, Ellegon reported. *So we'll try the next one.*

While Enkiar was militantly neutral, and the Home warriors were free to make camp in the forests to its west and north, the enforcement of that neutrality was sometimes more theoretical than actual outside the city proper. Though Lord Gyren's troops enforced the neutrality in the city itself, the discipline tended to fade toward the edges.

There were advantages to all that. Enkiar's neutrality didn't stop the Home raiding teams from gathering information. A few times, Home warriors had managed to parlay that information into the ambush of a slaver caravan. It worked both ways, though; once, slavers had managed an ambush of Frandred's team, an attack that had left twenty of his warriors dead. So Home raiders never camped twice in a row in the same spot, and always kept a good watch.

Rising on a pillar of smoke and flame, a signal rocket flared green ahead of them.

Nope. They're at number five, Ellegon said. *They have a dwarf standing guard.*

How could you tell?

Think about it. At this distance, the dragon said, *human eyes couldn't spot me against a night sky. Dwarves are different.*

The dragon's wings slowed as Ellegon swooped down, then broke into a furious flurry as the ground came up quickly.

"Torches!" a familiar gruff voice called from below.

Daherrin, what are you doing on watch?

"We was short of dwarves," came from the darkness.

Three shadowy shapes ran up in the darkness, holding bundles of unlit torches in front of them; Ellegon's flame flared briefly, judiciously, lighting the brands one by one.

Jason quickly unfastened himself from the saddle and dropped heavily to the dew-slick grass, flexing his knees to take up the shock.

As the torches cast their flickering light around the meadow, Jason found himself face to face with Daherrin and Mikyn. Mikyn was Jason's age; they'd been friends since early childhood. Now Mikyn looked older, a bit world-worn since Jason had last seen him: his sparse brown beard just a touch fuller, the hollows under his eyes darker, and the bones of his face more prominent in the flickering firelight. If Jason hadn't known better, he would have put Mikyn's age at perhaps twenty-five, maybe thirty. Old.

The big change was in his expression; Jason's childhood friend was looking at him as if he were a stranger.

"Jason," Daherrin said, his voice shockingly cool, no tone betraying warmth or anger. The dwarf hadn't changed in the many tendays since Jason had last seen him: a solid, seemingly unchangeable stump of a person, almost as wide as he was tall. While Daherrin's head barely came to the top of Jason's chest, his shoulders were every bit as broad as Jason's father's had been. Above a mouse-brown beard shot with gray, two beady eyes peered out over an absurdly aquiline nose.

The dwarf's lined face was unreadable in the flickering torchlight.

Then he broke into a smile so broad it would have torn apart a human's face. "Jason," Daherrin said, hugging him so hard bones threatened to break. "Jason, boy, it's good to see you." He released Jason and stepped back. "*Damn* me if you ain't a bit less skinny across the shoulders." His face sobered. "Heard about your father, and I'm sorry."

Jason nodded. "So am I."

Mikyn didn't say anything; he watched Jason.

The dwarf slapped Jason across the shoulder, almost bowling him over. "I also heard that you did for Ahrmin. Nice going." He smiled. Killing didn't bother Daherrin; it was by way of his business. "You sure the bastard's dead? I recall that your father thought he'd killed him once."

Jason returned the dwarf's level gaze. "I saw his brains."

"Good man. Betcha your mother's proud a' you." The dwarf started to turn away. "One more thing?"

"Yes?"

The dwarf turned toward the dragon. "Hey, Ellegon, keep a lid on things for a minute, would ya?" he called out, then turned back to Jason.

I'd rather you didn't—

"Chew on *this*, fucker," the dwarf said. A huge fist caught Jason on the cheek; the world came up and slapped him in the back, knocking the wind clean out of him. He tried to sit up, but curtains of darkness threatened to enfold his mind.

The distinctive clicks of rifles being cocked cut through the darkness.

"Tennetty, ta havath," Durine said. "I say ease up, all of you."

"Shove it up your ass," Tennetty shrilled. "You're ready to kill me for fucking putting my *hands* on him, and you're going to let—"

"Tennetty, shut up. Everybody put your weapons down, *now*," Aeia shouted into the night. "Ellegon!"

Everyone, be still. There's nothing going on that's worth dying over. Dragonfire brightened the sky, penetrating through the haze around Jason's brain. *He's fine. —Jason, get up.*

Mikyn looked down at him. "That didn't square things. But maybe, just maybe, it's a start." He offered Jason a hand.

Jason took it, and for a moment considered kicking his boyhood friend in the balls. Twice. Hard.

But he dismissed the idea and accepted Daherrin's and Mikyn's help to his feet.

"You coulda gotten half my team killed." The dwarf's nostrils flared as he gripped Jason's hand with painful strength. "I should give everyone a paddle and make you run the gantlet over bare coals, and if you was anybody but the future fucking Emperor, that's exactly what I'd do. But you are, so I can't, so we're all going to have to live with the way you fucked up.

"You can be Heir, or boy Emperor, or *his* son, or whatever you wanna be, but you never, never do that again, or what I'll do to you'll make you think this was like the kiss on the butt your mother used to give you when she was done changing your diapers. You hear me, Jason Cullinane?"

"I hear you." Jason released their hands and stood, wobbly.

Everybody, calm down. There has been no harm done.

Off in the darkness, Tennetty and Kethol still faced off against Daherrin's three warriors, Aeia and Durine standing between them. Guns and swords were drawn, but there hadn't been any shots fired or blood spilled, or damage done.

No harm done.

The dragon loomed above them all, whisps of smoke issuing from his nostrils. *Tell them that.*

"Ta havath." Jason raised a hand. "Everybody, ease up, eh?" He took a step and reconsidered. Except for his head; he had a bitch of a headache.

*   *   *

Close to a hundred warriors gathered around the campfire as Daherrin's quartermasters divided up Ellegon's supplies. The supplies were divided into three categories: clothes, weapons, and miscellany.

Clothes were plentiful. There was a change for everybody. Warriors would pick up fresh clothes and disappear into the night down the lamplit path to a nearby stream, soaping up, then shivering as they sluiced off in the cold water and changed into fresh clothes to return, damp and cold but clean, to bag the dirty laundry for washing at Home.

There was plenty of powder and shot to go around, and a few spare rifles to be exchanged for ones damaged beyond field repair.

Miscellaneous was, as Walter Slovotsky used to say, the largest category. There were: spare lamps, sewing kits, a few precious flasks of healing draughts, leather thongs, coils of rope, bundles of arrow stock and fletching equipment, a small bag of mail . . . but no food. While raiding teams were expected to buy staples and fodder locally, dried meat and fresh vegetables were a great treat on the road.

Not this time.

Daherrin swore softly. "An' it's real good to see you," he said to Aeia, his voice only a trace sarcastic, "and your noble baronship," he added, with a too-deep bow toward Bren Adahan, "and all that, and Durine's a real treat for the eyes. . . ."

The big man chuckled.

The dwarf expectorated into the fire and considered the sizzling gobbet of spit for a moment. "But I'd have rather had your weight in carrots and prunes than all of you."

His second, a lanky man who was missing most of his front teeth, shrugged. "Well, sho we shend shomebody in to town tomorrow to pick up shome more shupplies."

"We could. But—" The dwarf considered it for a moment. "I don't like facing the slavers if we don't have to."

Jason raised an eyebrow.

"Slavers in town." The dwarf spat again. "Big caravan—too big fer us ta take right now. But they are headed back toward Pandathaway, and I've got a runner off to Frandred; mebbe we'll join up and jump them around Metreyll, if they take that route."

A large caravan? Ellegon's wings fluttered nervously.

Large slaver caravans almost always meant a lot of dragonbaned crossbow bolts.

The dwarf nodded. "Yeah. Which is why, if I'm sending somebody into town right now, Enkiar being neutral or not, I'd like you to hang around until tomorrow. Fly up into the hills and get lost fer a day; but we might need some quick rescue."

Steam hissed from between the dragon's teeth. *But if I'm that far away, I can't mindtalk to anyone, and I can't even get distant thoughts and impressions from anyone except Jason.*

Thanks a lot.

"Jason." Daherrin toyed with his beard. "You got a problem with going into town?"

Not again, he thought. *I'll not run again.* "There's no problem, Daherrin." Jason shook his head. "I can handle it."

Tennetty nodded. "Right. I'll watch your back."

"No." Bren Adahan said.

Heads turned toward him in surprise.

'I don't recall asking your opinion, Baron," Tennetty said.

Bren Adahan waved her objection away. "You're too well-known. Anybody sees Karl Cullinane's one-eyed attack bitch and they'll start looking at who she's protecting. Jason will be safer if he's less visible—just him, and a few others. Jason will be just one of the crowd."

"The baron's making sense." Durine nodded. "Count us in."

"No." Bren Adahan shook his head again.

Kethol cocked his head to one side. "What's your problem with that?"

"Mixed teams. Do you like working with mixed teams? It's better if Jason is protected by a team that's used to working together. They're used to working in concert; they can read signals from each other that you and Durine and I would miss."

Kethol bit his lip, and then nodded. "You may be right. I don't like it, but you're right. Rather have Daherrin work with his own people—Jason will be safer that way."

"It's my call, not any of yours," Daherrin said. "I go in with my people, plus Jason. Jason, me, Mikyn, Arrikol and Falherten. Now, what do we call you? Any name you prefer?"

"Taren," Jason said. "I'm used to answering to it."

The dwarf raised his voice. "Okay, everybody—this is Taren. You all get used ta calling him that, and just that. Five extra watches and a twentieth-share penalty on the next haul for the first one who miscalls him. Double the penalty for the second. There won't be a third." He slapped his meaty hands together. "Okay. Let's get this shit unpacked."

CHAPTER 9

"The Warrior Lives"

Fundamentally, every bar is the same as every other one, if it's the kind you're drinking in, to end a sentence with a preposition, which I haven't.

—Walter Slovotsky

On the road ahead, a soldier at the guard station began working the wooden arms of a pair of signal flags. A tall, lanky man, he moved easily, as though the weight of his steel helmet and rusty chainmail didn't matter, or couldn't be allowed to matter. The red and white cloths fluttered madly as the long wooden arms clicked and clacked in the warm noon air, then halted for a few moments, only to start up again.

Jason, sitting astride a big brown gelding, caught Daherrin eyeing the motion intently. "Can you read that?"

Daherrin nodded briefly. "A bit, Taren." He shrugged. " 'Nough to know that's not one of their danger signals. Alarms tend to be short. We shouldn't have much trouble; Enkiar's an open city, remember?"

"We don't usually have any trouble in Enkiar, Taren,"

Mikyn said. Like the others, he was giving Jason's assumed name a thorough workout. Jason hoped that would all wear off before they ran into anybody; folks might wonder why it was Taren-this and Taren-that all the time.

"You still in touch with the dragon?" Daherrin asked.

Jason shrugged. It was hard to say. He *thought* he could feel Ellegon's distant presence, but he wasn't sure. Besides, it didn't matter if he could now; the issue was whether he could if and when things went sour in Enkiar.

A better question was whether that would do any good at all. It would take Ellegon at least a few minutes to arrive in response to even the most plainly heard call for help; it took only a moment to turn a live person into a corpse.

They rode in slowly, hands away from weapons, although none of them was heavily armed: each of the four humans carried only a beltknife and sword, while Daherrin sported a bastard combination of a short staff and a mace. There were five rifles in the flatbed wagon that Falherten drove, but those were props, not intended for use; real rifles weren't brought into Enkiar.

The outer guard station consisted of a pair of low stone buildings that might have concealed as many as twenty men each, no more. No more than a bowshot beyond that was the curtain wall surrounding the town, the only visible access an open gate.

Daherrin was known in Enkiar, certainly by one of the guards, possibly by the half dozen manning the station; it took only a few moments, a palmed coin and a handshake to get them inside, after the most cursory of examinations. They did have to surrender the guns, but since the only ones they were carrying were the five slaver blunderbusses that required the magically compounded slaver powder, leaving them behind presented no problem. Slaver powder wasn't particularly a secret, not for years; it was just horribly expensive.

"Besides," Daherrin said, tucking their whittled-bone claim tokens into his pouch as they rode through the gate and into Enkiar proper, "it gives 'em something to think about." His ugly face split in a grin. "Let 'em wonder if we're really using Home powder, or if that secret died with you-know-who's father."

That didn't make any sense, none at all. The making of gunpowder was an Engineering secret, known only to the Engineer and his most senior and trusted subordinate master engineers. All the other Other Siders probably knew something about it, but none of them except the Engineer knew the details of what everybody knew was an incredibly detailed and difficult chemical process.

He thought he was keeping his own counsel, but something must have shown on his face. Mikyn snorted. "I don't think so either, but there's lots of folks who think he could do anything."

"Maybe he could, Mikyn." Arrikol said. He was a tall blond Salke, his hair twisted into a single thick braid, seaman style. He clicked his tongue against the roof of his mouth as he reached across his waist, nervously pulling his sword a fraction of an inch out of its scabbard, then slipping it back, pumping the steel a few times like a piston before he caught himself and stopped.

Falherten, sitting on the narrow bench of the flatbed wagon, clucked at the horses and twitched the reins gently. "The market's the other direction, Daherrin; you're going the wrong way."

The dwarf smiled. "Gotta be sure that they know we're here, Fal. If we don't let them see how confident we are, they might get the idea that we're worried or something. Not that we are, eh?"

Falherten didn't return his smile.

Jason swallowed, hard.

The main streets of Enkiar, easily wide enough for two carts to travel in each direction, were paved with ancient cobblestones, their tops worn smooth, the spaces between them packed with the dirt of years. It was more like riding down a good dirt road than a cobblestone street: there weren't any ruts.

It was midday, and a pretty day, and the streets were filled with life. Seemingly endless crowds of ragged children played tag, weaving in and out of the streets and onto the sidewalks in a restless dance. A thickset woman in the ragged gray dress of a peasant walked down the road, a plump, nut-brown chicken struggling under either arm; her stringy hair was bound back with a kerchief of dissonant scarlet.

Over in the smithy, a fat man worked over his anvil, his face greasy, his bare chest and massive belly sweaty from the heat of his forge, the coarse black mat of hair covering his torso broken in perhaps half a dozen spaces where white scars peeked through, announcing that he had been clumsy or careless with hot metal perhaps half a dozen times.

At a nearby stall, a willowy woman crouched over her iron brazier, dipping a brush into a bowl of sauce. She basted the skewers of meat and vegetables on the grill, then exchanged the brush for a paper fan, gently fanning the coals. The scent of broiling lamb and onion and garlic spread across the air.

Two compact men in flat, broad hats leaned toward each other over an empty barrel of grain, one repeatedly shaking a small leather purse, the other shaking his head and repeatedly shouting, "Not for that, not for that," spraying the first with spittle.

Just a normal market day.

"Farmers Market's down this way, Taren," Daherrin said.

Beyond the last of the low stone buildings began a series of low pens for animals; it stank of cattle. Jason hated the smell of cattle; he'd ridden far too long downwind of it on a cattle drive from Metreyll to Pandathaway.

There was a leisurely sale in progress; a trio of brawny men Jason took to be innkeepers were spending as much time consulting with each other as they did bidding on the half dozen animals in the pen, little to the delight of the auctioneer.

Beyond the cattle pen were pigs; beyond pigs were the chicken cages. Beyond the chicken cages were three steel cages, each big enough to hold perhaps two dozen humans.

There were three guards at the door of the cage, none of them in the red and brown livery of Enklar's Prince Gyren. Slavers.

They didn't look evil; they just looked like three swordsmen in iron and brass and leather. Nothing unusual, unless you looked closely at the way one of them narrowed his eyes.

You couldn't always tell evil by looking at it. Maybe that was part of why Gyren of Enkiar kept Enkiar nonpartisan in the war between Home and the Slavers' Guild. Gyren the Neutral, he called himself—proudly, as if there were something to be proud of in being neutral in a fight between Good and Evil.

Well, maybe Good wasn't good all the time. Jason wasn't good, noble, right and proper all the damn time. He'd been a coward once, and been afraid a lot. But at least he didn't own people.

The middle cage was empty, the other two nowhere near capacity. One held perhaps ten glum men, ranging in age from early teens to middle fifties; the other contained five women, all plain and unadorned.

But could any of them be from Kernat village? Jason kicked in his heels and rode over toward the cages, calling out, "Are any of you from Kernat village? Any Biemish among you?"

One of the slavers reached toward the signalling horn at his waist, desisting only when another shook his head. "Ta havath," he said, holding up a palm toward Jason. "You're an Imperial?"

Jason nodded. "By origin, if not profession, at the moment," he said.

Behind him, Daherrin's horse pranced impatiently, snorting. "Ta havath, Taren," the dwarf said. "You're a Home raider these days, not an Imperial." The dwarf eyed the slavers carefully, his broad smile more than vaguely insulting. "My name's Daherrin, slaver. You heard of me?"

The slaver nodded. "I recognized you from descriptions."

The dwarf nodded back. "Then why aren't you sweating like that one is?" he asked, indicating another of the slavers with a jerk of his head. "Or shitting yourself the way your other friend's about to?"

"Because there's nothing to worry about." The slaver smiled back. "Never heard you were stupid, never heard you were stupid enough to start trouble in Enkiar and end up with the city being closed to you." He turned to Jason. "We don't have a problem, young Taren. These aren't Imperials; they're all from the Shattered Islands. I haven't seen any fresh merchandise from Holtun or Bieme for years." His words had the ring of conviction, and none of the sullen slaves seemed to be stifling an objection; possibly he was telling the truth.

Daherrin had been trying to catch Jason's eye, but Jason had been deliberately ignoring him. "Taren," Daherrin said, snapping out the word like a lash. "That's enough."

Jason turned his horse away, the others falling in beside him. "Sorry, Daherrin," he said as soon as he was sure they turned a corner and left the slave markets behind. "But I had to know."

"We can talk about it later," the dwarf said. "Later."
He shrugged. "No, damn it, we can talk about it now.
You don't *ever*," he said, "*ever* go independent on me
again. You're not in charge here; I am. If I'm out of it,
command goes to Falherten, then to Mikyn, then to
Arrikol. You're only in charge if you're all alone 'cause
the three of us are dead."

Jason's ears burned.

"What you just pulled, boy," the dwarf went on, "is
the sort of shit that your father always used to. But he
could get away with it. You're not him. He could have
taken all three of them all by himself; you couldn't."

"So?" Jason couldn't resist protesting. "It was my risk."

"Bullshit," the dwarf said. "Not when you're part of a
team. Part of *my* team. When you do something, you're
counting on the rest of us, just like we're counting on
you. There's plenty of room for independent thought,
but you don't act like you're on your own, 'cause you're
not."

They rode in silence for a minute.

"They're mostly ugly," Mikyn said. "Like usual."

"Eh?"

"I've always heard Walter Slovotsky talk about all the
beautiful women he'd freed."

"There is something to that. Aeia's awful pretty, for a
human," Daherrin put in.

"But most of them look like that," Mikyn said, jerking
his thumb toward the cage. There wasn't a beautiful slave
girl among them; they all looked like overworked domestics.

"Way I understand it," Daherrin said as they rode on,
"ugly humans hurt just as badly as pretty ones." The
dwarf clucked his tongue, once, twice, three times, urging his pony into a faster walk. "Not that there's shit we
can do about it here. Let's go buy some supplies."

*   *   *

It didn't take long to get the oats that they wanted—although Daherrin spent five times as long haggling over prices as Jason would have—and it took much less time to load the sacks of grain onto the bed of the wagon. That would have gone even more quickly if Daherrin had participated, but the raiding team leader didn't always make a practice of dirtying his hands.

The ritual was repeated at each of the stalls. Negotiate, pay and load. First the grains for the animals, and then a few sacks of dried beef and, finally, apples, carrots and turnips for both people and animals.

But, finally, the last copper was exchanged between Daherrin and an apple seller, the last sack opened and examined, the last sample apple removed (via a slit in the bag, from the middle of the bag, while the dealer's back was turned), then peeled, quartered and offered to the dealer, Daherrin seemingly by accident failing to put away the beltknife he'd used for paring the apple, the apple seller biting into the fruit without so much as a surprised glance, perhaps having dealt with a suspicious dwarf before . . . and then, with the apple seller's bite, munch and swallow, they were done.

"So. I guess we head back to camp," Jason said.

"You guess wrong, again. He used to call it 'showing the flag,' " Daherrin said, "even though he didn't like to do it. Scared him as bad as it scares me. Which don't mean shit." He looked Jason over carefully. "You're thinking that I'm about to take a risk, just like you did. The difference between what we're doing now and what you did a while ago is that I'm deciding this. Understood? Calculated risk, not an empty-headed impulse."

"Do what?" Jason asked, as Daherrin levered himself into his saddle and kicked his horse into a canter.

"What we're gonna do now, Taren," the dwarf said. "What I'm gonna do now. Can't let the traditions die."

. . . *With him.* The unspoken words hung in the air

between them. "There's a tavern, over this way," the dwarf said.

Falherten had a bit of trouble getting the flatbed turned around.

The tavern was a one-story wattle-and-daub building, differing from any of the dozen others on the street in, first, the huge pewter tankard, easily a quarter of Jason's height, that hung over the door like a boast, and, secondly, in the persons of the thirty or so soldiers in the livery of Lord Gyren, crowding the street in front of the tavern.

Their leader, a jowly man with a long, oily mustache that curled down the sides of his face and under his chin, held up a restraining hand as Daherrin dismounted, signaling for the others to wait.

Daherrin put an easy grin on his face. "Greetings, Captain . . . ?"

"Asklans. Greetings, Daherrin."

"Oh? We met before?"

The captain nodded. "A few years back. Some of my men and I applied to join the Home raiders. It is perhaps as well you didn't take us; this is working out acceptably. The pay isn't good, but there's less blood. We would like to keep it that way."

"Hey, Fal," the dwarf said, gesturing at Mikyn and Arriken to dismount. "You and Taren watch the wagon. We're gonna to buy the captain an ale or three."

Jason looked at Daherrin. *Relay, please: I'm not going to let you keep me out of things*, he started reflexively, then remembered that Ellegon wasn't close enough.

But the dwarf relented anyway.

"Belay that," Daherrin said. "Taren, you look too thirsty to be standing on the street."

Jason tried to feel at the corners of his mind. Yes, the

dragon was there, if need be, and perhaps was wondering something—perhaps how things were going?

He tried to broadcast a feeling of cautious reassurance, but wasn't sure that he was even capable of feeling that, much less transmitting it. Shrugging, he followed Daherrin into the tavern, Asklans and a half dozen of his soldiers following behind.

There was probably an exception to the rule about taverns looking the same—near as Jason could figure, there were exceptions to all of Slovotsky's Laws—but this one wasn't it: it was a dark and smoky room, too few lanterns sending too much smoke and too little light into the stale air.

It was crowded, too: there were easily forty men sitting on stools around the rough-hewn tables, most of them looking at Daherrin and his three companions, and at the soldiers following them in. Most of them were locals, some in the clean broadcloths of merchants, others in the rough gray tunics, breechclouts, and leggings of peasants, their tunics belted with rope, not sword belts—but a dozen of the men were armed, some with their swords belted on, some with them propped against the walls.

"I smell slavers," the dwarf said, sniffing loudly. "The Slavers' Guild doesn't need to make its members wear uniforms, not when slavers stink up a room."

The room got very quiet, very quickly. At one of the low tables, four peasants looked from one to another, then rose, leaving their ale and bread unfinished as they headed out the door.

One of the slavers reached slowly, carefully toward his sword belt, not pausing when Asklans held up a restraining hand, desisting only when another slaver shook his head twice, quickly, his face expressionless.

Daherrin seated himself at the nearest of the tables, his eyes never leaving the slavers.

The innkeeper—a thickset man with the customary beer belly and big hands—scurried over, wiping his hands on a rag. "Drinks? Or drinks and food?"

"Just ale," the dwarf said. "Four tankards. Go help him pour, Arriken."

"That won't be necessary," Asklans said, taking up a position behind the dwarf. No apparent signal passed from him to his troops, but the six men spread out, two of them taking up parade rest positions in a far corner, two others near the door to the kitchen, the final two walking to stand behind the slavers in the far corner of the room.

Daherrin didn't turn as he answered, "Maybe it isn't." But he didn't say anything to Arriken, who followed the innkeeper into the kitchen, returning with four pewter tankards, each brimming with foam. Arriken sipped each one in turn, setting the first in front of the dwarf, the second in front of Mikyn, the third in front of Jason, and taking the last for himself.

"Drink up, Taren," he said. "If things go to shit, you may as well have a last brew in your belly." He sat down next to the dwarf and gulped his own ale, the foam staining his full lips and beard.

Nobody in the room spoke for a long time, until one of the slavers stood. Daherrin shook his head fractionally, and Mikyn, who had looked as if he were about to launch himself across the table, relaxed to the same degree that Jason did: not much.

Jason didn't like it. Slavers were supposed to look evil—Ahrmin had looked like cruelty incarnate—but this one didn't. He just looked like a normal, twentyish man in the tunic, breechclout and leggings combination that was the common dress in the Eren regions. His sword was at the left side of his waist, the scabbard rigged to keep the hilt canted forward at a comfortable angle for a cross-body draw.

His face wasn't pinched; his eyes weren't sunken hollows. Just a normal-looking brown-haired man, with perhaps a too-easy grin on his broad face. But it wasn't much of a grin.

"Greetings," he said, seating himself opposite Daherrin, Jason and Arriken, both hands on his tankard. "Willem, senior journeyman of the Slavers' Guild. You are?"

"Daherrin," the dwarf said, returning the human's gaze levelly. "Home raiding team leader."

"Arriken, raider," Arriken said.

"Taren, raider," Jason said.

"Death," Mikyn whispered, his voice barely audible.

"Mikyn," the dwarf snapped, "ta havath."

"I'm your death," Mikyn repeated. There was a tight grin on his lips, a smile that wasn't at all reflected in his eyes. "I'm what you see before it all ends for you." He whispered the words gently, almost lovingly.

When just a child, Mikyn and both his parents had been taken by slavers. He and his father had been freed in a raid by the team headed by Karl Cullinane. His mother had never been heard from again.

"*Mikyn*," the dwarf repeated. "ta havath, I said. We're just here to show the flag," he went on in English, "not to get our heads broke in a fight. Ease off, boy."

Mikyn wasn't having any. "Remember me," he whispered. "Always remember me."

There was a metallic taste at the back of Jason's mouth: the taste of bile, the taste of fear. *Ellegon!*

There was no distant reassurance.

Asklans clapped his hands together three times. "So be it. Enough of this; we're not going to have a fight here." He nodded to one of his men, who stuck two fingers in his mouth and gave out a three-part whistle, which was repeated from outside.

Jason, Daherrin, Mikyn and Arriken found themselves quickly surrounded by easily a dozen soldiers, each with a drawn shortsword; across the room, the slavers were similarly surrounded.

"Enkiar is neutral," Asklans said. "Enkiar will remain both neutral and peaceful, if I have to butcher a thousand slavers and raiders. By the authority of Lord Gyren, you both are to leave Enkiar—Daherrin, you and your team will head out in the morning on the Home road; Willem, you will inform Master Lifezh that all of you are to leave tomorrow, heading toward Khar."

"Such was our intention," Willem said. "Such was our intention."

Soldiers began to crowd Daherrin and his group out the front door, while others pushed the slavers toward the back.

Then there was a low cry from one of the peasants in the dark of the room. "The warrior lives," the harsh voice whispered. "The warrior lives."

Jason couldn't see who said it, but he did catch a glimpse of Willem's face before the soldiers pushed him out the door.

The slaver's face was white.

The warrior lives? What did that mean? And why should it scare the slavers so badly?

"You'll be on your way by sunset," Asklans said. "By sunset, do you hear?"

"We hear," Daherrin said. "I'm not sure we understand everything, but we hear."

CHAPTER 10

Farewells

"My idea of an agreeable person," said Hugo Bohun, "is a person who agrees with me."

—Benjamin Disraeli

Arguing is one of life's greatest pleasures, even if you have to argue with yourself. 'Course, I could enjoy the other side of that argument, too.

—Walter Slovotsky

There's no enemy in range; I'm coming in.

Ellegon swooped down out of the late afternoon sky, the backblast from his fast-moving wings drawing nervous neighs from the horses and sending sparks from the dying campfires swirling off into the grasses.

That had happened before, and the half dozen of Daherrin's warriors on fire duty were ready for it; five of them stomped out the sparks, while the sixth wielded a canteen, for insurance.

The dozen Enkiaran soldiers down by the road had good discipline: although several of the horses pranced their nervousness, none of the horsemen let his mount get away from him. Enkiar's neutrality apparently applied to nonhostile dragons, too.

As long as none of them have dragonbane on their bolts, Ellegon said nervously.

I would have assumed you mindprobed them.

*Assume all you want. All I can tell is that none of them *knows* he has a poisoned bolt. I doubt that would do me a lot of good if their fletcher's primed one without telling them. Let's get in the air. Now.*

Durine was already tightening the dragon's rigging and helping first Aeia, then Bren Adahan into their places.

I'll be just a minute.

While the others got aboard, Jason took a moment to brace Daherrin. "What was that about a warrior living?"

"Who knows?" The dwarf shrugged. "Wouldn't make too much of that. Probably another freelancer put a scare into them, even if they have been scarce for the past few years. If so, he'll—most likely show up at Home, sooner or later."

Mikyn led his horse over. "I don't know about that. What say you send somebody on their trail to find out?"

The dwarf shook his head. "No. Just no. There's a full hundred slavers, and I don't like those odds at all."

"Then make it just me," Mikyn said. There was a strange note in his voice, a suggestion of something that could have been resolve, could have been fear. "I have to."

"No," the dwarf said. "The bastards've gotten better over the past coupla years—they been putting rear guards on their backtrail more often than not."

"Then set me up as a roving tradesman—we've got the traveling farrier outfit all ready to go—and let me go."

"Shit, Mikyn, we discussed this a tenday ago, and you said then that the traveling farrier disguise is wearing a bit thin, and—"

"Mikyn," Jason said, "what is it?" Jason had thought at first that Mikyn had just been trying to spook the slaver, but there was more to it than that.

"I remember the voice. It was his voice. When we were sold. I heard his voice."

The dwarf snorted. "Not bloody likely. That was twenty years ago; he ain't a lot older'n you."

"Then it's a brother, or a son, or a fucking *cousin*, or it's one of the bastards that just happens to sound like the one who. . . ." Mikyn's fists clenched. "But he's *mine*. You hear me, Daherrin? He's mine. You're right: the team can't take their trail. But I can."

Jason, we have to go now.

Just a moment. "Daherrin, it's your team, and I wouldn't think of interfering with how you run it . . ."

"Right." The dwarf actually laughed. "The usual Cullinane opening to interfering with how I run the company. You think he should go get his liver sliced open?"

"No. I don't think you should let him go. Not unless you want to, upon reconsideration." *Relay, please: but I think he will, no matter what you do, and you're better off giving your blessing than having a deserter gone in the night.* "And unless Mikyn promises to keep his head down. My father took out a lot of slavers when he died."

"He did, at that," Mikyn said, a thin smile peeking through his beard.

"But we'd all be better off if he'd lived." Jason gripped Mikyn's shoulder tightly. "All of us would be."

Mikyn hesitated, then nodded fractionally.

He's still going to go. But the dwarf says: 'Okay, kid. Get going; I'll pretend to think about it, and then let him slip away tonight, after we're moving.'

"Take care, Jason." Daherrin clasped Jason's hand.

"Hey, I know you're planning on settling down after this, but if you ever change your mind, I've got a job for you. Pay's low, and the working conditions range from bad to terrible, but at least the food sucks."

CHAPTER 11

Wehnest

Lord, give me the wisdom to distinguish between unnecessary brutality and brutal necessity. At least some of the time.

—David Warcinsky

Probably the most difficult decision real humans have to make is whether something is necessarily brutal or unnecessarily brutal. I wish there was something funny about that, but there you have it.

—Walter Slovotsky

Wehnest was usually Ellegon's last stop before Home. Partly it was because it was a solid day's flight from any of several of the usual rendezvous locations; largely it was because there were often extra trade goods remaining after the resupply runs, usually consisting of leftover Nehera-made blades that were marketable anywhere.

This wasn't a usual trip; but they stopped in Wehnest anyway.

* * *

The ground rushed up in the dark, more felt than seen; Ellegon's flailing wings battered the air so hard that Jason couldn't keep his eyes open, but he felt the ground coming up as though it was reaching up to knock them out of the sky, until, at the last moment, their downward momentum slowed and the dragon landed with a thump that rattled Jason's teeth.

Everybody down, the dragon said.

The all alighted in the dark. By arrangement, Tennetty and Durine slipped off into the trees, on watch.

Everyone was silent for a moment, then Ellegon snorted. *We can light a fire; there's nobody around.*

The clearing that Ellegon had chosen was just short of a thinning stand of tall pines and stumps; beyond the trees, a fallow field stood in the starlight, a ragged rug of weeds proclaiming its idleness. Over the rise in the other direction was Wehnest, but it would be safe to start a small fire anyway; the light breeze was blowing steadily into the forest, and the smoke of a fire wouldn't be visible before daybreak, still several hours away.

Jason smiled as they quickly gathered and stacked firewood. At least he wouldn't have to light it. Karl Cullinane had insisted that Jason learn to light a fire with flint and steel—a laborious and downright boring process. Lighting this fire would be easy, what with Ellegon around, but gathering wood took no less time.

I still say you should just skip Wehnest, the dragon said. *The purpose of this trip is to pick up Walter's daughters and wife, not to trade in some blades.*

Aeia stooped over a fallen tree, grabbing an out-thrust branch with one hand and neatly detaching it from the tree trunk with three quick chops of her hatchet. "The trouble with that is that we're doing more than one thing," she said. "We're also checking into the Kernat raid."

Jason dropped an armload of wood on the charred spot

near the center of the clearing. Aeia was right, as usual. Still, the chances of learning anything in Wehnest were minimal; Wehnest was one of Home's main trading partners, and likely the ground had been gone over repeatedly by Home traders.

But the difference between likely and certain was important; Jason would probably never learn what had happened to the people who disappeared from Kernat village, but he had to try. It came with the job.

As defined by your father, the dragon said. *Not every ruler thinks he has to look into everything himself.*

Firstly, it wasn't everything. Karl Cullinane had felt perfectly comfortable in sending Danagar, General Garavar's son, out spying—about this very matter, in fact.

But, secondly, Karl Cullinane had established the point that the Emperor of Holtun-Bieme wasn't going to be afraid to get his hands dirty, and that was rubbing off, much to the better. Bren Adahan was along on this trip only partly to chase after Aeia; he'd long since accepted Karl's notion that a ruler was supposed to be in contact with the world, not sitting in a castle in luxurious isolation.

Thomen Furnael had picked up on that, too, Jason thought with a smile. Although the last time Thomen had tried something clever, Father had sent him home with a groin kick that Gashier had described in glorious detail. The kick had been to teach Thomen another lesson: opposing Karl Cullinane wasn't a good idea.

All that's true, the dragon said. *But I don't have to like it. Getting too involved with the world is what got him killed. You Cullinanes aren't unkillable, you know.*

That was true enough. Although . . . there had been a time when it had been thought that Karl Cullinane was unkillable, that nobody could take him on. There were legends that had grown up around Jason's father, about the time that he had single-handedly freed his wife-to-be from a thousand slavers.

And, like all legends, there was a germ of truth in that: Karl Cullinane had freed Andrea. But it had been from a scant dozen slavers, and Walter Slovotsky had been along, softening them up with several crossbow bolts fired out of the night.

Filling a legend's boots was going to be hard. Piling firewood for Ellegon was a lot easier.

"I think that's about enough," Jason said, dropping a final armload on the pile. He stood back. Ellegon's cavernous mouth opened fractionally, and then a quick tongue of flame issued forth.

The wood only broke into a smoky smoulder; Ellegon tried again.

*It's too *damp*,* the dragon said with a petulant sniff. He raised his head again and exhaled a huge mouthful of flame that not only set the stacked firewood burning, but sent flaming embers shooting off into the night, some of them threatening to start minor fires which could, if unchecked, quickly grow into a major blaze.

Aeia stomped out one incipient ember; Kethol and Durine, both giggling incongruously, pissed on a second and third, while Jason ground out a fourth.

Nice going, Ellegon, he thought.

*I can't control *everything*,* the dragon said.

Still, it did make a good campfire.

Tennetty and Durine had first watch; Jason slept like a dead man.

The first thing to do the next morning was to head into Wehnest and get some horses. While Wehnest was smaller than, say, Biemestren, it was spread out, and some of the places Jason wanted to go to were a fair walk from each other.

Besides, it gave him the chance to look up a friend. Of sorts.

Pistols close at hand but not in evidence, Tennetty,

Kethol and Durine spread out, watching the street, while Jason, Bren Adahan and Aeia walked up to the stables.

He heard a distant mental question from Ellegon, and sent back reassurance. Everything was fine. The stables were better kept than they'd been the last time he was here; the straw covering the dirt floor was freshly changed, and while the place reeked of horse piss and horse shit, most of it seemed to emanate from the exercise yard outside, not the stables themselves.

The hostler was bent over, busy examining the left front hoof of a small brown mare.

"I'll need the use of half a dozen horses for two or three days," Jason said, slapping a silverpiece on the railpost. It rang brightly, a musical tone that announced that it was too much money by an order of magnitude.

The hostler, surprised, dropped the hoof and straightened, looking him in the face.

He was a short, fat, bald man whose eyes held traces of fear and pettiness, perhaps, but no cruelty. Or maybe Jason was just projecting; he had reason to know that the man wasn't cruel, was in fact more softhearted and sentimental than a hostler, or anyone else in this world, had any business being.

Maybe.

"*Taren*," Vator the hostler exclaimed. A smile broke across his face. "Taren, boy," he said, clapping his hands to Jason's shoulders. "Or should it be Jason?"

Bren Adahan stiffened, but Jason held up a hand. There was no reason to worry. Jason had fled as word spread that Karl Cullinane's son was on his own in the Eren regions, alone and vulnerable. He hadn't expected his cover to fool Vator then, and he certainly hadn't expected the cover to be intact by now.

As Walter Slovotsky would have said, you can't be just a little bit exposed.

Jason eased his rucksack from his shoulders and then,

practiced fingers undoing the knots in the leather draw-string, drew out a winesack.

"A drink for luck," he said, straightening, uncorking it. "Jason Cullinane, heir to crown and throne of Holtun-Bieme, wishes you well." He tilted back the skin. He hadn't drunk out of a wineskin for too long; some of the lukewarm liquid ran down the side of his cheek, down his neck, into his tunic. He handed the skin to Vator.

"Vator, the hostler, of Wehnest, wishes you well," Expertly the fat man tilted back the wine, then handed it to Aeia and Bren Adahan, who introduced themselves and drank.

"Now," the hostler said, "you want some horses?"

Jason nodded. "And saddles. Just for two days, maybe three," he lied reflexively. It would be one day at most, that was all the time they'd need, but it made sense to let even someone as trustworthy as Vator think that there was plenty of time to arrange a betrayal.

The hostler nodded. "The silverpiece will be fine," he said, tiredly, as though announcing his resignation to a long session of bargaining.

"Agreed," Jason said.

The hostler looked every bit as disappointed as surprised, but he turned to the stables, calling out, "Gachet, Gachet, where are you? Are you sleeping again?"

"No, master, no I'm not," floated down from the hayloft. "I was just cleaning up here."

"I should flay you within a handbreadth of your life, but just saddle six of our best—yes, yes, the white gelding, I said the best, didn't I?—just saddle six of the best and I'll forget it all, I'll forget it all."

A man in a ragged tunic and black iron collar clambered down from the hayloft and disappeared into the stables.

Jason felt the smile fade from his face; he looked the hostler over coldly.

Vator seemed taken aback for a moment, but then he shrugged.

He didn't have any reason to be afraid; while Home warriors were almost always willing to take on slavers, slave-owners were a different matter. Home couldn't afford to take on every slave-owner in the Eren regions; the policy was to not free slaves in the hands of private parties, unless the private parties were acting on behalf of the guild.

Aeia's smile seemed genuine. "Jason never mentioned that you were doing so well when he was through here."

Vator smiled weakly. "I arranged a trade, when some guildsmen came through here, looking for the boy from Home. I gave them his direction and they gave me a slave. An acceptable deal, eh? Of course, there was the problem of telling them where you'd gone. I had no intention of putting them actually on your trail, so I sent them toward the Healing Hand Tabernacle."

"Which is where I told you I was going," Jason said.

"Yes, yes," Vator said, with a nod, "but I knew you were lying." He gripped Jason's hand tightly. "I'd not betray you, Jason, then or now. —Let me help Gachet saddle your horses."

Their first concern had been the possibility of slavers in town, but there weren't any; the slave trade was at a virtual standstill around Wehnest, as the cost of hiring labor was so much lower than buying it.

And, since there was no sign of fresh slaves, there was therefore no sign of any slaves who had been taken in the Kernat village raid. That part of the mission was, so far, a failure.

Still, the Nehera blades had gone for a nice price, Jason thought, hefting the small bag of silver and listening to the coins tinkle pleasantly. He'd have to tell Nehera first off, once they got to Home; the dwarf would be pleased that authentic Nehera blades were still so valuable.

"It could be Ahrmin," Durine mused. "He was always tricky."

"If that little bastard was behind the Kernat raid," Tennetty said, the index and middle fingers of her free hand drumming a random tattoo on the front peak of her saddle, "it's not impossible that the people they seized were simply killed."

"Then why take them at all?" Kethol asked.

Jason nodded. That didn't make sense either. There was some Other Sider's principle that Walter Slovotsky had told him about, something about not making explanations any more complicated than necessary to fit the facts. Somebody's . . . knife, was it? No, not knife. But something similar. Knife, blade, sword, dagger, razor, cleaver. Cleaver. That sounded familiar. Beaver's Cleaver —that sounded about right.

"We don't get to understand it all," he said, as they rode back to the corral outside Vator's stables, dismounting one by one.

Gachet, Vator's slave, ran to take their reins and led three of the animals into the corral while Jason, Aeia and Bren Adahan led their own horses.

Jason's skin crawled. He hadn't had much experience around slaves—the only kind of slaves in Home and Holtun-Bieme were *former* slaves—and he didn't like it much. He remembered the Slavers' Guildhall in Pandath-away, and the crack of whips and parting of flesh.

Inside the corral he let the reins drop and dismissed the horse with a light slap on its solid flank. Not quite the animal that Jason's big gelding, Libertarian, had been— but not a bad mount, at least for the day.

The slave led the horse away.

Slave. . . .

Jason's fist clenched.

Jason. The distant voice held concern and alarm.

I'm fine, he sent back.

There was nothing he could do about it, then or now. Wehnest was neutral, and there were no slavers here; he could hardly take Gachet away from Vator.

That was the trouble, he thought, as Vator walked over to him, concern creasing his sweating brow. "Is there a problem, Jason Cullinane?" the hostler asked.

Beyond Vator, a few children and an overweight, stooped woman were working in the stables. The woman mucked out one of the stalls while one of the children brought fresh hay for the horses and another helped Gachet unsaddle and wipe down the horses.

It wasn't the same thing as in Pandathaway, Jason thought. Vator was the sort who would threaten to beat the slave within an inch of his life, but he wouldn't do it. He didn't mean it. Vator's wife and children probably worked every bit as hard as Gachet, and Vator himself surely worked harder.

"Gachet," Jason heard himself saying, "do you want to be free?"

The slave paled. He looked from Vator to Jason, then opened his mouth, closed it, opened it again, and then closed it again.

Over in the stables, the woman bent down to whisper to one of the boys, who took off down the road behind the exercise yard, bare feet pounding on the bare dirt.

Kethol looked over to Jason, as if to ask, *Do I chase him?*

"It's your play," Tennetty said. "Call it, Jason."

Durine looked from Jason to Tennetty to Kethol, and then nodded.

Bren Adahan took a step toward Jason, but stopped when Aeia grabbed his arm. "Leave it be," she said. "Pick us up, and hurry," Aeia muttered.

Don't do anything stupid, the distant voice said. *I'm on my way.*

Vator faced him. "There's no glory to be won here, Jason Cullinane, unless you can find some honor in six of you cutting down one unarmed man." He spat on the ground between them.

"Perhaps we don't have to do anything to the one unarmed man," Bren Adahan said. "Perhaps you will simply free Gachet of your own will."

For a moment, just a moment, Jason thought Vator was going to back down. It would have been the logical, the reasonable thing to do. Resisting didn't make sense; they had him outmanned, and Vator was no warrior.

"You'll not take what's mine, Jason Cullinane," Vator whispered. He had a knife in his belt; anyone who works around horses and stables finds a hundred daily uses for a knife. His hand dropped to its hilt.

Tennetty cocked a pistol with an emphatic click. "Don't even think about it." She extended the pistol and sighted down her arm.

"Lower your gun, Tennetty," Jason said. He was the center of everything, but he couldn't hold it all together. It was all falling apart, and there was nothing he could do about it.

Except try for a way out.

Come pick us up, and hurry.

Hang on, please, the distant voice said. *Just a few more moments.*

"Sure, I'll put the gun down. Soon as you draw your sword. I'm not going to have to tell your mother that I let him stab you to death while you stood there with a scabbarded sword."

"She's right, sir," Durine said. "Get your blade out. Please."

Compromise. There had to be a compromise.

Jason drew his sword. "Change your mind, Vator. Let him go, of your own free will."

"Go into the stables, Gachet," Vator said quietly, his eyes never leaving Jason's.

"As you are," Bren Adahan said, as he and Aeia each took one of the slave's arms; Gachet didn't resist as they moved him away.

"Dur—around the other side," Kethol said, breaking into a sprint for the stables. He came out a moment later; dragging Vator's wife by one arm and holding a crossbow in his free hand. "She was trying to load this."

Vator's eyes never left Jason's as a dark form rose above the trees. With a flurry of wings and a gout of flame, Ellegon's massive form appeared over the stables and hovered momentarily, sending dust and leaves swirling into the air before the dragon dropped heavily to the ground.

Vator's wife screamed; tearing her arm loose from Kethol's grasp, she fled for the stables.

Let him go, Vator, the dragon said. *There's no shame in being defeated by an overwhelming force.*

Vator's eyes never left Jason's. "You'll not take what's mine."

"Get aboard, everyone," Jason said, "Kethol, help Gachet get aboard."

"Let's move it, people," Tennetty said. "I can hear the hoofbeats from down the road, and even if they don't have dragonbaned arrows, my hide isn't as thick as Ellegon's."

Vator shook his head. "Not this time, Jason Cullinane. Not this time." He drew his knife and lunged at Jason.

"No!"

Two guns fired at once. One bullet missed entirely, another smashed into Vator's knee. The fat hostler opened his mouth to scream, but the blade of a thrown knife flew past his lips, becoming a hideous metal tongue.

The hostler fell dead at Jason's feet. A stench rose into the air as his body voided itself, leaving him without dignity even in death.

There was no need for it. Jason might not have been the swordsman his father had been, but even Jason could take on an overweight hostler wielding a utility knife. It wasn't necessary.

We have to get going, the dragon said. Tennetty scabbarded his sword, and then Durine half-helped, half-carried Jason up to his seat.

Fasten yourself in. Now.

Distant fingers buckled him into place.

"Let's get out of here, Ellegon," Tennetty said.

Wings flapping madly, the dragon leaped into the sky. Gachet screeched as the ground dropped away, stopping when Tennetty told him to shut up.

Below, a young boy, standing over the dead body of his father, looked up into the sky.

They flew in silence for a few moments, until Tennetty snorted, briefly. It could have been a laugh.

"What's so funny?" Aeia asked, her irritation audible.

Tennetty sighed. "Reminds me of the old days, that's all. Just remembering something the dwarf once said in the old days, about how we seem to leave most towns just ahead of the cops."

CHAPTER 12

Home, At Last

I judge impetuosity to be better than caution.
                                              —Niccoló Machiavelli

Niccoló Machiavelli was an asshole.
                                              —Walter Slovotsky

It was sundown when they landed in the front yard of the New House, the house where Jason had spent most of his time growing up, before the move to Biemestren.

As they circled in, a crowd of people gathered below, their elongated shadows playing across the grass: a few warriors from Frandred's team; some farmers in from their fields on business; Petros, the deputy mayor; and Lou Riccetti. The Engineer was grim as death as he stood, fingers twining impatiently, thin lips pursed perhaps in sorrow, perhaps in irritation.

There's news, the dragon said as he *thunk*ed to the ground. Ellegon's mental voice held a quaver of excitement. *About your father.*

"Jason," Lou Riccetti said, "quickly: how many did you leave behind you in Melawei?"

"Two. Ahira and Walter Slovotsky."

"Then," Lou Riccetti said, choosing this words slowly, carefully, "I think your father might be alive. I may have a lead on where he is. Come with me inside; we've got to talk to Aldren."

CHAPTER 13

"All Men Are Created Equal . . ."

We boast our emancipation from many superstitions; but if we have broken any idols, it is through a transfer of idolatry.

—Ralph Waldo Emerson

I find that we all get more legendary as time goes by. "Legend" means, basically, "bullshit."

—Walter Slovotsky

A trader had brought word of Karl Cullinane's death just the tenday before.

Lou hadn't been sure whether or not to believe it.

Then Aldren came Home.

"As far as I know, I was the last one out searching for you," Aldren said as they sat in the living room of the New House. "I was posing as a mercenary soldier looking for work." He sat back in the big leather chair next to the fireplace and drank more from his big pewter tankard of ale. In the light of the crackling fire, he looked ordinary enough: fortyish, gray hairs streaking a roughly-cut brown beard, a few scars on his hand and a few laugh lines around his eyes. "I must have hit Pandathaway about three tendays after you all left; and I figured that if you'd gotten as far as Pandathaway by the time Ahrmin left, you'd likely be chasing after Karl.

"Which, it seemed to me, made the search for you pointless. But, just in case, I headed north, up the coast, on the grounds that it might be a good idea to scout out Guild strengths in some of the coastal cities; we don't like to work that close to Pandathaway, but maybe we're going to have to, way pickings have been.

"In any case, I found that there were fewer guildsmen around than there ought to have been—skeleton crews everywhere, and they looked scared."

He drained his ale and signaled for more; Riccetti himself refilled it from the hogshead in the corner.

"I'm not the best swordsman around, and I'm not too good with a gun. But there's two things I'm real good at: I can blend into the furniture, and I can drink any two men under the table. I got a couple of them drinking, and then drunk. And they started talking.

"Seems that Ahrmin and all of his shorebound force died in Melawei."

That didn't surprise Jason; Walter Slovotsky had said that he wouldn't let anyone kill Karl Cullinane and live to brag about it.

"When their relief force got there, they were stinking in the sun. And there was a note left behind, pinned to one of the corpses, part of it in a language that the slavers didn't understand and part of it in Erendra. There were three signatures to the note. The part in Erendra read: *The warrior lives.*

"Scared the shit out of the slavers, but what could they do?"

Jason swallowed. *The warrior lives.* The same thing

somebody had said in the Enkiar tavern. He walked to the mantelpiece and ran his fingers along it, the heat from the fire beating against his legs, even through his trousers.

Outside, leathery wings rustled in the night.

What do you think?

I don't know. What do you think?

There was no answer as Aldren went on: "Then, about six tendays ago, a guildsman in Lundeyll woke up next to one with his throat cut. Another note, also with three signatures. The word is that a dozen men, several of them Mels—but not all of them—caught a ship out of there the next morning, just ahead of Lord Lund's proctors."

"Shit." Tennetty slapped her hand down on the arm of her chair and laughed. "He could be alive. Leaving town just ahead of trouble is the Cullinane family trademark, Jason."

Lou Riccetti's smile and nod were distant. "Lundeyll was the first town we fled from, on This Side." His smile vanished; he shook his head. "Your namesake died there," he told Jason. "He was my best friend." Riccetti bit his lip. "I'm sorry—go on, Aldren."

"Another note, also with three signatures." Aldren reached for a map. "In Wehnest, on the way back, I picked up news that it's happened again, on Menelet. In any case, the slavers believe that your father and his two comrades are somewhere in the Shattered Islands, or maybe on Salket. Every guildsman is either hunkering down, hoping they'll hit somewhere else, or trying to hunt them down."

Lou Riccetti leaned forward. "Aldren just got in yesterday. I was putting together a team to go hunting for them, too. But your arrival suggests another idea."

Kethol nodded. "With Ellegon to place us, we've got a

good chance of getting to them before the slavers do, particularly if we can figure out where they'll hit next."

Thanks for the vote of confidence. But it all depends on where they're going to hit next, and on how well we can guess.

Aeia smiled. Jason had to admit that his adopted sister was lovely when she smiled. "We know where they're going," she said. "Just draw a line. They're headed for Endell. Probably Ahira's idea; when they get close to dwarvish territory, they'll be safe. If the slavers don't catch up with them or cut them off first."

That seems to be generally true, but I doubt that Karl or Walter are going to draw a straight line for the slavers to follow.

"We have to know." Jason began to pace back and forth. "We have to tie it all down, and quickly."

Lou Riccetti raised an eyebrow. "Before the slavers get to them?"

"It's not that." Jason dropped heavily into his chair. It was like ripples on a pond, like the skipped stones. When Jason was a boy, his father had little time to play with him, and after they moved to Holtun-Bieme, that time had dropped off to virtually nothing.

But he remembered a day, when they were back visiting Home on some business, and an evening, as the sun set, when his father took him down to the lake and taught him how to skip a stone across the water. The trick was to pick the right stone, to curl your index finger around it, then throw it sidearm, just right, and it would bounce five, six, seven times across the still, flat water, each bounce sending out a circular, expanding ripple.

Word that Karl Cullinane was alive was spreading after the strikes, like the splashes of the stone that day.

"If he's alive, he can handle all the slavers in the world," Jason said. "It's not that; we have to nail this down, tight, before word of this reaches my mother."

He stood. "My father's death hit her hard." *Harder than any of you know, or are going to know.* "I won't have her hopes raised and then dashed. We have to settle all this and get back to Biemestren before word reaches Holtun-Bieme. We find out if my father's really alive, and we find out fast."

Ellegon spoke up. *I can drop you off along the coast and rendezvous later, but I have a run that can't wait forever. Daven's team is not going to be able to hold out without a resupply.*

And more; Ellegon might be needed to extract Daven's team, a few at a time.

There was another matter. *I want you to check in on my mother, and stay with her if necessary.*

Doria was a good—Doria *had been* a good healer, but she wasn't a healer anymore, and she couldn't read minds.

True. But I don't like picking her brains. It's not like with you.

Do it anyway.

Still, it shouldn't take many of them. They had more of a Walter Slovotsky job than a Karl Cullinane one: Locate, find, make contact and extract. Get them to a rendezvous with the dragon and get them all out. And back to Biemestren.

"Best to start from the other end," Tennetty said. "Endell; work our way south, hoping that we don't pass them by, or if we do, that we pick up a live trail."

Kethol nodded. "Just you, with Durine and me to keep an eye on your back. Small and fast. We find them, rendezvous with Ellegon and lift out."

"And me," Tennetty said, quietly. "You can't leave me behind. Not for this."

"And Tennetty," Durine said. He studied her with a curious intensity. "But that's all."

Lou Riccetti nodded. "That makes sense. Take tomorrow to rest up—there's some things I want to get ready for you—and you can leave the day after."

"No," Aeia said. "That is not all. I have to know. I have to go. He's my father, too," Aeia said. "Or isn't my blood Cullinane enough for you?"

"*Definitely* not." Lou Riccetti shook his head. "Not you, Aeia. You have to stay here. You're needed; the matter is closed."

As she opened her mouth, he raised a palm. "I can't—force you to stay here. But Ellegon won't carry you into danger—not this time. Until it's proven otherwise, we have to hope that Karl is alive, but assume he's dead. If Jason's going into harm's way to find him, then we have to consider who the Cullinane heir is. You think Andrea's likely to have any more children?"

Aeia shook her head.

"Then who else will produce the Cullinane heir, if Jason doesn't come back? Which is why you stay, too, Bren Adahan."

For a moment, Jason thought that Lou Riccetti was going to prevail, but then Bren Adahan shook his head.

"You may be correct, Mr. Mayor," he said slowly, choosing his words carefully, like a man picking his way barefoot across sharp stones, "that, if Jason dies, the Cullinane heir has to come from her womb—but I don't have to be the father. I would not be the father. I'm still a Holt. The Biemish barons would not stand for the father of the Heir being a Holt, or the son of a Holt." His fists clenched. "While I resent these private matters becoming subjects for public comment, let me point out to you that my only chance at having Aeia for my wife is to keep Jason Cullinane from getting killed. He will *stay* alive." His fingers curled around the arm of his chair, their knuckles white.

He looked Jason square in the face. "Which is why I

am coming along, Jason Cullinane. I will see to it that you stay alive, no matter what it takes."

Tennetty stood. "Everybody drink up, then hit the sheets. Tomorrow, we pack; we leave the day after."

Jason couldn't sleep. It would have been nice if there was somebody to hold his hand while he slept, but there wasn't, not anymore. Valeran was dead, and so was Chak. Mother was too dependent on him, even if she didn't know it. Doria wasn't here, and Karl Cullinane was dead.

Maybe. Maybe not.

Everybody died on him. Chak, Valeran, Father, even Vator. The bastard. Why did he have to die in a fight over a slave? Was it worth his life?

Shit. It just didn't make any sense. None of it made sense.

Jason sat in a weathered wooden chair on the porch of the New House, carving idly at a scrap of pine and staring out at the starlight, watching the slow pulse of faerie lights off to the west. Somewhere in the distance, dicalas chittered in the trees.

A dark shape passed overhead: Ellegon on the last leg of a patrol. The wards around the valley prevented anyone from bringing in magical implements, but couldn't react to creatures unencumbered by spells. While the dragon spent little time here these days, the resident raiders appreciated being able to reduce the guard on those few days when he was around. A night's sleep was a precious thing.

Are you out there? That didn't make any sense, either. If Karl Cullinane was alive, nothing in the world would have kept him from his wife. If he was alive, what were Walter Slovotsky and the dwarf up to? Sure, it made sense to prevent the slavers from returning to Pandathaway to brag of having seen Karl Cullinane's dead body—but they couldn't possibly be counting on maintaining that kind of deception. The word would eventually get out.

But maybe he wasn't dead. Jason hadn't actually seen his father die; all that any of them had seen was a wounded Karl Cullinane leaving them behind, and then an explosion.

Could he have triggered the explosion from far enough away to have survived it?

It wasn't impossible. Or was it?

He could be alive. In which case Jason wasn't going to have to take the crown, not yet.

That felt good. As if a weight had been lifted from his shoulders. Or as if, maybe, a weight was now being lifted; he couldn't tell, yet.

But it felt good.

The door behind him yawned open, light splashing through and pushing the edges of darkness away, although only a little. Jason turned to see Lou Riccetti, an undyed cotton robe belted tightly over a pair of Home jeans, a pair of wooden clogs on his feet. Riccetti had a wooden box and a mottled glass bottle under one arm; in his other hand he held a lantern. He set the lantern on a table.

"What are you doing up at this hour?" Jason asked.

"I was going to ask you that." Riccetti chuckled. "You should go to bed." He pulled out the bottle's wooden stopper with his teeth, then spat the stopper carefully onto the tabletop. He set the box on the table at Jason's elbow. "Maybe some of the Best will help." He tilted back the bottle, wiped his mouth with the back of his hand, then handed the bottle to Jason.

Jason sipped the fiery liquor out of politeness. It tasted horrible—but then again, he'd never developed the Other Siders' taste for corn whiskey. No, that wasn't fair. It wasn't just the Other Siders; Home was doing a modest trade in Riccetti's Best, although other distillers were springing up all across the Eren regions and into the dwarvish north and elvish east.

They sat in silence for a few minutes, passing the bottle back and forth.

"The council wants me to talk you out of doing business with the elves over powder," Jason said. "But will you listen to me?"

"I will listen, but I'll do what I think best. Don't count on persuading me." Riccetti shook his head. "You don't have the information I do. Or the feel for what happens next."

"You sound almost like Doria," Jason said, chuckling.

Riccetti laughed. "Maybe I do. Been a long time since I've seen her. When you get back, tell her I want a visit. Maybe she could bring your mother, and whenever Slovotsky shows up, we could all play some bridge."

My father played bridge, too. It was one of the Other Side innovations that just hadn't caught on. Like the shower.

"About the powder. . . ."

"Yeah. The powder." Riccetti opened the box and pulled out a small leather pouch. He opened it and tilted half a dozen tiny brass buttons onto the table. "Step the next. We strip the frizzen and pan off the long rifles and put on a metal nipple leading into the end of the barrel. Then modify the hammer to snap down tightly over the nipple. Nehera can do ten a day; lesser blacksmiths can do at least four or five.

"Come here." He picked up one of the buttons and walked a few paces off the porch and down to the first flat stone in the walk. He set the button down carefully on the stone. "Give me your knife."

"Eh?"

"Your knife, your knife."

Jason drew his beltknife and handed it over properly, hilt first.

The older man squatted in front of the stone. Taking careful aim with the hilt, he slammed it squarely down on the metal button. It flashed into a quiet snap of flame and a small puff of smoke that shattered in the light breeze.

"Primer. Hit it hard enough, it flashes into fire. Just like the priming powder in the pan."

They returned to the porch and sat back down, Riccetti laying Jason's knife down on the table.

Jason picked it up gingerly. The metal was blackened where Riccetti had struck the primer cap, but the carbon rubbed off on his thumb.

"Advantages: no hangfire; reloading goes a bit more quickly. Also more reliable—no more worry about breaking flints. That's what we do as soon as is politic, after we sell the secret of powder-making to the elves."

It made sense. Just stay a pace or two ahead of everyone else . . . but Jason still didn't like it. Eventually, the Nyphs could end up with guns. The barons wouldn't like that. And justifiably so.

"Not enough of a step?" Riccetti said. "You're right. I have a present for you." He tapped his fingers on the box. "This was going to be for your father, but I guess you inherit it, too." He opened the box. Inside was a plain leather holster, rigged in a peculiar way. Riccetti set it aside.

In the light of the lamp, the two nested guns looked strange, but even more strangely deadly. The pistols had unusually long barrels, but there was some sort of cylindrical thing over the trigger, where the frizzen and pan were supposed to be. The pistols were encircled by a square of brass pegs mounted in holes in the box.

Riccetti picked up one of the pistols and quickly did something with his hands that made the pistol click and the cylinder swing out to one side. "It's modeled on the old Colt Peacemaker—but I'm a better engineer than old

Sam Colt," he said. Jason wasn't sure how much the Engineer was talking to him and how much he was talking to himself.

"These are called cartridges," Riccetti said, pulling out one of the brass pegs. "Everything in one—bullet here. resting on charge, inside here, primer cap here." He tapped the gray tip of the . . . cartridge. There was a hole in it, like the head of a penis. "I've drilled about halfway through the bullet. When this hits meat it expands, mushrooms almost like it's exploding. It *will* do damage."

He worked the pistol; the cylinder slipped to one side. Riccetti slid the cartridge into a hole in the cylinder. "Fits in here like so," he said, tilting the weapon up, letting the cartridge fall back into his palm. "Six holes; six cartridges," he said, fitting five of them in, "but carry it with an empty chamber here, under the hammer. Don't want it going off when your horse takes a bouncy step."

He tilted the weapon back; the five cartridges slipped back into his palm, looking oddly innocuous and even pretty in the lamplight. "Save your brass. We can reload it here, if it's not too badly bashed up—and if it is, we can always use some scrap. If a bullet misfires, drop it to the ground and bury it shallowly, with the toe of your boot. Don't pick it up."

He snapped the empty barrel back into the gun and pointed the weapon out into the night. "You can pull the hammer back like this," he said, thumbing it back until it locked into place with a solid click. "The empty chamber under the hammer rotates out of the way, bringing a cartridge into line. Then fire slowly, squeeze carefully— it's easier than what you're used to; there's no perceptible hangfire." Riccetti smiled, lowering the hammer carefully.

"Or you can just pull back on the trigger. Double action, it's called."

The hammer rose, then snapped down. "Hammer rises, then falls. Hammer hits firing pin, pin hits primer, primer fires charge, charge shoots bullet. Different gunpowder—different principle. And when we sell the secret of the old stuff to the elves, it won't teach them how to make this kind—or how to make it safe when you do. But Ranella and I can do it."

Jason smiled. "I don't even know how the old gunpowder is made." It was something he'd have to be trusted with eventually, but certainly not until he took the crown.

Riccetti ignored him. "You'll find it smokes a whole lot less than you're used to. Smells different; not as much like the fires of hell. In any case, you pull the trigger again and the cylinder turns, bringing a new cartridge into line. Hammer hits firing pin, pin hits primer, primer fires charge, charge shoots bullet." He dry-fired four more times, quickly.

"Like five pistols in one," Jason said.

Lou Riccetti smiled. "Or better." He picked up a thin, flat, round piece of steel, about half again the diameter of a Biemish copper mark, but perhaps a fifth as thick, and fitted six cartridges snugly into it. He snapped a cover over the primer end of the cartridges, holding them tightly into place. "Break open the cylinder, like so, dump out your old brass and slip this in, tight." He snapped the cylinder closed; the cover went flying to the ground. "Loaded again. Fire six times more; repeat as necessary. Strip off your tunic."

"Eh?"

"Get to your feet," Riccetti said, doing just that. He picked up the holster. "Strip off your tunic."

Jason did just that, and Riccetti helped him shrug into the holster. "The rig fits around your back, regardless. It can go on over the tunic—a good idea, if you're wearing a cloak or coat over the tunic—or under, like this." He handed the gun to Jason; Jason slipped it into the holster.

It slid almost under his arm, but not quite, and hung with a comforting weight. The butt was canted forward far enough for an easy draw with the right hand, and a clumsy one for the left.

Jason reached across his waist to where his swordhilt would have been; the gun didn't interfere with a cross-body draw.

"It won't give you away—as long as you don't show it. A lot of folks carry a hidden knife strapped about there, and more and more slaver pistols are showing up."

He tapped a stubby index finger against the pistol. "Right now there's exactly six of these in existence, and only two thousand rounds of ammunition. In a year, Ranella is going to be making them in quantity in Holtun-Bieme; we'll keep the ammo manufacture here, where I can keep an eye on it. In ten years, not only will every Imperial soldier be equipped with long guns that can fire faster and farther than this pistol, but you'll have a limited number of weapons that can fire more than two hundred rounds per minute. You have the opinion of the Engineer on that." He smiled. "Now, how scared are you of a bunch of elves with single-shot black powder guns?"

Jason didn't like it—damn it, gunpowder was *their* secret, even if he wasn't privy to it yet—but the Engineer wasn't going to be deterred.

"I guess we do it your way," he said.

Riccetti knocked back another hefty gulp of Riccetti's Best. "You guess right, Jason Cullinane. Like your father used to say: 'All men are created equal. Lou Riccetti made them that way.' "

"I . . . don't understand."

Riccetti handed him the bottle. "You will, Jason. You will."

Jason took a sip, and then shrugged. "I'll take your word for it."

"Two more things. If he's alive, you find him and you tell him thanks from me." Riccetti hefted the bottle as though to drink from it, then set it back down on the table. "I don't think I ever got around to saying thanks to the big bastard," he said, shaking his head. "Damn it."

"He knew." *Or knows.* "And the other thing?"

"I'm not a warrior," Riccetti said slowly, deliberately. "I'm very good at what I do, I'm very happy at what I do; I'm as good in my way as your old man was in his.

"But just this once, I wish I was a warrior. So you do it for me. If it can be done—you do it." Riccetti picked up the pistol and placed it in Jason's hand, folding Jason's fingers over it. "This is an iffy sort of thing, but if your dad is dead, and if Slovotsky and the dwarf screwed up and didn't kill the one who got him, and if you get the chance—no heroics; don't get yourself killed—you take this pistol," he said, squeezing tightly, "you walk up to whoever killed him, you stick the barrel in his navel, you say to him, 'Lou Riccetti says hello, asshole,' and then you pull the trigger until all you hear are clicks. You blast his belly out through his fucking spine—you do it for me."

The Engineer's eyes were wet; he turned away.

PART THREE

THE SEARCH

CHAPTER 14

The Test of the Dwarf King

The nobly born must nobly meet his fate.

—Euripides

When the Black Camel comes for me, I'm not going to go kicking and screaming—I am, however, going to try to talk my way out of it. "No, no, you want the other Walter Slovotsky."

—Walter Slovotsky

At the end of the corridor there was another of the peculiar doglegs, this one more difficult than the last. As the passage jogged off to the left, the ceiling inclined sharply downward, leaving a narrow space that took a bit of doing even for a dwarf to fit through. That made it much more awkward for a human: Durine had to leave his weapons with Tennetty and Jason and worm himself through in an awkward half-squat.

Getting in to see King Maherralen of Endell was getting to be a definite pain in the ass, Jason Cullinane decided.

Jason handed Durine's combo belt through, then passed along the big man's shotgun and his own swordbelt. One of his pistols was inside his tunic, a comforting weight; the other, along with the gear that they had left behind, was outside the main entrance to the old warrens, under the watchful gaze of Ellegon, Bren Adahan and Kethol.

As Bren Adahan had put it, the locals were moderately friendly allies, but there was little point in tempting either their friendliness or their moderation.

That had made sense to Jason; besides, it gave Bren Adahan the chance to haggle with a stableman over the price of a few horses without Jason around. Jason didn't make a good haggler; he was too impatient.

"Watch your head, young sir," Durine said, perhaps too solicitously, as the big man accepted Jason's gear.

"Just move yourself along to keep up with Nefennen, human, and let us worry about those following," said Ketherren, the guard captain. He was a half-head shorter than any of the other of the dwarves, and perhaps two handbreadths broader across the shoulders.

Jason worked himself through, then straightened and stretched.

Again, the room beyond the dogleg was yet another one of what Durine had named "trap rooms." The wide, low door beyond was thick oak, its blankness broken only by three arrow loops; a man's height above, another stone-rimmed balcony loomed threateningly.

Behind the five of them, the rest of their dozen dwarvish escorts mumbled to themselves, while the three leading them waited impatiently in the room beyond.

Jason tried to reach out with his mind to Ellegon, but he couldn't read the dragon; they were too far away, too deep inside the mountain.

He hadn't known what to expect when the three of them were herded into the warrens, but it had been something roomier than this. The further they'd been led into the depths of the Old Warrens, the lower the ceilings had become, as though the long-ago ancestors of these dwarves had started tunneling as giants, shrinking as they bored into the cold stone.

The light breeze that always seemed to come from ahead of them was cool, but not uncomfortably so; it was the grim demeanor of the dozen guards that chilled him.

The hall ahead jogged right, then left again, the gloom more moderated than alleviated by the faint blue light of the overhead glowsteels.

Then the corridor widened and the ceiling retreated, until the passage was again comfortable for humans to walk through.

A few dozen yards down the corridor, a massive door blocked their way. The two guards in front of it bore short, thick polearms.

There was no exchange of passwords; the leader of their dwarvish escort ran ahead to whisper into the ear of one of the guards, who then rapped a staccato tattoo on the panel with his thick knuckles.

Rusty hinges protesting loudly, the doors swung slowly open; Jason's party was ushered into the room beyond.

"Your majesty," their escort announced in thick, guttural dwarvish, "Jason Cullinane and his party."

Tennetty snorted. "I think you like the sound of that too much."

"Shut up," Durine said, moving a half-step closer to Tennetty.

The ceiling of the hall of the mountain king was high, easily sixty feet over their heads. A roast was being turned slowly in front of the open fireplace at the far end of the hall, the smoke adding to the gloom.

There were a dozen dwarves gathered around the long table, although it could easily have accommodated twice as many. Unused plates of polished stone stood stacked, and waiting, while a trio of husky dwarf women prepared the meal. One basted the roast, another stirred a pot, while yet another used what looked like an oversized pair of tweezers to move twenty or so vaguely spherical objects, which looked more like stone loaves than anything else, around in front of the fire.

"Greetings," the dwarf at the head of the table said in thickly accented Erendra. He rose from his chair and walked toward them. "I am Maherralen, son of Mehennalen." The shortest of the dwarves, he was a barrel-chested creature, almost as broad as he was tall, but there was nothing small or insignificant about the strength of the oversized hand that gripped Jason's.

"The human does not look any too impressive to me," a bent-nosed dwarf sitting at the table muttered in dwarvish, as Maherralen released Jason and waved them all to seats. "Too skinny. Emaciated. Maybe they don't eat enough."

"You do not impress me, either," Jason answered in the same language, "with either your wisdom or your manners. Would you be happier if I made a few more insulting comments about you?"

There was a moment of silence, while the dwarves, including the cooks, looked to the king for a signal.

Maherralen smiled as he reclaimed his seat. "Perhaps you would impress him more if you did. But that would make you a poor guest."

"You speak dwarvish?" Bent-nose asked.

"It seems that he does, Kennen." Maherralen cracked a thin smile. "Although I can't place the accent. Heverel, perhaps?"

Jason nodded, reaching down to unclip his bowie from his belt, but not unsheathing it as he laid it on the table. "Nehera the smith taught me. That, and other things."

Another dwarf smiled. "A smith you are, too?" The way it had been explained to Jason, smithing was the most respected profession among the dwarves. It stood to reason: the tools that the smiths forged made it possible for the dwarves to tunnel through stone, both giving the dwarves a secure place to live and providing access to seams of hematite and the other minerals that they could turn into metal, the source of their stock in trade.

"I wish I could say I was." Jason shook his head. "I just know a bit of smithing."

Apparently that was the right answer; some of the frowns dissolved a trifle.

The day was dragging on outside, and there was a no-doubt-impatient dragon out there; Jason leaned forward. "In any case, we are here to—"

"Yes, yes, we know. Our messenger carried your request in," Kennen said. "But you are here, human, not elsewhere, and you will discuss things at a reasonable pace, not in an indecent human hurry."

Jason frowned. "I don't understand."

Maherralen nodded. "That's correct. You do not understand."

"We're just here to—"

"—take the Slovotsky women with you," Kennen said.

Well, that was true as far as it went; they were there to load the Slovotsky women on Ellegon-back, and dispatch them to Holtun-Bieme, as per Walter Slovotsky's instructions.

Jason said as much.

"But can we trust you with them?" Kennen said.

It's not your decision, Jason thought. It was Walter Slovotsky's. If Kirah or the girls wanted to go against Slovotsky, that was a family matter; Jason wouldn't try to force them to come along.

But they weren't here. Tennetty leaned over and whispered in his ear. "I get the impression that the Slovotsky women may not even know we're here."

"That is quite true," another dwarf spoke up, his deep

voice gentle. "I am Neterren, son of Kedderren. I request that you don't think so unkindly of us."

Jason nodded. "I will hear you."

"Ah." Neterren's smile broadened. "You know something of formal argument. To begin," he said formally, his gravelly voice taking on a sing-song quality, "I was with Kirah when she gave birth to Doria Andrea," he said, spreading his hands in front of him. "I held her when she took her first breaths. To continue, it is important to me that I know she is going into good hands."

"Or? Would you keep them here against their will?" Tennetty snapped.

Neterren smiled sadly. "No. We couldn't do that," he said. "We—"

"It's all I can do to understand the filthy idea," Kennen said.

"Sure."

"Tennetty, hush," Jason said, turning back toward Neterren. "To respond to your beginning," he said in dwarvish, pacing his words with traditional slowness, "your friendship with the Slovotsky family is noted, and accepted. To respond to your continuation, it is important to me, too, that the wife and daughters of my father's friend go into good hands. Walter Slovotsky designated mine."

Maherralen shook his head. "Your word on that is not sufficient, and I am yet unpersuaded. You must convince me. I'll simply not let them know that you are here, if we decide not to trust them to your hands." The dwarf spoke sadly. "I like few humans, but I've grown attached to these three. Four, if you include their father."

"They were left in our care, Jason Cullinane," Neterren said. "We'll not simply hand them over. Not without being sure that it is right." He stared at Jason unblinkingly.

It felt something like when Ellegon probed Jason, but there was no mindtouch; it was as though the dwarf thought that by looking at Jason he could judge his essence.

But the moment passed. Neterren shook his massive head. "I can't decide. Not just from looking at you."

"Then they will be tested," the king said. He snapped his fingers at the nearest of the dwarf women, who glowered back and vanished through the curtains, returning with two large, silver drinking horns brimming with foaming ale.

"I am Wellen, son of Gwellin." Another of the dwarves stood. "I drink." He took one of the horns from the dwarf woman, gesturing with it to where Jason and the two other humans sat.

The dwarf tilted back the horn and began to drink. Both his capacity and speed were amazing; only a few gills of the brew dribbled down the sides of his mouth, running into his beard as he downed it all. He tossed the drinking horn end over end, high into the air, then caught it, slamming its mouth down on the table.

"Nicely done," the king said.

The dwarf woman walked over and handed the horn to Jason.

It was huge. There was no chance that he could possibly down it all.

"Wait," Durine said. "Is the test just for him, or is it for all of us?"

Neterren smiled. "You pass the first test; you ask a good question. Yes, Durine, the test is for any and all of you. We shall decide what is success and what is failure."

"Not you," Kennen snapped.

Durine stood. "Then *I* drink," he said with a smile. "I can drink real good." He took the horn from Jason, then moved a few steps away. Durine tilted the horn back and drank.

The first few swallows went quickly, but then Durine seemed to flag, to almost choke on the no-doubt bitter ale, but the big man pressed on, finally lowering the drinking horn.

A brief smile flickered across his face, then he, too, tossed the horn into the air, the few drops of liquid that remained spinning off into the gloom.

He reached up to catch the horn as it fell, then slammed it down on the table just as the dwarf had. He stood, wobbling a bit, and belched hugely.

"Nicely done, Durine," Tennetty said. "What's next?" She patted her belly. "Eating?"

"I am Belleren." Another dwarf stood. "I wrestle," he said, stripping off his leather tunic and boots, leaving himself in only breechclout and leggings.

"You're mine," Tennetty said, standing, reaching for the laces of her tunic.

"We don't wrestle women," Kennen said. "It's embarrassing enough for Belleren to have to face a human in the first place."

Durine hadn't taken his seat. "I'll wrestle you," he said.

Jason stood. "No you won't. I'll do it." Durine wasn't drunk, but he would be in a matter of moments; that amount of beer on an empty stomach would go quickly to his head.

Jason stood and stripped off his tunic, then unbuckled his holster, handing it to Durine. "What are the rules?"

"Two falls out of three. Just proper wrestling, for me." The dwarf shrugged. "For me, grips only; for you, no weapons. Punch me, stick your fingers in my eye, throw me; anything. You can even keep your boots on and kick me. If I let you hurt me, I deserve it."

On grass, Jason would have kept his boots, but their leather soles could skid too easily on the stone; he sat down to take them off.

"Let me." Tennetty smiled as she squatted in front of him and unlaced his boots. "I think you've drawn the hard one," she whispered. "How much do you want to bet the next dwarf says, 'I fuck'?" She snorted.

Jason shook his head. Tennetty always found herself diverting.

"Watch your ass," she said.

He'd been right to take off his boots: the stone was gritty and cold under his feet; it was like walking on sandpaper.

There was the metallic taste of fear at the back of his mouth as they moved to a clear space on the stone floor and squared off. Jason knew that a human with normal strength had no chance of beating a dwarf. But that wasn't the test. Or if it was, he had already failed. He'd failed tests before; it didn't kill you. Jason worked the muscles of his shoulders.

It wouldn't kill him to fail this test unless the dwarf wanted to kill him. Once those hands closed on Jason, it wasn't up to him. The dwarf could throw Jason on his head—or just twist Jason's head off.

There was a derisive laugh from one of the dwarves.

Belleren moved in, reaching for Jason's arm.

He remembered Valeran going on about unarmed fighting. *You never have to be unarmed,* the old captain had said. *You've got feet and hands and elbows and a head—use them.*

He snapped a kick at the dwarf's groin, but one of his opponent's hairy hands clamped down on his ankle, lifting it up, pushing Jason off balance.

The dwarf smiled; there were several gaps in the rows of yellowed teeth. "Not good enough."

He lunged for Jason, but Jason dodged to one side, lashing out with his foot and connecting solidly with Belleren's knee. The dwarf staggered to one side, his vulnerable back to Jason; Jason leaped on him to finish him off.

The dwarf stank of the unwashed sweat that slickened

his back and bull neck. If Jason could get one arm around Belleren's throat and brace himself, he could choke the dwarf. Dwarves had stronger muscles than humans but that didn't make the arteries in their necks any more resilient. Cut off the supply of oxygen to the brain and—

—he was grabbed, lifted and slammed down hard on the stone floor, the force of his fall knocking the wind out of him.

He left a dark patch on the stone, where skin and blood had rubbed off against the floor. He clenched his jaw, turning his scream into a high-pitched groan and fighting for breath as he fought his way to his knees, bent over, trying as hard as he could not to puke on the cold stone.

Both Tennetty and Durine were on their feet. He knew he was supposed to, he was expected to wave them back to their seats, but it was all he could do to fight for his next breath, to force himself not to scream at the white pain throbbing up and down his back.

Belleren waited for him to get to his feet. He wasn't even breathing hard.

Jason could breathe again, a little; he forced himself to his feet, his hands clamped over his belly, trying to force more air into his lungs.

"As soon as you're ready, we start again," Belleren said.

"No, slam him down *now*," Kennen hissed. "Two falls out of three."

"As soon as you're ready," the dwarf said again, waiting patiently.

Still clutching at the pit of his stomach, barely able to breathe, Jason staggered toward the dwarf.

"No." Belleren caught him by the shoulders, not ungently. "I'll wait until you're—"

Jason gave the back-handed shot everything he had, and caught the dwarf solidly on the windpipe.

"Gack," the dwarf said, his fingers tightening on Jason's shoulders.

"I'm ready now." Jason hit him again, in the same place, harder.

"Gack." Belleren released Jason and staggered back.

Jason didn't have much strength left, but he reached down and fastened his left hand on the belt holding Belleren's breechclout, and then smashed his right fist as hard as he could into the dwarf's groin. And again, and again.

"Grmph."

Jason let go of the dwarf and tottered away, as Belleren fell first to his knees, then to his face, clutching his crotch.

"If your dwarf can't get up?" Tennetty asked. "Jason wins?"

"Yes," Maherralen said. "There was nothing said about the giving of quarter; he need not wait for Belleren to recover."

Jason staggered toward the dwarf, who had gotten to all fours. All he had to do was jump onto the dwarf's back and fix a chokehold before Belleren got to his feet. All he had to do. . . .

He couldn't. If it had been a fight to the death, that would have been one thing; if lives hung in the balance, he could kick a man who was on his knees.

But Belleren had given Jason quarter. He had to wait, even if that meant losing.

And it didn't matter if that was the right or wrong answer to the dwarves—it was Jason's right answer. He forced himself to stand straight.

"I'm sorry I hit you when you weren't expecting it," he said. "I'll wait for you, Belleren."

CHAPTER 15

Janie

Those not present are always wrong.

—Destouches

Being right all the time is a real expensive habit.
—Walter Slovotsky

A wet cloth lightly slapped his face.

The cool dark reached out with vague fingers for him again, and he reached for them. It was much better to fall back into the murk, much easier than dealing with all of the pain.

The cloth slapped his face again, harder.

"Go 'way," he tried to shout, but it only came out as a mumble.

This time it was a hand—not slapping him; tugging at his arm.

"Go *away*." He slipped back into the dark.

"That's the thing about Cullinane men," Tennetty's harsh voice said from a long way off. "They don't wake up easy."

Another voice laughed, a sound of distant silver bells. "So Dad used to say. Can you do anything more?"

"I have done almost all I can do," a deep dwarvish voice said. It took a moment for Jason to place it: Neterren, the least hostile of King Maherralen's court. "He needs sleep now."

"He can sleep in the air," Tennetty said. "If you don't want to wake him, I will." Metal slid against leather, flesh thunked against flesh and steel rang on stone.

The darkness swam toward him, but he pushed it away, far away, and forced his eyes open, swimming up into the harsh blue light of the glowsteel hanging overhead.

Durine had Tennetty pinned against the stone wall. The room was small, and crowded; the other two had backed away to give Durine room. Durine had both her wrists in one of his hands and—

"Stop," Jason shouted. It only came out as a harsh whisper, but that was enough. "Let her go."

Durine shoved her away, hard.

"That's two, shithead." Tennetty eyed him stonily. "I was just going to touch him with the knifepoint. Wakes you up real quick."

Stooping to pick up the knife, Durine shook his head. His eyes didn't leave hers for a moment.

Jason's first reaction was to reach for his weapons. His fingers went to his side, to where one pistol lay, wrapped in his tunic. He slid his fingers inside the tunic, letting them rest on the cool steel.

Naked from the waist up, Jason was lying on a mattress bag of some sort—much softer than anything he was used to—which rested on a wooden frame. He forced himself up on an elbow, and found to his surprise that he could.

Rising to his less than majestic height, Neterren smiled down at him. "Feeling better, young Emperor?"

Actually, he was. He reached his hand to where he'd

scraped half of the skin of his back off against stone, and touched only flesh. It was overly sensitive, like the skin under a scab that had just come off, but it didn't hurt at all.

"You're a healer?" he asked, as Neterren felt at Jason's wrist.

"A keen eye for the obvious runs in the Cullinane family," Jane Slovotsky said as she moved around to where he could see her. There was something unusually graceful in her walk, something like a warrior in a fighting stance.

He'd only seen that kind of walk a few times before: it was the kind of studied grace possessed by a few of the more prominent members of a traveling acrobatic troupe that had passed through Biemestren a few years before. Both men and women always walked with perfect balance.

It was the same kind of grace that Walter Slovotsky had. Balance ran in the Slovotsky family, it seemed.

She was dressed in leggings and a mannish brown cloth tunic, long enough to be more of a shift, belted tightly at her waist to reveal a slim but definitely female figure. Her light brown hair was cropped short, framing a face with high cheekbones, ever-so-slightly slanted brown eyes, and thin lips bent into a smile that was partly friendly, partly mocking. He knew that she was fifteen, about to turn sixteen, more than a year younger than he was. but her appraising look made him feel like he was being examined by somebody at least five years older.

"When you're done checking me out, maybe we can re-introduce ourselves," she said. "I don't know how well you remember me, but we were kids together ten years ago. I'm Jane Slovotsky."

He reached for something clever to say. "You grew up." That wasn't it.

She laughed again, and he wasn't sure whether she was laughing at him or with him.

Neterren released Jason's wrist. "You'll feel better in the morning; it would be best if you rest for the remainder of the day, though." He turned to the humans. "He could use some more sleep."

Jane shook her head. "I'll be short."

"Just a *little* time, eh?" Neterren smiled.

"Got a few things to talk over with Hero, Junior, here." She folded a blanket over into a cushion, dropped it to the stone floor next to the bed and seated herself on it, tailor-fashion.

Neterren's eyes twinkled. "Then I'll be sure you don't tire him."

Tennetty shrugged. "We might as well leave." She turned to Durine. "I'll keep an eye on him while you go tell the others, outside."

Durine shook his head as they walked to the door. "I'll be outside, young sir, if you need anything. Tennetty will brief the others." He closed the heavy wooden door behind him.

"How did I do?" Jason asked.

Neterren's brow furrowed for a moment. "Oh. The third fall. Belleren picked you up and slammed you down, in less time than it takes to say it. Bunged you up fairly heavily, too."

"I thank you for healing me, Neterren," he said formally, as he'd been taught to give thanks.

"You can thank him for the use of his room, too," Jane said. "Such as it is."

"I don't need much, Jane," the dwarf said. "The cell serves my needs."

"I mean," Jason went on, "did I pass the test?"

Jane snorted. "Think it through, hero. You were being tested, among other things, to determine if you're good enough to protect me. You lost—and to an opponent you could have beaten. Maherralen doesn't impress too easily, and that didn't do it."

But the dwarf king had said that if Jason didn't pass the test the Slovotsky women wouldn't even know that he was there. He said as much.

Neterren smiled. "Jane has run through these warrens for ten years; she knows them as well as any Endell dwarf does. She also knows the *hazvarfen*, the echo paths, better than anybody else." The dwarf gave her an affectionate pat. "She was listening. The Slovotsky women are free here, young Emperor. We aren't . . . constituted so as to be willing to hold them here by force. It is still my opinion that you shouldn't go, Jane," the dwarf said.

"To begin," she said formally, in dwarvish, only cheating a little on the gutturals, "I do not rely upon Jason to protect me. That big ox of his looks like he would be better at such a thing. To continue, if he does protect me, it's going to be with a gun, knife, bow or sword—I do not think that any matters of importance are dependent on his mastery of the art of wrestling, no matter how highly the Moderate People rank that art. To continue further, any issue of danger aside, it seems to me that I must go along. I invite discussion." She waited.

The dwarf nodded. "I respond to your beginning: I am concerned about your well-being. I respond to your continuation: I am concerned about your well-being. I respond to your further continuation: I am concerned about your well-being, and—"

"You are stalling," she said in Erendra. "You won't hold us here by force, but you would prolong the conversation forever." She threw up her hands in exasperation.

Neterren chuckled. "Very well, little one. I'll be back to check on you later, Jason."

The dwarf left, shutting the door behind him.

"So," Jason said, "you're going back to Holtun-Bieme with Ellegon?"

"That's what I wanted to talk to you about." She

shook her head. "No." She swallowed heavily. "Mom and Dorann are going there. I'm going with you."

There was something Father had once said about what he called his "command voice," about how if you said something, if you gave an order with perfect and complete faith that it would be obeyed, then it *would* be obeyed.

I will be obeyed; she will do what I say. "You are not," he said, willing himself to believe that he would be obeyed. "You will go to Holtun-Bieme on Ellegon's back. With the others."

She pursed her lips for a moment, then took a quick chew on her lower lip, and just for a moment he thought she was going to give in.

But then she shook her head. "Look, I don't like it any more than you do. Less—I'd much rather stay here, shooting blanks. But—"

"You will—"

"*You* will hear me out, shithead." She slammed her hand down, hard, on the bed. "No—I'm sorry. Wrong approach." She closed her eyes and formed her hands into fists, then relaxed them and her whole body. "Let's try it this way: hear me out, please?" she said, softly, her eyes resting on his eyes, her hand resting on his hand.

It couldn't hurt to listen. "Go ahead."

"You're going under the assumption that the three of them—both our fathers and Ahira—are alive and carving a swath through the slavers, heading this way. Sort of like that last run thing he used to talk about, except that it's an announcement that your father's alive. Correct?"

He nodded. "It's just an assumption."

She returned his nod. "But it makes sense. There's a lesser probability that this is some scheme of the Slavers' Guild to get you out of Holtun-Bieme and chasing after ghosts, but if that had been the case they would have been ready to jump you in Enkiar.

"It sounds a lot like your father. I've been re-reading his letters; Karl Cullinane has been champing at the bit for years, wanting to get out from under that crown. This is just the sort of thing he'd try to pull, particularly since he'd know he'd have to settle down after it."

"But what does that have to do with—"

"Listen to me! Think it through, damn it." she said. "Who do you think's running the operation? *Your* father? Look, I've been raised to think highly of the great and powerful Karl Cullinane, but if they've survived this long, it's because they're doing something tricky. A lot of tricky things—you think the slavers looking for them are all idiots? You think that they can't track a team consisting of a dwarf, a big man and a bigger man with seven fingers? It has to be something tricky.

"And tricky isn't something your father is. Or was. Ahira can be subtle, but this whole thing smells of craftiness." She dipped two fingers into her belt pouch and produced a copper coin. "Look," she said, slipping the coin into her right fist, then holding both fists out in front of her. "Quickly, which hand is it in?"

He shrugged. He'd seen the sleight before. If it had been done well—and it had—there was no way that he could tell which hand held the coin.

"The right," he said, picking one at random.

"Nope," she said, as she opened her first, revealing an empty right hand. "Guess again."

"The left," he said, then realizing that since she was letting him guess again, it couldn't be in—

"Wrong again." She held up an empty left hand. She picked the coin out of her lap. "You think like your father. I think like mine.

"This is my father's show. If you haven't latched onto that by now, it's because you don't think enough like

Dad. There are only two people I know who can follow his thinking, convoluted as it is. One of them's Ahira; he and the dwarf have been working together since before I was born." She shrugged.

"And the other one's you?"

"Good guess, Jason. Have Ellegon drop us off outside Elleport and we'll hire a boat and find them. Trust me, I'll find them for you. There's just one thing I want you to do."

"Yeah?"

"Keep me alive while I'm doing it." she said. She swallowed, hard. "You may not understand about this, but I've got to tell you that I'm scared shitless."

He knew something about being scared. He knew a lot about being scared. But it wasn't something he was yet brave enough to admit to a pretty girl, not if he didn't have to.

She stuck out a hand. "We got a deal, Cullinane?"

He took it. "We've got a deal, Slovotsky."

CHAPTER 16

Elleport

All the rivers run into the sea, yet the sea is not full.
—Ecclesiastes 1:7

There just isn't any pleasing some people. The trick is to stop trying.

—Walter Slovotsky

Ellegon dropped them off before dawn, near the Orduin just north of Findarel, a small riverfront village less than a day's ride from Elleport and the Cirric. They were too close to the dock area to risk a light, so it took longer than usual to unload their gear from the dragon's back, and then get Kirah, little Dorann and Kennen aboard again.

The dwarf didn't like any of it, and while they were unloading he stood by, explaining to all and sundry how much he didn't like it.

He loathed riding on dragonback, he abhorred the idea of Kirah going to Biemestren, he found idiotic the idea of Doria Andrea going to Biemestren, he thought the idea that he was going to Biemestren was detestable—

Why not just tell him to shut up or you won't take him to Biemestren?

Because I wouldn't mean it, the dragon said, *and I don't like making phony threats. If I don't take Kennen to Biemestren I would have to leave him with you. Either that, or abandon him. Abandoning him would not sit well with King Maherralen, and I'd prefer not to be met with a hail of bolts the next time I stop off in Endell. So I'll just bear up bravely under the weight of the irritation.*

And be a fine, fine example to me, Jason thought.

—and Kennen very particularly was not fond of the idea of Jane going off into who-knew-what kind of trouble with a bunch of spindly humans, and he loathed the fact that the saddles were rigged for these oversized excuses for persons, and he was angry that the lap-belt chafed him, and he thought it was absolutely ridiculous that it was taking so long to get everybody and everything unloaded and then get the three of them reloaded, and—

Shut up, Kennen.

The dwarf took a long look at the dragon and started complaining again.

—and it was incredibly stupid that Kethol couldn't work any faster than that, how the—

Shut up or I'll roast you, the dragon said, slightly parting his reptilian jaws, letting just a whisper of flame escape from between his teeth.

The dwarf shut up.

Oh. I didn't think of that. I should have said, "Try threatening to burn him."

Sarcasm ill becomes you. There was a distant, draconic chuckle that held the sharpness that meant it was only for Jason.

But, finally, Jane's mother, Kirah, and her sister Doria Andrea were strapped back into their places on the dragon's back, and so was the dwarf. All of the goods for

Jason and the company had been unloaded, while both the Slovotsky family possessions and the trade goods destined for Biemestren were safely lashed into place.

They were done. It was none too early, either; the blackness of the eastern sky was turning into dim darkness, threatening to brighten into a new day, and the dragon had to be away.

Jane's mother called down a last urging to be careful, her voice carefully balanced between her own fear for her older daughter's safety and the need to continue to reassure her younger daughter that there was nothing to worry about, and wasn't the ride on Ellegon's back fun? And wasn't it just wonderful that they were going to get to do it again now!

Three tendays, Ellegon said. *On Pefret. I'll be there; I hope you are. Preferably all of you, and our three friends.*

"Preferably." *Just keep things quiet.*

Ellegon shrugged. *We don't have much longer until word reaches Biemestren, but even when it does, we'll keep it from your mother, just as long as we can.*

"Please," Kirah called down, "be careful."

His pounding wings sending leaves and sticks and dust flying about, the dragon leaped into the air, leaving behind Kirah's gentle words to her daughter, Dorann's shouts of excitement, and a few stray oaths from Kennen.

Tennetty already had her rucksack on her back. "Saddle up, people," she said. "I want us to catch the first barge out of Findarel."

She could have passed as a trader, if you didn't know her. She had her glass eye in the empty socket, and it could pass a cursory inspection. Jason hoped she would pass; her identity was too good a clue to his own. The charm that the Spidersect cleric had placed on the eye kept it moist in appearance, and slaved it to the motion of her real eye.

Her sword was stowed with the common gear—women wearing swords were enough of a rarity to be suspicious—but she could protect herself somewhat with the over-sized bowie at her waist and with the two pistols she carried, one in a holster under her left armpit, the other tucked into the top of her right boot.

"Move it, people," she said.

Durine looked at her, long and hard, as though to say that she wasn't running things here, and that as far as he was concerned she'd never run things; but Kethol must have caught Jason's headshake out of the corner of his eye, and nudged the bigger man, who subsided.

Jason swapped a trade knife for passage for all six of them, and got the chief bargeman to throw in two meals and the use of his tent. Durine, Kethol and Bren Adahan were tired; they hadn't gotten much sleep the day before.

Tennetty was unimpressed. If she had been negotiating, the bargeman would have thrown in some local coin, and thanked them smartly for the bargain. Or so she said.

Jane, on the other hand, wasn't visibly bowled over by Tennetty's claim. She tilted her head toward Jason as they leaned against the forward rail, watching the river bend and turn in the distance.

"The other possibility, of course," Jane murmured, "is that Tennetty would have pushed him so far, so hard that he would have called for the local armsmen." Which was entirely possible.

Still, maybe Tennetty would have gotten a better deal. Space wasn't at a particular premium today: the bags of grain and barrels of dried beef weren't piled more than shoulder high anywhere on the barge. There were only a dozen or so chicken cages with their clucking birds idiotically eyeing the outside world as they floated gently toward somebody's stewpot. There was even enough room for the bargemen to have all four of their mules on board, carefully hitched and hobbled at the rear rail, instead of trotting along the mulepath on the riverbank, the same path they would take to haul the barge upriver.

Riding or walking, downriver was easy on the animals, although it was a bit trickier for the bargemen. Instead of using their poles simply to keep the barge far enough from the riverbank to avoid grounding it, the four brawny men, their torsos gleaming with sweat, worked in almost silent coordination to keep the massive craft well toward the middle of the river. The current was fastest there, and business waited for no man. Still, they had to keep the ungainly craft under control, anticipating the turns of the swollen Orduin.

Which were, granted, familiar to them. But the work was hard; all four of them were heavily muscled, and the chief bargeman's hand had been hard and strong when Jason had shaken it.

The day wore on, and with a changing of the guard it was Jason's, Tennetty's and Jane's turn to nap in the shade of the tent, with Durine posted just outside. Tennetty unbuckled her belt and lay down flat on her back, folding her hands over her belly as she shut her eyes.

Jason decided that he was tired; when Janie unselfconsciously stripped down to bare skin and slipped into her blankets, he barely noticed.

Just as he was stretching out and deciding that he really couldn't sleep, that he had a responsibility to keep an eye on everything, tiredness overcame him and he dropped off to sleep.

Durine woke him when they were only a short while out of Elleport; the other two were already up and out of the tent.

Jason rubbed the backs of his hands against his gritty

eyes and scratched at where the bugs infesting the tent had bitten him—all over, basically—and took a few moments to dress, again checking his pistols to make sure that both of them, the one in his shoulder holster and the one in his rucksack, were loaded, which they always were, and turning the cylinder until the chamber under the hammer was the one just ahead of the empty one, then dryfiring each pistol once to make sure that the mechanism still worked, which it did.

Valeran, his teacher, had taught him to handle firearms ritualistically; adapting to a new ritual wasn't difficult.

In only a few moments the pistols were checked and ready and stowed. He walked out into the afternoon.

As the barge rounded the final bend, the bargemen swung the craft out into the river to avoid a pair of barges bound upriver, then bent their backs and their poles to bring it back into the quiet water near the banks, so that it wouldn't be carried away into the Cirric.

Beyond the banks the fields stood idle, expanses of rotting cornstalks proclaiming that they had been harvested neither recently nor long ago, but somewhere in between.

"There's the docks, over there," one of the bargemen said, indicating a direction with a jerk of his chin as he once again bent his back to his pole. It took longer for them to maneuver the barge over to its berth than Jason would have thought it should, but only a few moments for the waiting dock crew to grab the expertly thrown lines, pull the barge in tight against the dock and tie it firmly in place.

Still, the sun was getting low in the sky as they left the barge, making their way across the floating dock to the shore, all of them staggering a bit as they got their land legs back.

Bren Adahan took the lead. "The first thing we should

do," the baron said, "is to find some lodgings for the night. Tomorrow we get to find out what's going on."

"Or," Jane put in, "at least what the locals think is going on."

CHAPTER 17

Questions and Answers

Kindness is within our power, but fondness is not.
—Dr. Samuel Johnson

A little gentleness goes only a short way. Ladle it out generously, and often, when you can.
—Walter Slovotsky

Jason, Jane and Bren Adahan made their way through the farmers' market, toward the docks and the Slavers Guildhall. Elleport wasn't exactly Pandathaway, but the markets had some charm.

Just goes to show that you can waste a lot of time and effort doing more planning than is necessary, Jason thought. As it turned out, "the Warrior" and his two companions were the talk of the market, and the rumors were flying thickly. Too thickly: the story was growing in the telling.

Jason and the others had made some changes to their appearance: with their gear stowed in their rooms under the watchful eye of Kethol, they could tolerate a careful search. Jason and Bren wore the raw leather of

157

Wehnest cattlemen, and Janie was in the ragged shift and rude iron collar of a slave. The fact that the collar had a secret catch that not only allowed her to take it off, but brought out a slim blade that could easily slice through leather or flesh, was not apparent.

That she had very nice legs, however, was. When they'd stopped to get directions toward the guild pens, they'd gotten several offers on her.

They stopped at an appleseller's stall, Bren quickly negotiating for three shiny apples, each about the size of his fist, then handing one to Jason, tossing the smallest to Janie, and biting into the third himself.

The appleseller was a short, wan man, vaguely toad-faced, yellowing teeth showing for just a moment as he eyed Janie in her shift and collar. Jason muffled a glower, while Bren Adahan shared the appleseller's smile.

"Had her long?" the merchant asked, while Bren Adahan eyed a basket of apples as though pretending to consider buying more.

"A while," Bren Adahan said. "I picked her up in Wehnest, to make the trip more pleasant."

"I can imagine."

Janie didn't blush, although she did lower her eyes.

"Cooks, too," Bren Adahan said. "But I've had better. I thought I'd sell her here, but I'm beginning to suspect that the market isn't good right now."

"Not from the guild," the merchant said, "although a private sale might bring you some good luck." He shrugged. "You might try Emmon the silversmith, over on the Street of the Dead Dog—he always seems to have some extra coin, and a keen eye for flesh. Though that ax-faced woman of his'd probably make him resell her."

"Not the guild?"

He shook his head, then shrugged. "The slavers are nervous about buying, what with the Warrior and his friends running around slitting their throats and then vanishing." He picked up and hefted an apple, the shiniest of the lot, and then polished it still further on his apron, before calling out to the baker across the way and tossing the apple in a practiced high arc that brought it almost exactly into the baker's outstretched palm.

The baker threw a quarter of a head-sized loaf back; the appleseller tore off a hunk and nibbled at it.

Jason forced a slow nod. "Where were they last seen?" He bit into his apple again.

The merchant looked him over thoroughly. "I wouldn't, young man. The hilt of your sword may be well-worn, but trying to take on Karl Cullinane isn't something for an amateur. Particularly not one who enjoys a good apple as much as you do." He raised his hand in a brief salute of dismissal. "I'd like your business again."

The three walked off.

"Too much information," Jane murmured.

The Warrior and his men had been spotted in Lundeyll, and on Salket, and on half a dozen of the Shattered Islands, and in Enkiar, and Nyphien. Slavers had been found dead in Pandathaway itself, and on ships bound for Ehvenor. There were three of them, armed with nothing more than swords and knives; there were a score of them on a stolen slaver ship; hundreds of them could appear at any time. They were nowhere and everywhere.

The rumors were just beginning to make a splash here. In a few days, or a few tendays, it would be old news, but now it was all flying fast and furious, and there was no way to sort the truth out from the noise.

If there was any truth to be sorted out.

Damn.

Janie had the only good idea that occurred to any of them all afternoon: since they wanted to know who was killing the slavers, the best place to go was the guild section of the market.

The Slavers' Guildhall was ahead; the steel pens outside held only half a dozen people, although there was ample room for a hundred.

Bren Adahan leaned toward him. "What do you say we skip this? We already have enough information. Too much."

Jason nodded. "Just what I was thinking."

"Then why didn't you *say* it?" Jane whispered, irritated.

"More beer, if you please," Durine called out.

There was no immediate response.

He pounded his fist on the table. Tankards and platters rattled on the battered wooden surface, spoons, knives and spicers dancing for a moment. "More beer, if you please," he repeated, his voice almost a whisper.

"My pleasure, sir. My pleasure," the innkeeper called back, scurrying out with two fresh tankards of what was probably the worst beer Durine had tasted in years. The stocky man across the table started to glare at him, but clearly thought better of it; he decided that the watery stew in his bowl was interesting to watch. "Your food will be ready in a moment, or right now, if you'd like," said the innkeeper.

"No rush," Durine said, sipping at the beer. Awful stuff. Was it as bad as the beer they'd had in the barracks a couple years back, from the barrel where they later found a drowned mouse? It was a close call.

Tennetty pursed her lips, inclining her head slightly toward the nearest of the three skinny men with seamen's pigtails who were seated together, down the bench from where she and Durine sat. Her ears were sharper than his; she'd heard something that suggested the sailor knew something of interest.

The dining room of the inn had probably been the outside not too long ago: the long room ran across the front of the inn, as though it were an enclosed porch; the door that led inside was large, thick and weatherbeaten.

At the far end of the room, a pair of ragged children of indeterminate sex—the older perhaps seven, the younger perhaps five or so—took turns slapping at each other and stomping on the treadle that turned the spit over the cooking fire. A heavily freckled, moderately pretty girl in her early teens occasionally paused in her dicing of carrots and onions to ladle some more brown sauce over the leg of lamb on the skewer, then waited a few moments for the sauce to burn in a bit before slicing off another few pieces of meat and stacking them haphazardly on a platter.

There was definitely some wild onion in the sauce; Durine could smell it from where he sat.

But just as the cook finished preparing a plate for the two of them, the sailor mopped up the last juices on his plate with a slab of bread, crammed the dripping slice in his mouth and stood, pushing his plate away, resting his hand for a moment on the shoulders of one of his comrades to steady himself. He turned to leave.

Tennetty tilted her head closer to Durine's. "He was saying something about 'the Warrior' and some island." She rose and he followed, ignoring the way the innkeeper looked curiously at them, then decided that it wasn't any of his business why they had decided not to eat the food that came with their rooms.

Durine and Tennetty followed the sailor out into the daylight.

The business district was crowded as they followed him toward the docks, through streets filled with sailors from the boats in the harbor; with merchants bringing dried meat and bagged grain down toward the docks, or returning from there with their hands pressed to the sides of their tunics, accompanied by a guard or two watching the crowd nervously for pickpockets or robbers; with ragged children playing their endless games of tag through the cobbled streets; with horses standing hitched in front of flatbed wagons, pissing noisily on the road.

Every city was the same.

"Try to look a bit less conspicuous," Tennetty said. "You're not built for following people."

"No," Durine said, "I'm not." He was every bit as tall as Karl Cullinane, and while his physique was the middle-heavy one of a wrestler's, he was heavy with muscle, not fat. He wasn't as pretty as the Emperor or Kethol were, or even as pleasantly ugly as Pirojil was—

But he wasn't supposed to be pretty, or inconspicuous. He was supposed to be large and dangerous. That was what the Emperor had kept him around for, and that was what he was good at: breaking things, and threatening to break things, whether the thing to be broken was a stout door or a thin neck.

Tennetty had a thin neck, and one that probably deserved breaking. But Jason had said not to, and even if the boy wasn't emperor yet, he was the closest thing to it. Besides, Bren Adahan had said she ought to be kept alive, and even if the baron was a fucking Holt he was a tame one, long as Aeia was leading him around by his—

He suddenly realized that he was alone, that while he had been woolgathering Tennetty had slipped away. He scanned the crowd for her, but there was no sign.

Still, the sailor was ahead, pausing at an alley to loosen the drawstrings of his trousers and relieve himself in the gutter. Fastening himself up, he seemed to see something ahead, and vanished into the alley.

Durine quickened his pace.

The narrow alley between the two three-storied buildings was nearly blocked by a man-high pile of dirt; there seemed to be some sort of excavation going on in the cellar of one of the buildings. There was barely enough room for Durine to squeeze by.

By the time he did, Tennetty already had the situation

well in hand. She was standing over the bound form of the sailor, who was making only quiet noises around the wad of cloth she'd jammed in his mouth. A nice decoy; although one would expect a sailor to know better than to follow a strange woman into even a well-lit alley. Then again, Elleport was a well-policed town, within its limits.

Durine bent over the man.

"We know you know about the Warrior," he said, talking quietly, slowly, patiently, knowing that when a man as large and powerful as he talked just that way it could chill the blood. "Let me tell you what is going to happen: I'm going to take out your gag, and you're going to quietly, quietly, answer all our questions." He dug two fingers into his pouch and came up with an imperial quarter-mark, a small silver coin the size of Durine's little fingernail. "After that, I am going to give you this, and you're going to walk away, and forget this happened, and never, never mention it to anyone."

Tennetty slipped her eye patch over her glass eye and smiled at the way the man's face whitened even further as he realized who she was.

"Take the patch off and go stand watch," Durine said.

She thought about it a moment, then moved off to do just that. He was getting tired of her habit of hesitating before complying, and he wouldn't have minded doing something about it, but Jason had said no.

Durine worked his fingers for a moment. It wouldn't be fair to take out his frustration on the sailor, so he just seized the man's face in his right hand, letting the sailor feel just a trace of the strength in his fingers. "Don't worry about her. Worry about me. If you don't do exactly what I've told you, if you lie to me, if you call out, if you ever tell anyone anything about this, I'm the one who's going to find you, wherever you are, lay hold of you by the back of your head, and grind your face against the palm of my other hand until you don't have a face anymore. Do you have any difficulty in believing me?"

The sailor tried to shake his head.

"Good."

From over by the mound, Tennetty laughed. "We are *not* nice people," she said.

The sailor talked at length.

The others had their ways; Kethol had his.

He followed the woman past the unblinking eyes of the house's bouncer, upstairs to her crib. The room was tiny, barely big enough to hold the pallet on the floor and a pitifully small wooden chest that probably contained all the whore owned. There was a large iron padlock on it, and he had spotted the poorly hidden pocket in the collar of her thigh-length shift where she kept the key.

She unbelted her shift and dropped it to one side. Underneath she was glistening from her bath; Kethol had insisted that she clean herself first. There was enough filth in the world, and on the road.

Damp and naked, she reached for his tunic, but he pushed her hands away. "I can undress myself," Kethol said.

For just a moment, her eyes widened. Perhaps she'd heard a trace of threat in his voice, and while there were limits to what he could do to her, he had rented her for the night and nobody would complain about a few bruises. That came with the rental, too.

He nodded his head toward the pallet, and she obediently slipped under the thin blanket.

He undressed swiftly but unhurriedly, folding and stacking his clothes carefully, leaving his scabbard on the floor where he'd be able to reach it in the dark, then blew out the lamp and joined her under the blankets.

She reached for him, but he gripped her wrists.

"Please," she said, "I'll do whatever you want. Anything."

"I've paid for the room, and for you, for the night," he said. "I decide what we do."

"Yes sir," she said as his grip tightened.

"First," he said, "you'll tell me how you came to be here."

She told him a long and rambling tale that began on Keelos island, where she was sold into slavery when her father lost the farm, and continued with her being freed by a Home raider team, and with her decision to try to return to her home, and how there was nothing there, and how she hadn't any skills, and what could she do, and. . . .

"And about the Warrior . . ." he said, interrupting.

While he held her wrists in his hands, she told him everything she knew. Karl Cullinane and his two companions—or maybe his twenty companions, or perhaps his hundred companions; nobody knew for sure—were everywhere at once. There had been raids throughout the Cirric and along the shore of the Cirric. Everywhere.

"That's all I know, sir, really."

His grip relaxed.

"How do you want me, sir? Do you want me to—"

"Shh," he said, letting her go. "I just want you to hold me. Gently. All night long." He was paying for the night; he could have whatever pleasure he wanted. Being held made him feel almost alive.

INTERLUDE

Laheran

Where the lion's skin will not reach, you must patch it out
with the fox's.

—Plutarch

The rooms in the Triple Hamlet Inn were clean, but
Laheran paced them like a caged beast. This was the
place to wait, but waiting came hard.

Salket was only a matter of time, Laheran had decided. The question was, where? Salket was a big island;
there were four guildhouses spread out across its length.

Cups-and-coins was not Laheran's favorite game. Children played it with walnut halves and walnut shells; in
the streets of Pandathaway, jugglers sometimes played it
for copper and silver and gold.

The principle was the same: put one coin of silver and
two of copper under three small, identical cups. The
juggler would move them around the polished surface of
the board he held across his lap, fingers dancing deceptively, until you were thoroughly confused. If you set
your coin, be it of copper or silver or gold, in front of the

166

cup with the silver coin in it, you won a coin equal to your bet; if you failed, the juggler kept your coin.

There were many swindles, of course. Sometimes you might think that you'd heard the *tink* of the silver coin against one cup, and gleefully set your coin in front to it, only to find a copper underneath; the clever juggler had merely tapped a ringed finger against the side of the cup, mimicking the sound of the coin.

Wherever you looked, wherever you *knew* the silver coin would be, it wouldn't be. If you guessed randomly, your chances were one in three; if you tried to guess wisely, you had no chance.

Laheran was tired of playing cups-and-coins. The writ of authority that Guildmaster Yryn had given him had been useful; Laheran had ordered the other guildhouses on the island shut down, leaving only the one house in the Triple Hamlet open. And well-defended.

Some of the defenses were obvious. Laheran and two dozen guildsmen had taken rooms down the street from the guildhouse, and were—some of them openly, some of them covertly—keeping a tight watch on both the town and the house.

Some were subtle; Cullinane wasn't the only one who could set a trap. The locks on the heavy doors to the slave kennels had been booby-trapped; turning a key to the left, the normal way to unlock a sprung lock, would release a deadfall that would crash through the ceiling from the room above, crushing whoever stood in front of the door.

Other precautions had been taken with the approaches to the rear, barred windows; the most important safeguards had been taken with the slaves themselves, with the poor wretches locked in the cage. It was hard, but guildsmen had to make sacrifices.

Laheran paced back and forth. The waiting was the hard part.

CHAPTER 18

Aboard the *Gazelle*

The dawn speeds a man on his journey, and speeds him too in his work.

—Hesiod

That glowing red ball hanging just over the horizon had damn well better be the setting *sun, bucko.*

—Walter Slovotsky

About the time that Elleport disappeared over the horizon, Jason came up on deck, one pistol seated firmly in his shoulder holster, a thong holding it firmly into place for extra security on the rolling deck. His sword was belted tightly around his waist, along with his Nehera-made bowie.

The real giveaway, though, were the Home-made shirt and button-front blue jeans.

It was a clear afternoon, the sun just beginning its fall toward the horizon, the ship rolling lazily as it quartered the waves. Jason's stomach didn't like the rolling gait, but it wasn't complaining emphatically.

Bren Adahan was stretched out on a blanket on the deck by the rail, sunning himself, wearing only a towel tied sarong-style around his waist.

"We didn't discuss this," he said, raising himself up on an elbow.

He caught himself. It really didn't matter whether they had discussed it or not, not anymore. A group of a half-dozen people traveling to Klimos to exchange trade knives for nacrestones might be well-armed—given that Klimos wasn't entirely civilized, they'd better be—but it was unlikely that they'd have both guns and Home apparel . . .

. . . unless they were from Home.

No longer lolling idly at the tiller, Thivar Anjer's eyes widened. His creased face, walnut brown in the bright sunlight, wrinkled into a scowl as he started to turn toward Bothan Ver, the grizzled old sailor who was the *Gazelle*'s only crew, but stopped himself.

"A time for truth, it seems," Anjer said.

"So it seems," Durine said. He was seated cross-legged at the stern, near the captain. Stripped to the waist, the big man dipped the bathing ladle over the side and into the water, then brought it up and poured the water over his head, giving himself a sketchy sponge-bath. His thick hands rubbed at a hairy torso crisscrossed with pink scars, rivulets of flesh through a forest of hair.

"Durine," Jason called out, sniffing at the cake of soap he'd retrieved from his rucksack. It was real Pandathaway soap, made from Mel copra and who knew what else, smelling of flowers and sunshine. "Catch." He tossed the cake to Durine, who quickly wiped his left palm dry on the deck and reached up to let the soap smack into his palm.

Durine smiled a quick thank you, then began to lather his massive chest and belly.

Kethol was stretched out on the narrow free space at

the bow, shaded by the jib, his eyes closed, hands folded over his stomach, apparently asleep. "Makes it easier," he said, his eyes still closed, not moving, "not to have to keep up a disguise."

Which was why Jason had done it. Besides, if he didn't, Tennetty was going to.

Tennetty came up from below, squinting in the daylight, now in her leathers, her hands patting her guns and the hilts of her sword and knife as though for reassurance. Balancing easily on the deck, she eyed the horizon, then reached down to help Jane Slovotsky up through the hatch. "Too bad," Tennetty murmured, "that Ganness wasn't in Elleport."

"Avair Ganness?" Jane Slovotsky raised an eyebrow. She was wearing a white blouse and a tight pair of Home denim shorts; incongruously, she had heavy shoes on her feet. Nice legs, though. Maybe a bit too skinny. But not much.

Another wave broke below the bow, spattering them all, making the metal cooking box hiss. Jane raised a hand to wipe the sea water from her face, the light, golden hairs on her forearm glistening with sun and spray. "Tennetty, you really expect that any time we need transportation by water, Avair Ganness is going to be around?"

"You haven't ridden with Ganness."

"No, but I have heard about him. Cullinanes and their friends seem to keep getting him in trouble, costing him ships."

"They do, at that." Tennetty laughed.

Jason liked that. He hadn't seen her laugh, not much, not since that night on the Mel beach, the night that Father died, or didn't.

The wind caught the peak of another whitecap, spraying them all again.

The rear deck was crowded, and Thivar Anjer didn't like it much. He glared at them while Bothan Ver went forward to where the half dozen needle-nosed rapentfish their nets had scooped up that morning were grilling over the steel cooking box.

"So. We're seeking Karl Cullinane," the captain said, not really a question. "What will happen when we find him?"

Jason opened his mouth to say something about how all the captain would have to do was drop them off at the rendezvous with Ellegon, but Bren Adahan beat him to it.

"You will go your way, and we will go ours," Bren Adahan said. "We'll use his transportation."

"If he and his friends have any," the captain mused. "Very well—I'll go my way with double the money, and all of the trade knives."

"Oh?"

"I used to know an Avair Ganness, captain of the *Warthog*. He used to talk at some length about how dangerous it is to get involved with Cullinane. I don't mind taking risks, but I won't do it for a few silvers. Nor will I do it without you all swearing on your blades that my ship and I will be released unharmed, and that you won't stop me running in the face of a fight." He gestured around. "I'm no warrior; this is not a warship."

"You'll be free to go. If you don't betray us. Or try to," Tennetty said.

"Agreed. Have we a bargain?"

"Yes, you have a bargain," Bren Adahan said.

"No. Not you." Thivar Anjer turned to Jason. "Young Cullinane, have we a bargain?"

"We do."

"Cullinanes don't break their word, do they?"

"No, we don't," Jason said.

Jason couldn't sleep. The hold was dank and musty, redolent of rotting fish, decaying wood and a distant, acrid stench that Jason couldn't quite identify. The smells, combined with the constant, albeit gentle rocking of the boat, had him vaguely nauseated.

He dressed and climbed the ladder, clearing his throat as he did so that Kethol would know it was him and not be surprised. That was one of the many things Valeran had taught him: never surprise a guard accidentally.

Bothan Ver was half-asleep next to the bound tiller, only occasionally coming half-awake to take a quick glance at the sky and water, perhaps make a slight, drowsy adjustment to tiller and sheets, and then stretching out again in his steersman's chair.

The night was chilly. Kethol crouched next to the cooking box, warming his hands over the banked coals. Straightening, he handed a waterskin to Jason, who took a quick swig for politeness, then handed it back.

Klimos lay ahead, somewhere off the bow. Just another of the Shattered Islands, a cluster of dirt-poor islands in the Cirric, where the people supported themselves by fishing and farming in good years, by selling off their children in bad years. They'd evolved a complex set of rules as to when and why some children were saleable and others weren't, but it still sucked.

Tennetty, sleeping lightly in her bag belowdecks, had been born on one of these islands, sold into slavery by her parents.

Jason shook his head.

Some problems didn't admit of easy solutions; Home raiders didn't often travel into the Shattered Islands. Being caught at sea by a slaver ship was always a possibility; like the Pandathaway-based Slavers' Guild, the Home raiders hadn't established themselves in the Outer Kingdoms, on the other side of the Cirric.

Besides, what could you do? Kill all parents who would sell a child? And what then? Pull food and money from the air?

He knew what Tennetty's answer was to that. Killing was her answer to everything. But Jason didn't know what his was. Not yet.

"At least I didn't get left behind this time," Kethol said. He knit his fingers together and cracked his knuckles.

"Eh?"

"Your father left the three of us in Ehvenor. The three of us who survived. The trip cost us some good men, sir."

And the trip wouldn't have been necessary if Jason hadn't panicked the first time he'd been around shots fired in anger. He wanted to lash out, but the rebuke was justified.

Kethol looked at him, then shook his head. "Not what I meant. Not what I meant at all. Would have happened eventually. You keep juggling knives, you're going to get cut. We all juggle knives."

Kethol had another swallow of water, and the two of them were silent for a while, watching the dark sky and the sea.

Far off, toward the horizon, a ring of perhaps a dozen faerie lights pulsed excitedly in sequence, blue chasing red around and around, the blue becoming brighter as it closed in on the red, fading when the red took on a tinge of orange and speeded up. And then, without warning, the lights stopped cooperating and spread across the sky, their pulsing color changes becoming random, lethargic.

"Do you think he's alive, Kethol?"

The lanky warrior took a long time answering. "Yes. And no. And maybe it doesn't matter, young sir." Kethol shook his head slowly, blunt fingers toying with his beard. "Yes, because he's what he was. Fastest man with a weapon I ever did see. Didn't matter what weapon—sword, staff, bare hands, anything. There maybe was a better swordsman here or there, and maybe somebody as good with a staff, but your father was a . . . wizard with everything.

"So: yes, he's alive, because of what he was, and because the Empire needs to be held together by somebody who knows what he's doing, and I'm not sure you do, not yet." The way he looked at Jason wasn't either friendly or hostile, just appraising. "No, that's not true. I'm sure that you don't, yet. You don't know when to be hard and when to be soft—which your father did. I don't think you know when to be direct and when to be subtle—which your father didn't. Doubt you've got the strength of will and the strength of body to carry off being direct all the time. Which he had.

"So yes, he's alive. We need him." Kethol leaned forward on his elbows and sighed. "But, no, I don't think he's alive, because nobody could have lived through that explosion that you and Tennetty described. Perhaps it doesn't matter, because perhaps it's all for nothing anyway."

He chuckled, a thin laugh that rattled in his throat like small, dry bones. "Only one thing I'm sure of, young emperor-to-be, and that's that you'd better decide who you are. If you're going to be just one of the fellows, then you'd best not expect us to follow you blindly into combat. If you want to be above us, keep yourself apart."

"And if I don't?"

"Well, then you'd better hope that your father is alive. In either case, you'd best not spend the night asking a simple soldier what we'll find at the end of the trail.

"Go to sleep, Jason."

CHAPTER 19

Klimos

A timid person is frightened before a danger, a coward during the time, and a courageous person afterward.
—Jean Paul Richter

Slovotsky's Law Number Thirty-One: Get scared right away; avoid the rush.
—Walter Slovotsky

Elleport to Elevos, and there were nothing but rumors; the markets were full of them. The Warrior had just struck at Menelet, but he'd been killed there. Or was it on Millipos?

Or he hadn't been killed. And it wasn't Millipos. It was Bursos. Besides, did you see that thing that flew overhead last tenday? It looked like a dragon, perhaps, and what are dragons doing in the Eren regions?

The trade in dragonbane was brisk.

The Warrior? Who cared about the Warrior when something, some *thing* had struck on Heshtos, leaving half the village dead, before it slipped into the sea? The village wizard? He was among the dead. The surviving villagers had sold two dozen children to the Slavers' Guild for the hire of a Pandathaway wizard, promising lavish treatment, anything, if he would only live among them and protect them.

The Warrior? No, not Heshtos. No, he and his dozen companions had raided Millipos, or was it Deddebos? It couldn't have been Filaket; perhaps it was Salket? No, it wasn't Salket, or Salkos, but maybe it was Bursos, and it was a hundred companions. No, two—another human, and a dwarf. A dwarf at sea? Don't be ridiculous. Dwarves don't sail; if they were to fall overboard they would sink like stones. Idiot.

There was a guild factor in residence in the only village on that tiny island, but they kept Tennetty on the *Gazelle*, and Kethol, Bren Adahan and Durine maintained a disguise as bounty hunters, seeking the Warrior, and they let the slaver's man live.

Elevos to Millipos, and as night fell Bothan Ver's sharp eyes saw something in the sky, something large and black, flying. But it was flying west and they were sailing north, the sun was setting and they couldn't quite make out what it was.

It wasn't Ellegon, that's all that Jason was sure of. It wasn't Ellegon.

Landfall at Millipos, and there were nothing but rumors. Yes, the Warrior had struck at Klimos, but he had disappeared. There were too many hunters on his trail; he had vanished into the air. No, he hadn't vanished into the air: he had attacked the slaver factor there, but had been driven off.

There was a tavern in Millipos that catered mainly to sailors, some drinking up their pay between trips, others looking for work. Kethol and Bren Adahan bought drinks, and listened.

Nothing since Klimos. But did you hear about . . . ?

They passed up the first rendezvous; they were a good three days' sail from Pefret, and there was no reason to hit Pefret. Next rendezvous, they hoped.

But now it was Millipos to Filaket, and there were nothing but rumors.

Try Klimos. He was there, and there hasn't been any rumor of him since. But he's still around; he kills slavers in their sleep, and he has two—no, twelve, no, a score of companions.

Slavers, *here?* With the Warrior about to step out of the night and skin anything resembling a slaver? Are you mad? Well, yes, we had a factor here, but look at the rice in the granaries—we don't have to sell anybody. What kind of monsters do you think us, that we would sell our children when we don't have to?

The smudge of smoke on the horizon grew as they approached Klimos, the *Gazelle* pointed high, running close to the wind, heeled over hard.

As he stood by the rail, there was a coldness, a tightness in Jason's belly, as though the bread and cheese he'd eaten earlier had changed into stone.

"Okay, people," Tennetty said, clapping her hands together for attention, "enough looking around. I want all guns loaded, all pans primed, all hammers on the half-cock. Bren Adahan and Durine, load your crossbows; Kethol, get your longbow strung."

Bren Adahan shook his head. "We are at least—"

"Shut your mouth and do as you're told," she said. "I've got more experience in running a raiding squad than anybody else here. So that puts me in charge of everything and everyone, which includes you, Baron Adahan."

Jason found all of them looking at him.

It's not fair, he thought. *I shouldn't have to make this kind of decision just because I'm my father's son.*

And why not? Why was Tennetty making a fuss when they were easily an hour from the island? The smoke indicated some possible danger, sure—but why bring things to a head now?

He thought about that for a quick moment, and decided that if there had to be an argument over who was in charge, now was the time for it. Maybe Tennetty wasn't quite as crazy as everybody thought.

Everybody was still looking at him.

What would his father have done? That was easy: Karl Cullinane would have trusted Tennetty. But Karl Cullinane could have relied on Tennetty. Jason didn't know any such thing.

He'd pretend that he did. He tried to keep his voice level. "You're in charge, Tennetty. Everybody load up, prime and half-cock."

"Oil patches, everyone," she added. "Save your spit. And, Durine," she said, "use a slug load in the big smoothbore."

"Mind if I overload it a bit?" the big man asked, as he carefully tied his short-barreled shotgun to the railing, then reached for the smoothbore.

"It's your face it'll blow up in."

"It's not much of a face, anyway." Durine tipped a heavily-rounded measure of powder down the muzzle of his big shotgun, pushed a hunk of wadding after it, then took a greasy bullet almost the size of his thumb out of his pouch and shoved it down into the barrel.

Jason belted his second holster tightly around his waist, then got his other revolver out of his bedroll gear, checked to see that it was loaded and that the empty chamber was under the hammer, and strapped it tightly into the shoulder holster.

He slipped the lacing out of his tunic front, leaving it open to his waist, tying the leather thong around his forehead partly just to put it someplace, partly to see that he didn't get any stray hair in his eyes. He was beginning to need a haircut, but this wasn't the time to do anything about that. He took out his kit and started working on his rifle, pleased to see that his fingers were faster at it than Bren Adahan's. At least there was something he could do better than the baron.

"This is not a warship," Thivar Anjer said, considering the smoke. "That appears to be trouble ahead."

Bren Adahan had finished priming his pan, and snapped the frizzen down into place with a sharp snick. "You've been here before," he said to Thivar Anjer.

"Yes, yes, of course I have, but—"

"Where does it look to you like the fire's coming from?"

"It's damn clear where the fire's coming from—it's Lehot's Village, over on the lee side of the island, and it's burning. It looks like your Karl Cullinane has been here again."

Tennetty snorted. "Everything that goes wrong anywhere in the Eren region is Karl's fault? Besides, we knew that he was here, that he killed some slavers here some tendays ago—you think he'd be stupid enough to come back?"

Jane opened her mouth, then closed it. Jason squatted next to her.

"What is it?" he asked. As they talked, his hands kept working at his rifle: wrap the bullet in an oil patch, seat the patch firmly with the short-starter from his pouch, slip the short-starter into his belt while he trimmed the patch with his beltknife, put the knife back in the scabbard, take the short-starter back in hand and seat the bullet firmly, replace the short-starter in his belt, slip the ramrod out from underneath the barrel to ram the bullet solidly home, replace the ramrod, take the vial of fine priming powder out of his pouch, tip a measure into the pan, snap the frizzen down.

She shook her head. "Tennetty's right, but for the wrong reason," she whispered. "I don't know that your father might not think it was tricky to double back and hit the same location twice. But *my* father's too clever for that. The slavers will have to worry about the possibility, anyway. That means that they'll have to watch out at places that the three of them have already hit—and Dad isn't going to let your dad hit them where they're watching."

"So?"

"So if the reports are right that the three of them hit the slavers here, then whatever this is, it isn't them. I say we get out of here," she said. "I don't like it."

Bren Adahan gestured at the smoke. "If you bring us around to the windward side, come around the island, and then cut across the path of the smoke, can we make a fast escape if we have to?"

Thivar Anjer shook his head, his mouth creased into a contemplative frown. "Better to sail straight in, in any event; I should be able to sail two, three points closer to the wind than a warship, if we have to run. But I am not willing to bet my ship and my life on that."

Bothan Ver studiously pulled in the mainsheet, as though a thumbs' breadth more or less slack was an important difference.

Bren Adahan licked his lips. "We have to investigate. This is our best clue to Karl Cullinane."

"Ah, a clue," Thivar Anjer snorted. "What will you have to suggest should the clue consist of a three-masted slaver raiding ship?"

"Don't worry about it," Jason said. "We can outrun a

warship if they've taken some sail damage. Jane, would you dig up a couple of the signal rockets and the launching rod?"

"Sure." She smiled. "You're thinking like a Slovotsky, and I like it." In a few moments she was back on deck with two of the slim, short-finned cylinders and the launching rod.

"This is supposed to be set in the ground to launch a signal rocket," she said, "but we can tie it to the railing, pointing backwards, and fire it off at any ship chasing us. If we can hit their sails—and if you can steer your ship, I can hit their sails—they'll be too busy dealing with their burning ship to give us any difficulties."

Durine rested his hand on the captain's shoulder. "Besides," he said, "it would make Tennetty very unhappy if we ran away from no threat at all."

The captain frowned. "Your logic has persuaded me."

All the preparations for fight-or-flight seemed unnecessary when they pulled around the island. There were no ships to fight or flee from, just a dozen or so small boats, none more than two-thirds the length of the *Gazelle*— fishing boats, suitable too for traveling to close islands, not really big enough to travel out in the Cirric.

But something had happened.

Two of the boats had been capsized; another lay on the sand with its mast splintered. What had been houses and sheds up at the edge of the sand were now just smoking ruin; pilings like blackened matchsticks stood where the dock had been. Black smoke still hung over the trees, almost obscuring the path up from the water.

Thivar Anjer spoke up. "It would seem sensible to leave. Whatever has done this is dangerous."

"You've got another lead to Karl Cullinane?" Jane Slovotsky asked gently.

"Does that mean you think we ought to check it out?" Jason said. "I thought you were for skipping this island."

"Any law against changing my mind?" She shrugged. "Either check it out real quickly, or not at all. I wouldn't want to wait in the dark for whatever did that."

"The dock is gone," the captain protested. "I will not ground my boat."

"There's a rowboat over there, still looks whole," Tennetty said, not taking her eyes off the water as she stripped down to her bare skin, belted her bowie around her naked waist, then tied her hair tightly behind her.

There was nothing even vaguely lewd about her naked body; it was all muscle, skin and scars. "I'll get it. Jason, keep me covered." She vaulted over the side, splashing feet-first into the water, then swam for the rowboat with swift, sure strokes.

He ought to say something constructive. "Durine, if you see anything in the water near her, shoot it." He could almost hear Ellegon in his head, saying something like, *Sure, sure. He would have, like, yelled boo otherwise.*

But there had to be something else to have them do. He reached up to his shoulder holster and drew his pistol. It had a faster rate of fire than anything—but Kethol's longbow would be a good second. "Kethol, use your bow."

"A good idea, young sir." Kethol smiled as he set aside his rifle, lashing the barrel to the railing with a practiced slipknot. "I've done some bowfishing, too. Remember, you've got to aim long. Things under water seem closer than they are."

He worked his shoulders under his tunic, then nocked an arrow and drew it back experimentally, the feathered shaft held easily in his knuckles. He slowly relaxed the tension on the bow.

"I'm ready," he said.

What next? There had to be some useful order to give, to remind everyone—particularly Jason—that Jason was in charge.

But nothing happened as Tennetty swam to shore, retrieved four paddles scattered across the rocks and sand, and threw them in the flat boat before launching it and paddling out to the *Gazelle*.

There was easily room enough for six people, even with weapons. He should go first, Jason decided, tying it fast as it scraped against the *Gazelle*'s side.

"Okay," he said, "after me."

"Like hell," Tennetty said, half-dressed already. Her damp hair clung to her face like black vines. "We do this in two transfers. First Durine, the baron and me establish a position on shore, and then I paddle back for you, Jane and Bothan Ver." She wiped her nose on her arm. "Kethol and the captain can stay—"

"We have your *word*!" Thivar Anjer hissed. "I will not send Bothan Ver ashore with you, and I'll not come with you myself."

The captain was right. Jason had given his word, and the word of a Cullinane wasn't to be taken lightly. "No, Tennetty. They stay here."

Tennetty shook her head vigorously, flinging drops of water. "That was before we—"

"No," he said, trying to speak with his father's voice. "No, Tennetty." She would have listened to his father; he tried for Karl Cullinane's command voice, speaking each word slowly, emphatically: "They stay here."

"Shit." She spat on the deck. "We don't have time to argue. Kethol, you stay on watch, and don't drink or eat anything. If there's trouble, send up a signal rocket and get out of here. Send up another one when you want a rendezvous."

"Understood, Tennetty." The redheaded man smiled,

teeth starkly white against his red beard. "Although you'd think we don't trust our new friends here."

"Hey, guys?" Jane Slovotsky raised a hand. "If somebody's going to be left behind, I wouldn't mind if it's me. I can light a signal flare real good, and my Dad's explained to me that Slovotskys don't like to stick our faces in the way of the ax. Although I could have worked that out myself," she added.

Durine and Bren Adahan smiled at that.

Tennetty snorted. "I've been watching the way these two have been watching you, and I'd sort of like to be able to introduce you to Karl as at least one woman of our acquaintance who hasn't been raped. We do it my way."

Getting ashore was tense, but uneventful. In just a short while they were all on land, the boat carefully beached.

Nothing stirred around them. It was still, the silence more accented than interrupted by the gentle slap of the waves on the rocks and the crackling of the smoldering wood.

"Keep it quiet, people," Tennetty whispered. "Let's move out."

There was only one clear path off the shore: a wide dirt road leading up, into the woods.

With a quick hand signal, Tennetty had them spread out. She took the point herself, with Durine on the right side of the road, behind her, Bren Adahan on the left, his rifle slung, a two-pronged fishing spear in his hands.

While everyone carried an extra pistol or two, Durine practically bristled with weapons: his heavy saber dangled from the left side of his belt; he carried the big smoothbore shotgun in his hands, a short rifle slung over his left shoulder, a rucksack over his right. The wooden butt of a flintlock pistol stuck out of his boot, and there was another brace of them in his belt, on the right side, leaving room for him to reach across his belly for the saber on the left.

Jane Slovotsky, the most lightly armed of the party, was in the middle, carrying a flintlock rifle and a single pistol, while Jason brought up the rear, his own flintlock heavy in his hands.

The wind changed, bringing more smoke their way, stinging their nostrils, carrying distant sounds to them; the crackling of the fire and something else, a dull roar that Jason couldn't quite make out.

Ahead there was a break in the trees. "Should be a village there," Tennetty said as they gathered around her. "In this part of the world they tend to keep trees between themselves and the Cirric; helps to break up the wind. There was—"

A distant scream cut her off. It was high and ululating, a cry of agony.

"Slow and easy, people. Slow and easy," Tennetty said.

They crept around the bend.

Where the trees broke, there had been a village. It was now burning and smoldering; some of the wooden houses had been smashed, and that had probably set off cooking fires, the sparks leaping from house to house.

There was another scream and some more cries; their source was clearly further down the road.

"Easy, easy," Tennetty whispered as they rounded one of the few remaining houses.

"Oh, shit," she said.

The cleared area beyond had apparently been the center of the village, where folks came to talk and trade together. Now they were even closer together; in the very center of the clearing, a hundred men, women and children huddled tightly.

Except for one: a short, wizened man in gray tattered robes stood between the humans and the creature. His left arm hung limp and bloody by his side, but his right arm was thrust out in front of his body, as though supporting the mass of light that stood between him and the creature.

The light and the lightning pushed it back, but the creature launched itself in the air for the wizard, only to be knocked back again.

It was a huge black beast, its body covered by tight fur that gleamed blackly in the sunlight. It was easily twice the size of a horse, its flat, triangular head vaguely lupine.

It had been wounded, at some point; a dozen arrows stuck in its shoulders and flanks, like feathers in an almost-plucked goose. Dirt matted a raw wound on its right foreleg; something had managed to cut through its hide.

Again it lunged, and again light and lightning issued from the cloud, knocking it back.

It crouched and screamed its defiance while it gathered its breath.

Maybe he tripped, or perhaps he panicked, but one of the villagers stumbled away from the rest, and then started to run when he realized he was alone and exposed.

The creature leaped and growled as it snatched at the fleeing man, pinning him to the ground with one paw, then dipping its head to pick up its victim, shaking its head like a dog shaking a rat, then flinging the now-limp form into the air. Then the monster turned back to the wizard.

Screams and cries filled the air, along with the deep growl of the creature as it tried and failed to reach past the cloud of light and fire.

Still, with each bolt of lightning, each blast of light, the glow seemed to dim marginally, as though its power were being drained whenever the creature slammed into it.

Jason had never seen anything like the monster before; but he remembered rumors of strange things coming out of Faerie. Could this, whatever it was, be one?

It didn't matter. He couldn't let it kill a village full of people. He cocked the hammer of his rifle and brought it to his shoulder.

"No," Tennetty hissed. "It's not our fight."

"Yes," he snapped back. "Would my father run away?"

"You're not your—shit, shit, shit," she said. "Fucking Cullinanes never listen." She brought her rifle to her shoulder and fired, all in one smooth motion.

Perhaps the bullet hit, but all that Jason could see was the creature dropping to all fours, then turning to face the new threat.

He took careful aim, trying for the base of the creature's neck. A head shot was risky; if you got the angle wrong the bullet could just ricochet off the creature's skull.

But if you could tear open any of the arteries leading to the brain, if you could smash the trachea. . . .

A gun crashed to his right, and then one to his left.

One shot missed, but the other became a splash of blood over the creature's right eye and a bestial scream of pain as its huge mouth sagged open, and it turned to see where the sound and hurt had come from.

The bullet had torn a gouge across its skull, but the creature wasn't seriously injured. It turned and leaped, covering half the distance between itself and Jason, settling its hind claws into the ground as it braced itself to spring and rush.

As it pushed itself into the air, Durine's smoothbore went off with a bang and a cloud of smoke, smashing the creature's right eye into a bloody mess, leaving it half-blind and fully maddened.

It fell to the ground only a few meters from Tennetty, who calmly fired one of her pistols into its side, only to be batted aside by a massive paw as she dropped her hand to her waist to grab another pistol. She tumbled through the air, falling to the stones, battered, broken like a child's discarded toy.

Bren Adahan, his pistols empty, his fisherman's trident lying bent on the ground, held his saber out in front of him with both hands, as though that narrow needle of steel could deflect claws and teeth. The monster batted him to one side, then stooped to bite, stopping only when gunfire from somewhere to Jason's left shook its body.

It's up to me, Jason thought.

It was just like in Melawei. It was always up to him, and he wouldn't fail, he couldn't fail, not when it counted.

He placed the sights on the creature's throat as it raised its head to snarl at him, then squeezed the trigger slowly, carefully.

The creature's remaining eye glared balefully at him as it braced itself for another leap.

The hammer sparked down on the frizzen; the butt of the rifle slammed into his shoulder; and a gout of flame from the barrel of the gun tore blood and flesh from the side of the animal's neck.

But the animal didn't slow, didn't stop, didn't fall down and die like it was supposed to.

Jason dropped his rifle to one side and snatched at the pistol in his belt holster.

"It happens sometimes," Valeran had once told him, the old man's eyes glazed, his voice slurred with drink, "that when the whole world is going to shit around you, time does funny things. Freezes, like ice, and you've got from now until forever. Don't smile, boy. There's nothing good about it." The battered old warrior leaned back and took another long pull on his bottle. "Only trouble is, you're fastened into place, too, like a roach frozen in an ice chip. Won't do you any damn good. Doesn't ever do you any damn good."

The monster didn't stop; it leaped at him. Jason took it all in, sights, sounds, and smells: the woody scent of smoke in the air; the musky reek of the creature; the cries of the villagers; Jane's shrill shouts from behind him; the pop of a pair of pistols, and the blood and gore splattering the creature's side; the tight fur on the creature's muzzle, terminating in a wet, leathery snout.

His peripheral vision was clear as fine crystal and the light was heady as wine, taking on an almost golden glow. In that glow Bren Adahan was on his feet again, blood streaming from his mouth and nose, his saber in his hand, all skills and training forgotten as he raised the sword over his head, as though preparing to hack down on the huge beast.

Durine had his rifle up to his shoulder; his brow was furrowed in concentration, his bottom lip caught in his teeth.

Jason bent time, forced his slow right hand up and pulled the trigger, once.

Fire and smoke nipped off a corner of the creature's ear, that was all.

And then lightning spoke, once, from his right, and the world crashed down on him.

He wasn't sure if he'd been unconscious, but the world was a black pit of pain. He tried to breathe, but the black mass crushed him down against the ground, blinding him with the weight of the stinking fur, the immense burden grinding the mass of the pistol in his shoulder holster into his chest.

There was blood and grit in his mouth. He forced a

little air into his lungs, feeling broken ribs grate, moving in his chest in sharp, agonizing counterpoint.

From a distance, he could hear them.

"Move it, move it, get it the fuck off him," Tennetty said. "You—use that spear as a lever. All of you there, push."

A single shot rang out, and Jane Slovotsky's clear contralto cut through the sound and pain. "Do it, now, please," she said.

The weight lifted, marginally, and he felt strong hands clawing at his ankles. When they pulled on his left leg the pain in his knee drew a scream from between his clenched teeth, but they didn't stop dragging him painfully across the rocky ground. Bones ground in his knee.

He tried to gasp for breath, but couldn't draw any in.

Somebody forced the mouth of a bottle between his lips, glass knocking hard against his teeth.

The too-sweet taste of Eareven healing draughts washed the taste of blood from his mouth, giving him enough strength to swallow.

He did, and as the liquid warmed his throat and chest the familiar miracle happened again: he healed.

One of his ribs had shattered, broken in half a dozen places, splinters of bone ripping into his flesh with every breath. The splinters became pieces and the pieces snapped into wholeness with a flurry of sound like corn popping.

He could breathe again and the air, even though it tasted of blood and dirt and shit, was sweeter and richer and tastier than a fine puff pastry.

Bruises unbruised; as he brought his right hand up before his face, a deep gash across his palm closed, ragged edges sealing themselves together until what had been slash became a red line that turned pink and vanished before his eyes. His broken right knee closed in on itself, blood vessels expelling tendons and bits of bone, ruined nerves reasserting themselves, while ruptured muscle, tendon and bone knitted and strengthened.

Dozens of villagers crowded around as he lay on the ground, next to the mountain of fur and flesh.

He could see Jane Slovotsky and Bren Adahan out of the corner of his eye; she stood arrogantly apart, one hand on her hip, another holding a cocked flintlock, while Bren Adahan leaned against the vast bulk of the dead creature, tilting back the bottle of healing draughts to drink from it.

"Durine. . . ." It felt as if he were shouting, but all he could hear was a thin croaking. Recovery was draining; there was a limit to what the healing potion could do.

The big man knelt at his side. "I'm right here, young sir," he said. Tennetty stood next to Durine, the left side of her face caked with blood.

"Ten? Are you—?"

She smiled through a mask of blood and dirt. "They got to me first with the healing draughts. I'm all right."

"She's fine," Durine said. "Everybody is fine, young sir."

"Your bullet?"

Durine nodded, as he rested the butt of his rifle on the ground, leaning on it. "Best shot I ever made. Cut right through the spine, killed it instantly."

"Luckiest shot you ever made," Tennetty said. "Or were you really aiming between the vertebrae?"

A sense of strength and power hummed in Jason's head, like strong whiskey; he rolled to his knees, waving off a score of helping hands.

He forced himself to his feet, but his new legs wouldn't support him; if Durine hadn't caught him, he would have fallen.

"Who . . . ?" he tried to say, he couldn't get the words out. "Are all of us okay?"

"We're just fine," Durine said.

Jason had failed, but they hadn't failed. "Bren?"

The baron was quickly at his side, smiling broadly, although the front of his tunic was bloodstained and he was mopping at his bloody face with a wet cloth that a villager had provided.

"We're all alive," he said, his voice quietly triumphant.

They were surrounded by a hundred smiling villagers, ranging in age from a scattered few infants to the old wizard who stood apart, watching them.

Something pulled at Jason's tunic. A barefoot, brown-haired little girl, five or six years old, dressed in a torn shift that had been made from a grain sack, held his pistol with one hand and tugged at his tunic with the other. "Is this yours?" she asked. "Sir?"

He accepted it, and stored it away in his belt holster, patting once at his other gun. "Yes, it's mine."

She smiled up at him, quickly hugged his waist, then vanished into the crowd.

Something caught in his throat; he couldn't speak for a moment.

Tennetty snickered. "Very nice, very nice. But is it worth getting killed?"

"Shut up."

Other villagers had gathered together their gear and piled it on the grass, not far from the dead beast. What had terrorized the villagers was now just a pile of fur and flesh. Two boys, one maybe ten, another perhaps a year or two older, were poking at the body of the beast, one with a short wooden stick, another with the hilt of a broken sword.

Bren Adahan's scabbard was empty. Jason drew his own sword, rapped the flat of it smartly against his now-solid knee, hard enough to make the steel ring with the distant sound of bright bells.

"Borrow mine," he said, reversing his grip and holding it out to the baron, who gave a quick salute with it, then slipped it into his scabbard. It was a loose fit; Bren's preferred saber was longer and heavier than Jason's.

The gray-robed wizard stood apart from the rest of them, watching them with eyes that didn't seem to blink. "I am Dava Natye," he said slowly. "We are in your debt."

Tennetty snorted. "Bet your fucking ass you are." She gestured at the beast. "What was that?"

The wizard shook his head. "I do not know. Traders have brought rumors of strange things coming out of Faerie. The Warrior spoke of—"

"The Warrior?" Jason asked. "He was here?"

"Two tendays ago," the wizard said.

"Describe him," Tennetty hissed.

The wizard shook his head. "I only saw him for a moment, outlined against the flames of the burning shack of the slaver, Nosinan. A big man; I can say no more. He told me to be gone, that this was a matter between him and the guild.

"He left a message, and then he vanished." The wizard spread his hands. "I never saw his boat, nor his companions. But they were here; and now they are not."

"The message," Tennetty said, taking a step toward the wizard, then stopping herself. "He left a message for us?"

"Not for you. For the slavers. He shouted at me, 'Tell them,' he said, 'tell them that the warrior lives, and tell them I am coming for them.' Then he shouted at his companions to meet him and the boat, and gave the body of Nosinan a final kick . . . and then he was gone."

Several of the villagers nodded in unison; one of them, a thin pock-faced man with deep-set eyes, spoke up. "It's just as Dava Natye said. It's just as we told Laheran, of the guild."

CHAPTER 20

Comfort

Be cheerful while you are alive.

—Ptahhotep

Grab what comfort you can, however you can, whenever you can. The ride gets real rocky 'way too often.

—Walter Slovotsky

Bren Adahan had decided that Jason and Tennetty, still recovering from the shock of their wounds and the healing, needed a good night's rest. Jason wasn't in the mood to protest.

So they spent the night ashore, explaining to the villagers that it would not be a good idea if anybody from the village came up on them at night. They camped out on the grassy fringe just above the rocks, in clear view of the *Gazelle*, where it floated at anchor. The others preferred to sleep under the stars, but Bren Adahan and Jason each pitched a small raider tent.

Jason was asleep when something touched his foot. He woke suddenly, reaching for his pistol.

"Easy, Jason," Jane Slovotsky's voice whispered from the mouth of the tent. She tapped him on the foot again. "You were crying out in your sleep."

There was a bitter taste in his mouth, and his head felt as if someone was regularly jabbing a dull icepick into the back of his head. He brought himself up to his elbows.

"It must have been a dream," he said. But the dream was gone now. Something about wading through knee-deep rivers of boiling blood, holding a crying baby girl over his head. It had been distinct, sharp as the edge of a knife . . . but now it was gone.

He wiped sweat from his forehead and stretched, his blankets damp and musty around him. "Thanks for waking me." Her outline was vague in the dark, and then it was gone. She was gone.

His mouth still tasted sour as he checked his weapons. There was no waterskin near his head; he'd forgotten to put one nearby. As far as he knew, Tennetty had the only bottle of Riccetti's Best on the island. He needed a drink of something, and his bladder was full, tight as a drum.

He didn't like waking Tennetty. Not only did she need her rest, but she always came awake armed. Two or three times the *Gazelle* had taken an unexpected pitch or roll and he'd found himself bumped up against Tennetty, the slim woman coming awake wide-eyed, a knife in her hand.

He had slept in his jeans, but unbuckled the waist for comfort; he buttoned himself up, slung his holster over his shoulder, then crawled out and stood up in the night.

Tennetty was asleep a few yards to his left and Jane had returned to her blankets and sleeping canvas, to his right.

Tireless Durine was on watch, sitting on a rock down by the water. The big man raised his hand in greeting.

Bren Adahan's tent was a stone's throw from Jason's, and beyond that was the forest; Jason took the traditional twenty steps beyond the farthest sleeper and urinated against the nearest tree. He buttoned his fly and walked back toward the camp.

Beyond the charred bones of the waterfront buildings, beyond where gentle waves stroked the shore, the *Gazelle* stood at anchor, supported by a sea that seemed built more of reflected starlight and faerie light than of water. It caught the twinkle of the million points of light overhead, and mixed it with the pulsations of the distant faerie lights.

There were light footsteps behind him—bare soles on dirt.

Jane Slovotsky cleared her throat. She stood there in the dark, wearing loose drawstring pants and a shirt, holding a pair of clay bottles. "Pretty, isn't it?"

"Yeah."

"Which do you want? Whiskey, water?"

"Both," he said, accepting the whiskey bottle first.

"You're not exactly your father," she said. "He wouldn't have let me sneak up behind him."

"I heard you."

"Sure."

He uncorked the bottle and took a swig. Lou Riccetti's corn whiskey might not have been as important a development as guns and gunpowder, but it had its points. Still tasted like horse piss, though.

"Easy on that," she said. "You had a bit of a shock today. Don't push yourself."

His first reaction was to bristle, to tell her that he was capable of judging how much he should drink and that it was none of her damn business . . . but she was right.

"Good point," he said. He exchanged bottles with her, and she took a quick swallow before recorking the whiskey.

A cold wind blew out of the west, but her smile was warm in the darkness.

The water was cold and fresh. It tasted good, particularly clean and bright tonight. Valeran had once said something about the value of almost getting killed: it did tend to sharpen the senses.

He handed her the water bottle. "Thanks."

"Mind if I ask a question?" she said as he started to turn away.

He shrugged. "Go ahead."

"Why haven't you made a pass at me?" There was a curious lilt in her voice, a note he hadn't heard before. "Is it me, or is it you, or is it some combination?"

"Has every man you've ever known tried to get you to sleep with him?"

She smiled. "Almost. Since I turned fourteen."

He looked down the slope toward the others, and she nodded.

"Sure. All three of them. Durine was kind of cute about it. Bren's being kind of a nuisance."

He shook his head, once. "Bren Adahan says he wants to marry my sister," he said coldly. "I'm not sure I like that."

"No harm done." She snorted. "I said no. Besides, I didn't know that it fits in only one," she said. "Yours shaped like a key?"

There wasn't anything to say to that, but he did anyway: "Do you have to talk like that?"

"I don't know." She shrugged. "Runs in the family. A lot runs in my family. . . . Did you ever ask yourself why my father sent you after me?"

"Because he wanted you and your mother and your sister to relocate to Biemestren," he said.

She snorted. "You *do* need a keeper. Didn't it occur to you that he thought that the two of us might pair off? Or don't you have all the parts?"

"No." It hadn't occurred to him. He swallowed. Why was she bringing this up? Just to make him uncomfortable. It should have occurred to him, though. Back in Biemestren, around court, there had been constant subtle pressure from most of the barons to pair him off with a baronial daughter. Any baron who had a daughter had no difficulty seeing her as the next empress. Why should Walter Slovotsky be all that different?

"Oh, that's too bad," she said half-mockingly. "You don't have all the parts, eh?"

"You know what I meant."

"Yes, I do."

He didn't remember her putting down the bottles, or moving closer to him, but suddenly she was in his arms, her hands locked behind his back, her mouth warm on his.

After a while she let go of him, moved a few inches away. "About time, Cullinane."

Durine had been watching the whole thing casually from his place by the water. Jason wasn't sure, but he thought he saw Durine smile before he turned away.

"He knows," Jason said.

She shrugged. "So what? Doesn't your tent have enough room for two?"

"Y-yes," he said, biting his lip in frustration at the way his voice shook for a moment. He was the man, damn it; he was supposed to be smooth and sophisticated. "But, why?"

"Didn't your father ever tell you not to look a gift horse in the mouth?" She laughed quietly, then kissed him gently on the lips when he frowned. "No, no. I'm not laughing at you. It's because, like, you're irresistible, maybe?"

"Try again." His smile didn't feel entirely genuine. Maybe Jane Slovotsky saw herself as an empress at court, too, eh?

"Who knows?" As though she was reading his mind, she nodded. "It won't bother me that from the morning on, it'll get easier to keep Bren's hand off my ass. That's getting real tiresome. But mainly it's because of my father."

"Your father?"

"Something he said. Something about what almost getting killed does. Or doesn't it make you horny, too?"

CHAPTER 21

To Salket

The logic of the heart is absurd.

—Julie de Lespinasse

Lying, like eating, can be overdone.

—Walter Slovotsky

Klimos to Geverat, and they hadn't been there, but maybe on Menelet? No, no, the raid on Menelet was tendays ago. It was Klimos. The three of them, the dozen of them, the hundreds of them, had struck on Klimos, burned everything to the ground.

And did you see that thing fly by last tenday? I don't know if it was a dragon, but you wouldn't have any essence of dragonbane to sell, would you?

Geverat to Heshtos, and Jane thought that might be it, so they fired off a signal rocket that night and lay anchored offshore for a night and a day, supposedly rerigging the mast.

A boat came out to investigate, but it was only some

local fishermen: Did you see those strange faerie lights last night? And have you heard about the Warrior? He could be anywhere—I hear the slavers are pissing down their legs any time they hear a loud fart.

They went ashore, but there was nothing but rumors.

Jane Slovotsky knelt by the map. "Salket," she decided, tapping the parchment, then resting her hand on Jason's leg. "It feels right." Her hand was warmer than it had any right to be.

"Two days," Bothan Ver said, hauling in the mainsheet, nail-bitten fingers directing the rope precisely, delicately, like a puppeteer pulling on the strings of his marionette. "Perhaps."

"If the wind holds," Thivar Anjer added, leaning on the tiller, squinting at the distant horizon. "Which it might."

"We'll find him there," Tennetty said, stropping her bowie against a whetstone. "And maybe only one or two of us will die."

"Everybody dies," Kethol said quietly. "Some of us a little piece at a time."

"It's your play, Jason," Durine said. "You're the Heir."

"That you are," Bren Adahan said. "And may one inquire why you're glaring at me?"

"You and I will have a talk about my sister," Jason said. "After Salket. And give me back my damn sword."

INTERLUDE

Ahira

The world is a vast temple dedicated to Discord.
—Voltaire

The dwarf was tired, dirty, and sore as, still on the back of his gray pony, he was hurried past the guard stations, into the inner bailey of Biemestren castle. The tendons in his thick neck burned like hot wires and a hot gray film had taken up residence behind his eyes. His right shoulder was a constant dull ache. It never went away, not even when he slept. The skin around the edges of the wound was raw and red.

After he had been picked up near New Pittsburgh, riders had been sent ahead, bringing word that he was on his way. So it was no surprise that they were waiting for him on the grass.

But it was still good to see them; it had been too long.

He dropped heavily to the ground and tossed his weapons to one side.

Kirah, D.A. in her arms, ran over to him. She dropped

to her knees, burying her face against his good shoulder, and wept.

"Ta havath, Kirah, ta havath," he said, awkwardly patting her on the back. "Walter was fine, last I saw him." But that was too damn long ago.

He'd taken a bolt in his shoulder three weeks before, but he ignored the pain as he scooped up little D.A. She balanced easily on his forearm for a moment, then planted a wet kiss on his wet cheek.

"I love you, Uncle Ahira," she said, clear as a bell.

He folded the little girl in his arms and held her gently, carefully, in arms that could, that *had* snapped a man's ribcage like matchsticks. Fingers that had crushed, fingers that had destroyed, fingers that ripped flesh, toyed with her pageboy-length hair. "Got a new haircut, eh?" he said.

She nodded and smiled, practically bubbling. "Aunt Doria and Auntie Andy did it."

They surrounded him, Doria, looking as she did in his dreams sometimes: young again, if you only looked at the arms and neck and face, and didn't quite notice the eyes.

Still holding D.A. in his right arm, he wrapped his left around her waist. "It's good to see you, old friend," he said, damning the quaver in his voice. "Is Ellegon here?" he asked, although he'd been shouting with his mind for the dragon for hours.

"No." Doria shook her head. "He's trying to rendezvous with Jason and the rest in Mipos. He'll be back— maybe with them—in a day or two. I hope." She bit her lip.

Thomen Furnael stood a few yards apart, his face creased in concern. He was dressed informally: trousers, a light shirt, a black robe tucked over his arm. "We have to know, Ahira: is he alive?"

Andrea's face was a mask of grief. She didn't have to ask.

God, she looks old.

The dwarf shook his head. "Of course not. He blew himself up in Melawei, just like Jason and the others must've told you. Get me a drink, and get me into a hot bath, and we'll talk about it. We've got a day or two before we can do anything. If we can do anything."

The water was already hot in the officers' bath, over by the barracks. Ahira crouched in the oaken vat, the water up to his neck, steam rising from the surface.

It had been forever since he'd had a hot bath.

He sat back and tried to ease his muscles; he was strung tight as a lute's treble strings.

It had made sense, when Walter had proposed it on the beach at Melawei.

"Look," Walter had said, "he's dead, and there's nothing we can do about that."

"Except gather together what we can for burial," Ahira said, kneeling in the hot sun over Karl's hand.

It was Karl's left hand: the three outer fingers were just stumps.

Miraculously, the hand had survived intact, severed almost cleanly at the wrist, although it had been thrown easily a hundred yards from the center of the explosion.

Ants were already crawling on it, but Ahira couldn't force himself to reach out and pick it up, or brush them off.

Damn it, damn it, damn it.

"We can't bring him back to life," Walter said. "But we can keep him from dying."

"You're getting clever, Slovotsky," the dwarf said. "Sounds like a bad idea to me." But he didn't mean it, not really. It was just a reflex, after so many years.

"First thing we got to do is bury the hand, plus any

other parts of him we can find. Or parts of the slavers that might be him. We can't let the Mel see that hand, and work it out. The official story is that Karl left."

"And then?"

"We've got to kill us some slavers." Slovotsky's smile was broad in the sunshine. But it wasn't really Walter Slovotsky's smile.

It was Karl's.

"When the Mel came back down from the hills, we— well, Walter, actually, lied his head off. Karl had left aboard Ganness's boat, we said, and we were to follow, once the slavers were dead.

"Old Wohtansen wasn't any too happy about that—I think he still remembers the time Karl punched him— but some of the Eriksen men volunteered.

"Didn't like the trip much. If anybody ever asks you if you want to face a storm on the Cirric in nothing more than an outrigger canoe with the sloppiest lateen rigging the universe has ever seen, tell them no.

"We hit them in Ehvenor. And then Lundeyll, and then Erifeyll, careful to leave evidence of three of us at all times.

"Walter and I split up in Erifeyll. The next part of the plan called for some time at sea, in the Shattered Islands. I'd be too conspicuous. A dwarf sailor? No; better they look for two humans and a dwarf. And just in case the legend of Karl Cullinane were to reach here, and raise false hopes, I was to hie myself back, fast as possible."

Ahira leaned back in the water and toyed with a cake of pear-scented soap, blunt fingers gently stirring up lather on its translucent surface. He tried to loosen his tense muscles, but that didn't happen. He fastened his hand around the bar of soap and squeezed. The soap flowed between his fingers like wet clay.

"I ran into a bit of trouble. Tell you about it sometime."

Doria felt at his shoulder, dry, practiced fingers touching impotently at a wound that was only partly healed. "We've sent for a healer," she said. "Spidersect."

He shrugged. "Walter's hopping among the Shattered Islands now, working his way—as indirectly as possible—to Elleport, then back up the Orduin toward Endell. He may head there, or he could change his route and head toward Home."

"Islands?" Garavar's voice sounded like gravel.

"Yes, yes, islands. He hires on as a sailor, and spends some time in the taverns across the islands, talking up the Warrior, and how he's been heard of here, there and everywhere. With his two, or twenty, or two hundred sidekicks. He should be finished soon; by now there'll be far too many hunters on the Warrior's trail, and Walter won't want to run into them." The dwarf sighed.

"Or, maybe he won't be finished. Not if he sees a Home signal rocket. He'll have to investigate that, which means that he's going to be looking for the kids just as hard as they're looking for him. Say, about half as hard as the slavers are looking for the Warrior."

Doria's fingers gripped his with surprising strength. "I'll come with you."

The dwarf shook his head. "No. Just me and the dragon. We'll try the next rendezvous that Jason and Janie set up, and if that doesn't work we'll try to find him."

"No," Andrea said. "No. It's you, Ellegon and me. I can find them."

"How do you expect to do that?" Doria was angry.

"I have my methods, Doria. Magic." Andrea muttered a few quick syllables that could only be heard and forgotten. She held out her right hand, and sparks danced between her fingers. "I know you think I use too much magic, but don't you think it's worthwhile for this? For my son's life?"

The sparks grew more violent, more frenzied, snapping like whips between her thumb and forefinger. Andrea's skin flinched where the sparks touched her, but she didn't shrink from it. Her lips moved silently, and the sparks grew louder, the flashes brighter and sharper, until with a quick flick of her fingers she dismissed the light and sound into nothingness.

"I know a bit about magic." Doria pursed her lips. "Sure, you can make a model of Jason, but you can't break through the protection spell of his amulet, no matter how much power you use. Magically, he isn't even vaguely similar to any form, not while he's wearing it."

"You're quite right." Andrea smiled thinly. "I can't. And I can't find Bren Adahan, or Tennetty, or Walter. Not while they're wearing their amulets. But Kethol and Durine aren't wearing amulets, are they?" She stalked out of the bath house, her skirts flaring as the breeze caught them.

And then she was gone.

"I don't like her using magic," Thomen Furnael said. "But I don't see any good way around it."

Or of stopping her, Ahira added silently.

Doria kept her thoughts to herself.

There was nothing to do, for the moment, but lean back and soak in the hot water, and rest.

He closed his eyes.

CHAPTER 22

Steer's Head Inn

All hell broke loose.

—Milton

Tell me again why it's a good idea to take a lot of chances.
—Walter Slovotsky

The storm moved in as the day was moving out. The sun hung just above the horizon, but the sky was dark with oncoming thunderheads. The damp wind whipped grass and leaves into the air around Jason as he stood on top of the hill.

Jason shivered and pulled his cloak around him, then bent to pick up the signal rocket. "Set the launching pole," he said.

Durine firmly shoved the thin metal pole into the bare ground, canted just a bit into the wind.

Jason straightened, then carefully slipped the rings on the side of the signal rocket along the launching rod. He knelt to unwrap the base of the rocket; it had been covered in waxed paper to keep the damp out.

It seemed to have worked just fine; his fingers couldn't feel a trace of wetness. The roll of fusing he took from a canvas bag was another matter. Something or other had gotten to it, and it was soggy.

It would probably burn, but perhaps not. Best not to fool with it. They had already taken that possibility into consideration; Jason had a flintlock pistol stuck into his belt, its tamping rod protruding from the barrel.

Dragging the heel of his boot to carve a shallow trench in the dirt, Durine kept his eyes on the road below.

Down there, Bren Adahan waited with their rented transportation: two saddle horses and the flatbed wagon, drawn by a pair of ragged mules. Janie and the others were a day's ride away, at Tesors, the port village, with the boat.

Durine handed him a powder horn, and Jason carefully tipped a trail of the powder into the trench, leading up to the signal rocket. He finished up with a heaping spoonful under the base of the rocket.

That ought to get it going.

"Okay, now, head on down there. I'll be with you in a moment." He could move faster than Durine, and while it was unlikely that the rocket would blow up, there was no sense taking a chance on it.

He waited for Durine to get to the base of the hill, and noted with approval that the big man had the horses' reins held firmly in his hands.

Standing at the far end of the trail of gunpowder, Jason took the tamping rod out of the pistol and stuck it carefully in its slot below the barrel. He primed the pan, then snapped the frizzen down, cocking the pistol before he aimed it carefully at the snaking trail of black powder.

Why was he aiming? He didn't need to aim. He knelt and set the muzzle against the end of the trail of the powder, and pulled the trigger.

The flintlock pistol spat fire, lighting the trail of gunpowder, sending a line of fire sizzling toward the rocket.

Jason didn't wait to see if the rocket would launch safely; he was already partway down the slope, out of line of sight of the rocket.

A vast cloud of smoke billowed from the base of the rocket, the reek of sulfur sending Jason huddling into his cloak, in a coughing fit.

He straightened, his eyes tearing, as the rocket roared away, leaving behind smoke and sulfur. Rising on a pillar of smoke and fire into the darkening sky, it climbed faster and faster, the fire growing more and more intense, as though challenging the brightness of the dim stars themselves.

The rocket's propellant charge burned out. The flame died, only to be replaced a few seconds later, a few degrees higher in the sky, by a bright green flash that expanded into a globe of fiery points, and then was gone.

Jason climbed back up, donning his damp leather gloves so he could pull the launching rod out of the soil. Heated by the flames of the signal rocket, it hissed against the gloves.

By the time he made his way back to the road, the others were saddled up. Bren Adahan had finished nailing a piece of parchment to the tree. They'd thought of using paper, but the parchment ought to wear better.

They'd thought about the date, too. With the increasing popularity of English numbering over the Erendra addition-based notation, it was entirely possible that somebody might decode the date. So they'd spelled that out phonetically, and followed it with a short message in English, similar to other notes that they'd left in various places across Salket over the preceding tendays.

It read:

Mother's health delicate; it's important that you abort this and reach Holtun-Bieme before word reaches her. We

*are heading into the Triple Hamlet; others waiting aboard
a single-master, the Gazelle, at Tesors, until this Tenthday.
Rendezvous, with Ellegon on Mipos, next Ninthday. Next
rendezvous, with Ellegon, two tendays later, outside of
Elleport.*

> *Be there.*
> *—Jason*

Jason tossed the launching rod into the back of the
flatbed, and stripped off his gloves.

"Let's go," Bren Adahan said. "I want to be a good
ways away from here before we make camp for the
night." They'd be in the Triple Hamlet tomorrow, and
see what could be found there. Apparently that was the
only Slavers' Guildhall left on Salket; the others had been
closed down.

If Karl Cullinane, Walter Slovotsky and Ahira were
hunting slavers on Salket, they'd be hunting them there.
If.

"You're too impatient, Baron," Jason said. The baron
wasn't the only one who was too impatient. As Jason
climbed into the saddle, his mare whinnied and took a
prancing sideways step. He tightened the reins firmly,
then patted her gently on the neck as she settled into a
slow walk.

"You think they saw it?" Durine asked Jason.

Why was Durine asking him? What did Jason know?
"I hope so," he said. "Even if we had another rocket, we
wouldn't get any benefit from setting it off, not with that
storm moving in. And I hope they're here, and if they're
here, I hope . . . I just hope."

He shrugged it away, and gave another hitch to the
reins.

The storm had long since broken when they rode into
the Triple Hamlet of Kalifeld, Bredham, and New Runsek.

While lightning flashed across the sky and thunder

crashed in his ears, cold rain clawed at Jason like an animal, icy fingers clutching at his face, his neck, his shoulders. Rivers of water ran down his back; he hunched forward, over the pistol under his tunic, trying to shield it with his body. He doubted that it was working, but maybe the rounds in his saddlebags were dry.

His trembling fingers, twisted tightly in the reins, were wrinkled from the wetness, and his jaw ached; the only way he could stop his teeth from chattering was to clamp his jaw tightly.

He was thoroughly cold and thoroughly miserable. But he couldn't complain. Bren Adahan and Durine, every bit as utterly water-logged as he was, didn't say a word. They just rode on, Durine stolidly ignoring the water that ran down his neck, Bren Adahan pulling his sodden cloak around him, a single hand emerging to handle the reins of the flatbed.

The road had been dirt; it was now a treacherous, clinging, stinking mud that clawed at the legs of their tired mounts, pulling the horses down.

Only the mules seemed unaffected. Despite the way the mud threatened to cover the iron-rimmed wheels up to the hubs, the mules simply put down their heads and trudged on miserably.

An oilskin tarpaulin covered their gear in the flatbed; Jason hoped that the water hadn't gotten to everything important, although he was sure that the rifles were soaked, and would have to be carefully dried and oiled when they stopped, lest they rust through their blueing.

Thankfully, at the crossing leading into the villages, the mud turned to cobblestones, and the horses' steps ceased to be a sullen, leaden plodding. Their hooves, cleaned somewhat as they walked through the pools and rivulets and streams that coursed over the cobblestones, actually resembled hooves now, instead of muddy stumps.

But the rain intensified, almost blinding him.

"Ahead, there," Bren Adahan called over the crash of thunder, and, sure enough, Jason could see the sign of an inn ahead, a piece of hammered silver that waved in the wind, beckoning them. It looked like a silver mushroom.

Across the road and further along it, another tavern's sign, this one a mounted cow's head, seemed to nod at them. But the Silver Mushroom Inn was the closer, and that was where Bren Adahan got down from his horse, tying it to the hitching rack.

Jason and Durine were quickly at his side. The three of them walked up the steps, and on to the covered porch, out of the rain.

Jason had been fantasizing about getting out of the rain, but it didn't help much. He was still wet and shivering, and thoroughly miserable.

The thick door was closed. Durine lifted the heavy brass goathead knocker and slammed it down twice.

There was no answer, but warm light peeked out through the shuttered windows, and Jason fancied there was a distant whiff of hot soup in the air. He tried to dismiss it, but his mouth began to water.

The door swung partly open; a fat, red-bearded man stood there, wearing a pullover cotton tunic, blousy pantaloons and a grease-spattered apron. He eyed the three of them for a long moment before he spoke.

"There's no room at the Silver Mushroom," he said. "Try the Steer's Head, down the street."

Bren Adahan started to turn away.

Voices whispered inside. "There's three of them, but the big one's kind of fat. N' if one of them's a dwarf, it's the biggest fucking dwarf I ever saw."

"We'd best be sure. About all of them."

"Hold one moment." The innkeeper swung the door open and beckoned them in. "The lad is shivering. You should at least come in for a mug of hot wine," he said. "I wouldn't want you to think unkindly of the Mushroom."

They walked inside. The entryway of the inn was a conventional mud room, barely lit by an overhead lamp; boot scrapers mounted on the floor to make a first pass at the mud, grass mats further in to catch the remnants.

Jason was shivering; he stood on the stone floor, water running off him in rivulets. Bren Adahan, his finery a sodden mess, leaned against a wall, brushing his hands down his arms, trying to get some of the water off.

Only Durine seemed unmoved: he stood to one side, silently, indifferently, methodically scraping the mud off of his boots, looking more like a corpse fished out of the river than anything else.

Two men walked quickly through the inner door, one holding two pairs of steaming silver tankards; the other, a tall, slim blond man, held only his own tankard.

The first was almost a caricature of a guild slaver: he was a sullen, thick-jowled man, a crop tucked into the left side of his belt, a truncheon into the right, his bulging belly threatening to slop over both weapons.

The other, a small-boned man who stood half a head taller than Jason, smiled gently at Jason and Durine before turning his attention to Bren Adahan.

"My name is Laheran," he said, striking a pose. He was slim, and studiously elegant, from the silver pin stuck through the collar of his short cape, down to the polished, pointed toes of his boots. A light rapier hung from the left side of his waist, and while the scabbard was trimmed in silver and shell, the weapon's basket hilt was wound with simple cord and brass; it was a weapon that advertised itself as something that was to be used, not merely displayed.

Jason kept his hands away from the hilt of his sword as Laheran set his tankard down on a dressing table, then passed out the steaming mugs of mulled wine.

"I th-thank you," Bren Adahan said, his teeth chattering. He stripped off his leather gloves to accept a mug of spiced wine, then started to raise the mug to his lips.

"*No*, Trader Hofna," Jason said. "Durine. Mix them, if you please."

Durine blankly accepted the mug from Laheran, then walked over to the table and picked up Laheran's, pouring wine from his tankard into the other's and then back. It was very quiet for a moment while Durine offered Laheran a tankard.

The slaver smiled as he accepted it, then drank. "Laheran wishes you luck," he said. "Although your precautions are excessive," he said, tilting his head to one side, as though idly considering the matter. "The guild doesn't drug or raid here."

"Durine wishes you luck," the big man said, "although I try to make my own. Perfunctory apologies," he said, "but Taren and I have been hired to guard the trader, here, and we do our job." He accepted the tankard from Laheran.

"So I see."

"Taren wishes you luck," Jason said, drinking.

"Why did you do that?" Bren Adahan hissed as soon as they were back outside, in the rain. "If you thought that the wine was drugged or poisoned—"

"I wouldn't have accepted it at all," Jason said. He hadn't been warned about that; the locals wouldn't let the slavers simply go around poisoning or drugging travelers at random. The time Uncle Chak had been tricked was a special case; he and some other mercenaries had been decoyed away from Pandathaway, off the trade routes, and then drugged, chained and sold. "I didn't want to seem to be too eager to please," he said. "They're already suspicious there; that would have raised their suspicions."

Durine's massive head nodded slowly, heavily. "It was just the right move."

The three of them sat on the floor facing the fireplace, each with a steaming mug of tea next to him.

Jason reached up and felt at his hair; it was only slightly damp. He was finally getting dry. It would be good to be dry, if only for a short while.

Their room in the Steer's Head Inn was cold and drafty, the air smoky, the straw-ticked bedding musty and bedbug-ridden, but the fire was hot and so was the tea. It tasted mainly of sassafras, Jason decided, although there were definitely overtones of ferique and cinnamon. Too much honey, though. Still, on a cold, wet night, who was going to complain about that?

The thing he liked best of all was the private bath off the room, the kettle-like tub elevated over an iron stove that vented to the outside. A hot bath would be wonderful.

It had once been a more elegant place, perhaps long ago. The oaken beams at all four corners of the room were carved to resemble towers of dwarves, each standing on the shoulders of the one beneath. Under the smoky residue that covered the walls, Jason could make out the outlines of ancient murals depicting deer frolicking in a woody glen.

The chill was relieved by a massive fireplace on the wall opposite the glass-paned doors to the balcony; the fireplace was crammed full of blazing logs. To the right of the fireplace, their clothing, both what they'd been wearing and what had been in their bags, hung on a cast-iron drying rack. Jason could actually see wisps of steam rising from his sodden jerkin.

A blocky iron rested on a heating plate by the fireplace, and a heat-scarred oaken ironing board stood in front of a woven-grass kneeling mat, but none of them had used it, either to press the clothes or to finish drying them.

The clothes could wait. Their gear had all survived, but it was all soaking wet; it would be late evening before they'd be finished with it all.

Durine looked more silly than threatening as he sat on a floor cushion, the hair on his face, chest and belly sweaty from the fire, his skin reddened, a woolen blanket wrapped around his waist, his big smoothbore on his lap as he worked over it with a few handfuls of cotton batting and a mottled green bottle of olive oil. The latter was one of the nice things about Salket; olive groves stood all over the island, and there was always good oil, reasonably cheap.

Jason had finished oiling the second of his revolvers, and had it pretty much squared away. But the cartridges, spread out on the blanket like nuts fallen from a tree, were a problem. Water wasn't going to harm the lead bullet, or the brass casing, and the built-in igniters were sealed, too, but the powder itself was suspect.

Would it fire? Best to be sure.

He took a pair of pliers from the tool kit on the floor between him and Bren Adahan, and setting a round backwards in a quickloader for leverage, carefully pried the bullet out, then tipped the powder on the worn floor boards in front of him.

It didn't look a whole lot different from the usual Home powder, although it was finer. Just black dust, seemingly dry.

He took a spare flint from Bren Adahan's kit and, taking his now-oily bowie from the blanket where it rested, stroked the flint down the length of the knife. The bowie was awfully oily; it took three strokes to get a spark.

The powder flared into fire and smoke and then was gone, leaving behind only an acrid smell and a lot less smoke than Jason would have expected if he hadn't fired a few rounds at Home.

Bren Adahan and Durine were all eyes, but neither of them said anything. Everybody knew that the Engineer had given Jason some new pistols, but they'd been secret, up to now.

They were for his use. And *his*, if he still lived.

Jason shook his head. That didn't make sense, not now. The purpose of guns was to kill people who needed killing, not to be a Cullinane family secret. Both Durine and Bren Adahan were trustworthy, within their limits; Ellegon had sworn to that.

"You said my instincts were good when we braced the slavers," Jason said.

Durine nodded. "Yes. They were. Some of him has rubbed off on you."

That was arrant nonsense; Valeran had a lot more to do with how Jason turned out than Karl Cullinane did. But maybe the old soldier had taught Jason well—before he'd fallen to the ground, the smooth wooden hilt of a throwing knife projecting from his eyesocket.

"Then they'd better be good now. I want to lend you these. If I don't come back, they're yours to use. Return them to the Engineer; he'll decide what to do with them." He checked to make sure that the cylinder was still empty before he clicked it into place, then dry-fired the gun half a dozen times, the barrel carefully pointed away from either of them. "They are operated like this—"

"Excuse me?" Bren Adahan's brow furrowed. "You're giving us your guns?"

"I can't risk any gunshots, so I shouldn't take them with me." Jason shrugged.

"You don't mean to say that you're going out into the rain?" Bren Adahan shook his head. "To what end?"

"Think it through, Baron," Jason said. He was glad that Adahan had missed the obvious; it gave Jason a chance to lecture him. "Salket has been left conspicuously alone by this warrior and his men. Jane—and she knows her father better than anybody else—thinks Salket is next.

"So do the slavers; they've closed down their other houses on the island, leaving this one as the only target. This whole place smells of a trap within a trap. We ride into town, and the largest inn is completely taken over by slavers, who are advertising who they are, in case we missed it. Can't you smell a trap?

"And we've put them on guard, brought their alertness 'way up. You think they haven't noticed the signal rockets? Whether he's seen our notes or not, the rational thing for Father to do under the circumstances would be to give Salket a bye.

"Now, somebody real subtle would let them rot here forever, waiting. Let them spend tendays waiting here for an attack that'll never come.

"But Father's not that subtle. He's always figured that the right way to scare slavers is to kill them. He'll go for it. Somebody's got to see where the trap is."

"Walter Slovotsky is with him," Durine said. "He can do a better job of reconnoitering than you can."

Jason shook his head. "But not if he's not here yet. Tonight I've got a storm to hide in; tomorrow he won't." And Jason might not have too long to hide in the storm, at that. A storm that moved in fast could move out fast, too.

Durine nodded, rummaging through his gear for a moment before coming out with a long strip of black cloth. "You'd best blindfold yourself until you go; give your eyes a chance to adjust to the dark."

Jason nodded. "Good idea."

Bren Adahan shook his head. "You're going back out in that? To see if you can find where the traps are?"

No, Jason wanted to say. *I'm seventeen years old, and*

I'm so fucking scared that it's all I can do to not shit all over the floor. But the first time I ever faced real danger I ran away, and I can't ever let myself do that again. I've got to be Karl Cullinane's son, and that means that I do what's necessary, in cold blood, whether it's hacking a rebellious baron to death or putting my own ass on the line.

His father was a legend. A legend was, above all, a lie. And Jason was the son of a legend. But maybe lies could become real, maybe you could twist the universe, bend it to shape, and make the lies real, if you could only keep your voice from shaking, your hand from trembling.

"Of course I am, Baron," he said, as he stood, drawing the damp, smelly, woolen blankets around him as though they were robes of state. "I am a Cullinane."

The baron didn't quite know how to take it, so Jason forced himself to meet his gaze until the baron looked away.

"I guess you are," Bren Adahan said.

CHAPTER 23

A Tap on the Shoulder

Am I a god? I see so clearly!
—Johann Wolfgang von Goethe

His clothes had been uncomfortably damp until he stepped out into the rain, but his belly was warm, his tongue and throat still aching with the taste of a last cup of almost scalding tea.

Now his clothes were simply soaked again as he splashed down in the waterlogged grass behind the Steer's Head Inn, then stepped back into the cover of the balcony.

Between the flashes of lightning the night was dark, the darkness broken only by lamps in the windows of the buildings that vanished into the distance in the rain and the gloom. Most places, that was enough light to see by, but just barely.

He stood silently next to the shingled side of the building. Wiping the back of his dripping hand across his eyes, he took a moment to get his bearings.

The inn was to his back and to the south. Immediately to the east were the inn's stables, where their horses waited under the none-too-watchful gaze of the stable-men, both of whom had reeked of cheap wine. To the west, further up the street, were three residences, clearly of upper middle-class merchants, and then the stables of the Silver Mushroom Inn. The Mushroom itself was across the street from its stables.

Two streets over and three down was the Slavers' Guild-hall. That was Jason's ultimate target for the night, but it was hours away, at least. When you're on a stalk, move slowly and carefully, Walter Slovotsky had said. Move not at all, if possible; wait for the prey to come to you.

Well, that wasn't possible here.

He'd have to keep away from open spaces. Dressed as he was in wet, dark clothes, he would be invisible in the shadows, but in a flash of lightning he could easily be seen if somebody happened to be looking the right way.

On the other hand, immediately after a flash of lightning would be a safe time. He closed his eyes and waited. When brightness flickered through his eyelids and thunder crashed in his ears, he opened his eyes and stepped off into the night, adjusting the coil of thin climbing rope that ran diagonally over his left shoulder.

With every step, his boots would sink ankle deep into the muck. That did no harm, but they made sucking sounds when he pulled them out. Nobody would be able to hear it very far, not over the sound of the rain, but it did carry a few yards.

Jason hid in the lee of an old oak tree, leaning against it, the wet bark painfully rough against his back even through his tunic. He pulled off first one boot, then the other; he tied them together with a thong from his belt pouch and slung them over his shoulder, then used another thong to tie them to his chest.

A stone bit into the ball of his right foot with his first step; the edge of a rock cut into the side of his left foot when he hopped to one side.

Shit. This wasn't going to make it. He leaned back against the tree and felt at his toes. This had the makings of a disaster, but you had to do the best with what you could. That was the rule.

Rinsing his feet off as best he could in the muddy water, he untied his boots, then pulled them back on, mud squishing between his toes. With his first step, something gave beneath his right foot; he tripped and fell flat on his face in the mud, the fall knocking the wind right out of him.

Some hero.

Face down in the mud, he fought to get his hands underneath him and push himself out of the mud, struggling both to not breathe in the cold goo and to get some air.

Finally he was able to force himself up to his hands and knees, and draw a jagged, shuddering breath, before he almost fell over in a coughing fit. He knelt again and wiped as much of the mud from his mouth, eyes and nose as he could.

There was nothing to do but press on. He staggered to his feet and off into the night as quietly as he could, a taste of mud and grit between his teeth, shivering, miserable, exposed, cold, dirty and utterly alone.

The first four buildings he checked turned out to be just what they had appeared to be: the homes of middle-class merchants, or noble merchants—it was hard to tell which, in Salket. Jason guessed that one was an iron-monger, another an olive dealer, the other involved in the sale of dried fish, but he could have been wrong, and couldn't guess what the owner of the fourth house was.

What the houses weren't were barracks, and that was what was important.

Was the rain starting to ease, or was that just his imagination? As if in answer it beat down harder on his head, the wind picking up, driving the icy water into his face.

He moved on.

The Silver Mushroom Inn had been built primarily for comfort, not security; each of its several suites seemed to have its own balcony, lower than those of the Steer's Head Inn. Ladderlike trellises supported trails of ivy.

Above his head, a narrow shaft of light from a gap in the curtains cut into the night; laughter and the rattle of dice in a cup suggested what was going on. Jason waited under the balcony until he could count at least four different voices, although he thought it was probably more like half a dozen. He moved on to the next balcony; the window above was dark.

He thought for a moment about climbing the trellis, but that was just too tempting, and too dangerous. There could easily be some sort of trap, some sort of alarm cord hidden beneath the dripping leaves.

Still, that was the sort of thing that it was best to find out about. He stooped to check one of the rungs of the trellis, one at his knee level. He carefully inserted his fingers in the gap, gently probing for anything suspicious. Nothing. He stiffened his fingers and arm, and then rested part, then all of his weight on it.

The rung didn't give at all. Not surprising; the Salkes were known for building things to last. Still, the wood was old and splitting. He thought about splinters, and about pulling on his climbing gloves, but decided that good touch was the better part of valor here.

He tested another rung, and then another, and then slowly, carefully began to climb. He reminded himself again: patience on a stalk wasn't preferable—it was essential. You had to master time, not let it be your master.

Haste was dangerous.

It was fifteen rungs to the balcony; slowly he put some

weight on it, until he was standing on the ninth. He reached up to close his hand on the railing and pull himself the rest of the way up—and then he caught himself. He couldn't see it, and he'd better see it before he put his weight on it.

He put his hand on the top rung, and started to draw himself up, but it gave fractionally. Slowly, slowly, he withdrew his hand, then felt around, slowly, carefully. Pretend that there might be sharpened razors hidden behind the trellis, at any moment, that was the trick. There might be.

He didn't find any razors, but his fingers found a hinge on one side of the trellis rung, and a cord running from the other side. Some sort of alarm.

He pushed a vine aside far enough so that, in the dim light coming from the next balcony over, he could see that the floor of the balcony was empty. There was nothing but water there, and not much of that; the floor was ever-so-slightly convex, like the lens of a magnifying glass, allowing water to run off the side and into the vines.

His probing fingers found nothing on the rain-slickened marble of the railing. Not a likely candidate for some sort of pressure switch; he pulled himself up and over the rail.

The panelled glass doors to the balcony were locked, and probably stronger than they looked, perhaps constructed like the panelled doors to the balconies at Castle Biemestren: what appeared to be criss-crossed wooden support members were actually wrought iron covered by thin wooden slats.

He unstrapped and drew his bowie, and tested the point against one of the criss-cross members; the sharp point sank easily a quarter-inch into the wet wood, but touched metal beneath. Just like home. There was no easy way inside, at least not through this balcony.

Jason slipped his knife back into its sheath and tied it into place.

He moved to the other side of the window; the curtain didn't quite cover there. Beyond the wet glass, light came into the room through the door leading to the bright hall beyond. He could see four tightly crowded sleeping pallets, two of them containing dim forms, and a rack of eight rifles, certainly slaver-powder rifles, set up near the door. It was a fair bet that this was a sleeping room for at least eight slavers. Multiply that by the six other balconied rooms in the inn, and he could guess that there were about fifty slavers in the Silver Mushroom Inn alone.

The next step was to—

A creak from inside the room froze him solid. His hand dropped to the bowie at his belt, but that was silly. There was nothing he could do with a bowie that wouldn't reveal him.

He stood next to the door and unwound the twin wooden handles of the garrotte from his belt. The thought of killing again made his hands tremble, but if the door opened he'd have to. Slip the thin strand of woven sinew over the neck, tighten and pull, and then ease the body to the ground and get the hell out of here.

His fingers tightened on the grips when there were low murmurs from inside the room. He couldn't quite make out the complete sentences, but caught a few fragments: "Your turn . . . awake this time . . . yeah, sure, if it don't rain."

Pressing his ear to the door, he could hear the sounds of somebody dressing, then stomping out of the room, while somebody else undressed, boots hitting the floor.

Then the thump of somebody dropping, dead tired, to a sleeping pallet. Jason waited until all he could hear were snores before climbing gingerly down the trellis. The rain was still coming down hard enough to make him miserable.

*   *   *

The Silver Mushroom Inn stables were next. There were only twenty horses in the stable, which wasn't in accord with his estimate of fifty slavers in the house. But there you had it: twenty horses, and one drunk stableboy sleeping up in the hayloft.

Next would be the guildhouse itself, and he'd have to be very careful there. It was only two streets over and three down, but walking down the cobblestone streets wasn't a good idea, dressed as he was. If they had any watch out at all, he'd be spotted.

He stuck to the service alleys behind the rows of houses. They were muddy, but there were more places to hide.

This business was miserable and dull, and when it wasn't dull it was dangerous. Something slippery under the mud behind one of the houses shot his feet out from him, landing him on his side, something biting into his back, just below his right shoulder blade.

He reached back, and pulled a piece of wood from his flesh. It was a splinter as long as his finger, and his back hurt like hell where it had gone in. He had a small metal bottle of healing draughts in his pouch, but it wasn't for minor injuries; he had to save it for something that really hurt.

While the wind was getting colder and colder, the rain was starting to ease up, and, from the top of a hill, he could even see the stars through a distant break in the clouds. If he was going to check out the Slavers' Guildhall, he'd best hurry.

Standing in the lee of the wall surrounding the Slavers' Guildhall, it occurred to him that there must not have been a lot of warring going on in inland Salket, not for a long time. The houses, once they'd gotten away from the port area, had seemed to be designed for comfort, not security: there were windows at many levels, albeit often barred; few of the homes were surrounded by a protective wall. While the houses of the poor were of the familiar wattle-and-daub, the homes of the wealthy were built of brick, not thick blocks of stone.

The Slavers' Guildhall, though, was an exception, as were the buildings to either side.

Just to the west of the slaver compound was a wooden stable, more of a barn, really, probably property of the slavers: there was a covered walkway between the two. To the east was what had been a stately, three-storied home, but it had suffered fire damage. While the local lord's firemen had clearly put out the blaze before it spread, the house was ruined and hadn't yet been repaired or replaced; part of the facade was ripped clean off, up to the third story.

The slaver compound hadn't been damaged by the fire. It was two-storied, built of stone, not brick, and completely surrounded by a ten-foot-high wall topped with a railed walkway, with two guardposts at the rear corners of the wall, although neither of them seemed to be occupied at the moment.

It wasn't a castle; it wouldn't withstand a siege, or a large-force assault, but it was intended to stand up to anything less than that.

It was reasonably new, too; the edges of the stone were still sharp, not worn smooth by hundreds of years' exposure to the elements, as were the walls at Biemestren Castle. Jason would have been willing to bet that it had been built out of fear of an attack by the Home raiders, and only finished perhaps ten years before.

But it could be taken. You could take anything, if you had the means. Batter hard enough against any wall and it would come down. Fire enough bolts, enough arrows, enough stones, enough bullets into an enemy mob, and they'd run or die.

The slavers had gone to the expense of mounting mirror-backed glowsteels on poles at each of the four corners and halfway down each of the walls, and while their blue glow was dim—either the spells were initially weak or they badly needed refreshing—it was enough to see by.

The slavers hadn't thought of everything, though; a huge oak tree spread its leaves and branches almost against the west side of the wall. He walked to the side of it and checked carefully around the bark for anything out of place, some tripwire, some pressure plate. There wasn't anything.

He shrugged. Could they have left such a hole in their defenses? At the same time as they were beefing up their defenses by stashing anywhere from twenty to fifty extra armed slavers at the Silver Mushroom Inn? That didn't make sense. Still, from where he was he could see that there wasn't any other tree near enough to overlook the wall.

Best to take a quick turn around the wall before he tried anything. He wouldn't want to risk checking out the streetside door, but that left three sides of the square.

Staying near the wall, though, was probably not the best idea. He crossed to the other side of the alley and, his back to the wooden fence that ran along the edge of the neighboring property, he worked his way toward the next corner, moving slowly and silently in the rain.

There was a slaver in the guardpost at that corner, after all. Muttering something or other under his breath, a dark form leaned out into the night.

Jason froze.

In seconds that felt like minutes, like hours, the guard leaned back in. He hadn't heard anything. Jason waited a dozen heartbeats, then moved on.

As he turned the northwest corner, something touched his shoulder.

CHAPTER 24

Walter Slovotsky

He who has patience may compass anything.
—François Rabelais

Valeran used to say something about how, in a combat situation, it was about sixteen times better to do something useful and violent right away than to wait and figure out something even more useful and violent later.

Jason spun on the balls of his feet, his left arm coming around to block, while his right hand snatched at his belt, his fingers falling on the wooden handles of his garotte, not his bowie.

It didn't matter; better something than nothing. He struck out—

—and let his fist drop.

Walter Slovotsky was standing a few feet away from him, dropping a crooked stick to the ground.

"Easy, kid, easy," Slovotsky whispered, beckoning him into the shadows. "Just your Uncle Walter, who doesn't want to get killed. Now or ever."

Jason could see enough of him in the light of the

glowsteel to see that he looked different: thinner, older, more shopworn. His beard was thicker and longer than it used to be; a shock of graying hair that badly needed cutting framing his lined face.

But it was still Walter Slovotsky; his all-is-peachy-keen-in-any-universe-clever-enough-to- contain- Walter-Slovotsky-smile was intact, although barely.

"What the *fuck* are you doing here?" Slovotsky whispered.

"Where are the others?" Jason looked around. "Ahira, Father—"

Walter Slovotsky's brow furrowed. "Your *father*? We need a long talk," he whispered, "and this isn't the place. You got a place around here?"

The rain had started to let up; as though bidding a farewell, a flurry of distant lightning bolts crackled to the ground.

Jason nodded. "The Steer's Head Inn. Two—"

"—streets over and three up." Slovotsky nodded. "You want to lead the way, or want me to take it?"

"Me first." It wasn't just that the rain was letting up; it must have been getting warmer, too; Jason didn't feel quite so cold anymore.

So Father was dead. He felt as if he should be crying, as if he was supposed to be crying, but he didn't feel like it. He had already mourned his father once, and perhaps once was enough.

Or perhaps not. Maybe the tears would come later. It was hard to tell about things like that. Try to lay down a rule, try to reduce what you do feel, should feel, ought to feel, will feel. . . . You try to turn that into some sort of formula, and you fail; emotions just didn't work that way.

Damn, damn, damn.

"Shit, folks," Walter Slovotsky said quietly, his hands

cupped around a steaming mug of herb tea, "you weren't supposed to buy the bullshit." He frowned at Jason. "You were *there*, Jason. Nobody could have survived the explosion, and Karl couldn't run far." He shook his head, then tossed it to clear the stringy wet hair from his eyes. He had called the toss, and won the first bath.

There were lines at the corners of Slovotsky's eyes that Jason didn't remember from before, and his eyelids were puffy and red from lack of sleep. "Yeah," he said. "I know I look like death warmed over, and not too well warmed over, at that." He sipped his tea. "The only reason I sent the dwarf off toward Holtun-Bieme was to get him out of the way. I couldn't take to the Cirric with him along, and he's every bit as much of a potential martyr as your dad was. Always has been, from well before we faced The Dragon."

He looked like he was going to say more, then decided not to. There wasn't anything they could do about Ahira right now, and right now was the problem.

"How firm's your rendezvous with this *Gazelle* of yours on the tenth?" Slovotsky asked.

Durine shrugged. "They'll be there."

"Good. Then you be there, and I'll see if I can make it to the next pickup. Got to finish this, first." He chuckled. "That daughter of mine is something, isn't she? She's right that I wouldn't have insisted on finishing things off with Salket—this is a tough nut—but Karl would have. Particularly if he had a couple of dozen men with him." Slovotsky smiled. "They're ready for a major assault. They're not ready for me. There's both too many of them and not enough of them."

Bren Adahan shook his head. "From yours and Jason's description, it sounds too difficult. Even if you can climb in by way of that tree—"

"Which you can't. It's booby-trapped—there's at least four tripwires hidden on the branch you'd use to get to the top of the wall. Jason, didn't you see the other stumps?"

"Stumps?"

"Fucking Greek chorus—yes, stumps. They cut down all the other trees near the wall and left that one. Didn't you see?"

Jason was going to protest that he had been about to do a full recon, and that he would have noticed the stumps, but that would have sounded like an excuse.

Besides, Walter Slovotsky, himself an inveterate liar, wouldn't have believed him anyway.

"You can't do anything about it, so get out of here. It's mine." Slovotsky shrugged, his shoulders working their way out of his blanket. He pulled it tightly around him. "Those damned signal rockets of yours have the slavers stirred up like a bunch of angry bees."

"Perhaps your killing them has something to do with it as well," Durine said gently.

Slovotsky laughed, but it was a tired laugh. "It might, at that. I don't see any way to get all the slaves out, but I can take out the watchers in the two other houses on the street. . . ." He raised an eyebrow. "You *did* notice that they've got watchmen in the loft of the barn, and in the garret of the burned-out house?"

"Don't be silly. Of course I did." Jason forced a smile to match the lie. "Would I miss something as easy as that?"

"You are your father's son, at that. Sometimes I forget." Slovotsky smiled back. "Okay, so I take them out, get inside, leave behind a few deaders, get the cages open, and then start enough of a fire, create enough of a distraction to give some of the poor bastards a chance to get away, and then vanish. I don't need you around for any of that; you can't disappear into the woodwork like I can. Even if they hadn't seen you, which they have."

Most of the escaped slaves would be rounded up by the

citizenry, of course, which was one of the reasons that Home raiders eschewed the cities—much better to get the slavers where there wasn't much of a local population to handle, either way—but some might be able to grab clothes and weapons, and perhaps enough money to buy themselves passage at one of the ports. Salket, like many areas in the Eren region, was a loose federation of small baronies, the barons meeting occasionally to settle internecine disputes, but without a unified government. It was in everyone's interest that, say, a hostler in the Triple Village return to Beteran of Tesfors a horse whose lip bore his tattoo; it was another thing to return an escaped slave who might, at least in theory, be related to the hostler.

But there was one problem with Walter Slovotsky's plan.

Jason leaned forward. "And what are you going to do when twenty to fifty slavers—armed with rifles and whatever else they can get their hands on—run over from the Silver Mushroom Inn, surround the place and shoot whoever or whatever comes out the door or over the wall?"

Slovotsky eyed him coldly. "I didn't know about them. You didn't tell me."

"I didn't think you'd miss something as easy as that." Jason smiled. "Besides, you were too busy talking."

After a long moment, Slovotsky smiled. "I was, at that. Let me think it over for a moment." He sat and drank some tea, staring into the flickering flames in the fireplace, as though he could find some wisdom there.

Finally he shook his head. "Can't be done. Shit. There's somewhere between a dozen and eighteen of them inside. We could probably kill the watchmen and a few of the guards and be gone, but we don't have anything near the manpower or the firepower to knock down a dozen quickly if it all hits the fan." He raised an eyebrow. "How're you fixed for money?"

Jason shrugged his shoulders. "We're fine. Why?"

Slovotsky scratched at himself. "Well, tomorrow afternoon see if you can rent about half a dozen horses, and station yourselves a ways down the road. I'll catch up with you, and we can get well ahead of any pursuit by switching mounts a lot. We should be able to make it to your boat half a day ahead of any chase, and be over the horizon by the time the slavers show. We hit the rendezvous with the dragon, and hit the air." He rubbed at his eyes with the back of his hand. "I'm burning out, boy. This shit takes a lot out of an old man."

Jason sat back and watched the older man carefully. It wasn't supposed to be like this. The Other Siders were supposed to be special, particularly Walter Slovotsky, a man who tossed off clever sayings like Lou Riccetti spun off new inventions: carelessly, casually, easily.

Walter Slovotsky was supposed to be something special, something more than just an exhausted old man, growing more tired and older by the moment. Slovotsky was into his forties, practically ready for the grave, and he looked every year of it as he drained the last of his tea and then staggered over to a sleeping pallet, dropped first to his knees, then to all fours. He sagged down into the straw mattress, seemingly asleep by the time he was fully horizontal.

Bren Adahan stood and stretched. "I would prefer it if you take first watch, Durine."

Durine nodded. "Very well."

Jason went over to the bath room and tested the water with his hand. It was warm, and that'd have to be enough; his eyes were sagging, and he didn't want to go to sleep filthy. Durine had washed his cuts, so they weren't in much danger of becoming infected, but it felt as if the grit Jason had slopped through had worked its way into every pore of his skin. He dropped his filthy clothes to the floor and mounted the step ladder, then lowered himself gingerly into the water.

Walter Slovotsky's plan would have to do, he decided. They didn't have the fire—

He stood up straight. "Walter, wake up—Durine, wake him up," Jason said, quickly rinsing himself off and getting out of the tub.

"What the fuck is it?" Slovotsky said after Durine had shaken him awake. He rubbed the back of a hand against reddened eyes.

Jason held out the two revolvers. "You said we didn't have enough firepower," he said, flicking open the cylinders. "You know what these are?"

"Where did you? —fucking Lou," Slovotsky said, holding one of the guns in his hand, cradling it like it was a child. He bit his lip for a long moment, and then straightened. "Fucking Lou," he repeated, his voice firmer, younger. "That hairless son of a bitch did it again." He didn't seem so tired, not anymore. "Yeah. I know what this is. How many rounds you got?"

"Two hundred. No, one-ninety-nine. Now, have we got enough firepower?"

Slovotsky stood silently for a long moment, so long that Jason was going to speak up, but thought better of it.

"Yeah," Slovotsky finally said. "That we do." He cocked his head to one side. "Your father used to get more mileage out of people than I would have thought they had in them. Including me, come to think of it. Looks like you inherited that from him, too." His eyes twinkled. "Get some sleep. Tomorrow we write the note, the one that says the Warrior lives."

Durine smiled. "I didn't think you wrote them on the scene."

Slovotsky laughed. "Hope I don't look that stupid. We write the note and rest up tomorrow, and tomorrow night, and the day after." He smiled, his face framed with a beard that somehow didn't seem quite so gray, not anymore. "And then we hit them." He cocked his head to one side. "Jason, you look like there's something you don't understand."

"I guess it's not important."

"Give it a try. You've got a problem with the assault plan?"

Jason shook his head. "It's not that. What I don't understand is about all the rumors. It took years for the story about you and Dad taking on Ohlmin and the slavers to, well, inflate like it has. But all this stuff about the Warrior running around with dozens, sometimes hundreds of men—those rumors have exploded."

"And you're wondering why?" Slovotsky nodded. "Couple of reasons. For one thing, your father was already legendary; these new rumors have just piggybacked on his legend. There are already dozens of stories of Karl Cullinane floating around; for the Warrior to build on them wasn't difficult." He rummaged through their gear and found the clay bottle of Riccetti's Best, pulled the cork, and took a heavy swig. "The stories would have spread quickly, even without the other thing."

"The other thing?"

"Well," Slovotsky grinned wolfishly, "I've been hitting damn near every tavern and hookshop in the Shattered Islands. I've been doing my best to spread the rumors myself."

Jason laughed. If anybody could find something heroic to do in every tavern and bordello in the Shattered Islands, it would have to be Walter Slovotsky.

CHAPTER 25

In Cold Blood

My men, yonder are the Hessians. They were bought for seven pounds and ten pence a man. Are you worth more? Prove it. Tonight the American flag floats from yonder hill or Molly Stark sleeps a widow!

—John Stark,
before the Battle of Bennington

The way Walter Slovotsky explained it, most of the problems were front-loaded; if things went to hell early, they should be able to break off and get out before it all fell apart.

Two days of rest had Jason feeling human again as he crouched near Durine, hiding in the dark next to the fence, with the walkway to his left. The slaver compound was behind him. In front of him was his target: the stable next door.

He was stiff, and his knees and lower back burned with pain; he longed to straighten up, but it was almost twelfth-hour and the guard should be changing shortly. That was the time to hit the slavers; it gave Jason and his companions as much leeway as possible.

With a creak of protesting hinges the door opened and a blocky man marched quickly toward the stable, someone behind him closing the door. He was dressed in a metal cap and chain mail, a slaver rifle and pike over his left shoulder, a hooded lantern held high in his right hand.

He passed perhaps fifteen feet from where Jason and Durine hid, and it was tempting to take him now, but it would have been wrong; his relief would be watching a marked candle burn down, and would be both expecting him and would be expected shortly by whoever was on the other side of the door.

They let him pass.

After waiting to be sure that the door to the compound was closed, Jason and Durine rose and followed the guard into the stable. Best to let his light lead the way.

The stable was as Walter Slovotsky had described it: a three-story building, two partial floors surrounding an open space. At each corner of the building, stairways led up to the top level, where another man waited for the slaver they were following. It smelled of rotting straw and old horseshit.

The horses could smell them; a large roan threw back its head and whinnied, its hooves beating a heavy tattoo on the floorboards. They ducked into an empty stall, knowing that the two slavers would attribute the sound of the horses to the disturbance by the relief watchman.

Jason took a deep breath and let it out. "Wish me luck," he more mouthed than whispered as he crept off toward the stairs.

Walter Slovotsky had done a thorough recon of the stable the night before last; and he had tested Jason's memory on which stairs didn't squeak.

Jason worked his way up the far stairway to the second level while the relief watchman called out a password that he couldn't quite make out. He seemed to take the responding grunt from above as a matter of course, and then put his weapons in a wooden box that was suspended from the ceiling via a rope and pulley arrangement. He pulled on the rope, raising them. The pulley needed greasing; it made enough noise to cover any sound that Jason would have made going up the stairs, although he was only able to get halfway up the second staircase before the weapons carrier reached the top.

The slaver pulled it in with a long crook. The rattling sounds suggested that he was replacing the new guard's weapons with his own; it was enough noise to cover Jason's careful creep up the second set of stairs, avoiding the eighth, eleventh and twelfth steps.

Finally he was on the top floor. He waited for the weapons carrier to creak and shudder its way to the ground, and then he drew his garotte.

And waited, while the sound of the retreating footsteps of the off-duty watchman diminished, then disappeared.

The watchman over by an unshuttered window had been waiting, too. As soon as the other was gone, he set his metal cap down on the floor and then took off his chain mail overshirt and dropped it to one side, chuckling to himself as it clanked and clicked to the floor. Mail is heavy stuff; he sighed as he worked his shoulders, then picked up his pike and leaned on it, looking out into the night.

Jason was right behind him and quickly, gently, slipped the noose of his garotte over the slaver's head, jerking it tight, dragging the man backward to the floor as he kicked and shuddered, then voided himself with a horrible flatulence and an awful stench.

Jason held the garotte tightly while the slaver gave one final jerk and then went limp.

Jason stood over the body for a moment. It was strange. He didn't feel anything; this was just another slaver who had gotten in his way, and now it was a dead slaver. It just didn't matter.

He whistled twice, softly, and was relieved to hear three short whistles back. In a few moments Durine was at the top of the stairs, lowering his gear to the floor: four heavy crossbows and a windlass to wind them, plus a dozen bolts. While Durine quickly loaded the crossbows, Jason put on the dead slaver's steel helmet and stood in front of the window, holding the pike.

Across the way, the garret in the burned-out house was dark. Jason wondered if Walter Slovotsky had done his job and taken out the other guard.

Apparently he had; there was something moving in the dark under the far guard shack on top of the wall.

"He's fast, that one," Durine whispered, handing Jason one of the crossbows and taking the other for himself. They were just backup; if everything went right, Walter Slovotsky would take out the guards on the wall. If everything went right.

If he hadn't been looking for it, Jason wouldn't have seen the rope snake up and around the pole supporting the glowsteel and mirror next to the guard station. Jason dipped the pike twice to the left, and then to the right.

At that signal, Walter Slovotsky climbed quickly up the rope and disappeared over the side. There was silence for a few moments, and then a dark form slumped out of the window of the narrow guard shack at that corner.

"Guard," Durine hissed. There was movement at the near guard shack.

The door to the shack opened and the guard stepped out onto the walkway.

"Now." Two bolts hissed into the night, vanishing in the darkness. Jason was sure it was Durine's that pinned the slaver's throat to the wall of the shack.

The man struggled feebly and Durine put another bolt into him, this one piercing his chest squarely.

"Let's get downstairs," Durine said, quickly reloading the crossbows, then tying the windlass and a quiver of bolts to his belt.

It was a bit awkward walking down the stairs with a cocked crossbow in each hand, but in a few moments they were at the rear door. It slowly opened, just far enough to admit the two of them.

Walter Slovotsky stood there, smiling in the dim light of the overhead glowsteels. He hitched at the pistol at the right side of his waist.

"Now?" Durine asked.

"Now, we go kill some slavers in their beds."

Sick to his stomach, Jason returned Slovotsky's smile.

They stood in front of the locked door to the slave pens while Jason fumbled with the keys.

It had all gone bloody, but well; they'd killed six sleeping men, Walter Slovotsky slitting their throats while they lay in their sleeping pallets, while Jason and Durine had stood in the doorway, ready to put a bolt in anyone who woke up.

But none of them woke up; Slovotsky had slit six throats, with no sound except for gurgling gasps.

They'd walked through the sleeping room, the floor slick with blood and shit, and through a swinging door into a kitchen, where five men, sitting around a table, drinking wine and talking, had sprung up, only to fall beneath hissing bolts and swords.

Three of them had shouted and leaped to their feet, reaching for weapons. One had whimpered as he tried to parry Slovotsky's lunge, only to be spitted on a sword, and another had thrown up his hands and begged for his life; Durine had hacked through his neck like a woodsman chopping down a tree.

Just numbers. That was all they were: six men sleeping, five men sitting, three shouting, one whimpering, another begging, eleven men dying. Just numbers.

Finally Jason found a key that fit into the lock of the knobless door. Durine stood behind him, ready to kick the door open if necessary.

Walter Slovotsky's brow furrowed; he held up a hand. *Wait*, he mouthed, running his fingers along the frame, up to the top of the door.

As his fingers tested the oak timber above the door, his face broke into a smile.

He gestured Jason to move away. Slovotsky took a small metal rod from his pouch and inserted it into the hole in the end of the key, tying the lockpick into place with a quick twist of string. He tied another length of string to the end of the pick, took a few quick turns around the key, and stepped back.

Slovotsky beckoned the two of them over. "That timber above the door isn't a timber," he whispered, his voice barely audible even inches away. "It's a deadfall. My guess is that if we turn the key counterclockwise, the way you usually would, it'll slam down. But I want to hedge my bet; it might be set to fall when the door opens, so when you do the door, Durine, get your leg out of the way, quick."

Durine nodded, and took up a position in front of the door, no longer quite below the timber.

Jason drew his pistol, opened the cylinder and thumbed a cartridge into the empty chamber, while Slovotsky did the same. If there were other slavers behind the door, this was a place for guns; a sixth round in the cylinder might make a difference.

Slovotsky pulled on the string. Slowly the key turned in the lock. Something *snick*ed inside.

Durine, his sword in his right hand, his left arm wrapped

in a cloak and left hand holding a lantern aloft, drew back his foot for a kick.

Slovotsky nodded. Durine's booted foot kicked the door, hard; wood splintered and shattered as it slammed inward.

Missing Durine's foot by only inches, the deadfall timber slammed down on the stone floor, splitting lengthwise with a pistol-like crack. Hopping over it, Slovotsky was first through the door: he broke left as he skittered inside in a half squat, the pistol held out in front of him.

Jason followed him in, breaking right.

There were shouts and cries, and Jason brought the pistol around, looking for targets.

There were targets in front of him: behind the bars, half-naked men crouched and shouted, some of them flinging hands up in front of their faces.

His wrist wavered, seeking a target. His finger tightened on the—

No. Those were the slaves in the cages; there were no slavers, no targets in the room.

Durine was smiling. "We're all set." The big man hung the lantern on a hook by the door, and left. He'd be keeping watch for a midnight relief party of slavers from the Silver Mushroom Inn.

Slovotsky was already straightening. "Ta havath, all of you. Shut *up*. You're being freed, assholes," he said, sticking his pistol into the front of his belt. He drew his knife and rapped on the bars with its hilt. "There's clothes upstairs, and you're welcome to what money and weapons you can find," he said, as Jason tried to stop the pounding of his heart.

Jason sagged against the coolness of the stone wall while Slovotsky released the slaves, ten unsmiling men in collars and filthy, ragged breechclouts, some of them standing in the front of their cage as though not sure what to do next, some of them still inside. They didn't appear to be ill-fed, but the slave kennels reeked of unwashed sweat; it was almost as bad as the charnel house outside.

Jason's lungs ached for the taste of fresh air.

"You'll find tools over there for getting the collars off," Slovotsky said as he worked the keys in the lock of the second cage. "The Warrior's next door, finishing off the guards in the stable. Help yourself to horses and saddles. I'd suggest you grab some food and weapons, and then get out of here. You're on your own."

One of the slaves, a skinny man, nodded briefly at another.

There was something very wrong here. The metallic taste of fear filled Jason's mouth, clutched at Jason's gut with icy fingers. Jason stepped away from the wall.

One of the slaves was having trouble getting up; Slovotsky took a step into the cell.

"No."

A black-bearded man reached out and pulled Jason off balance while strong fingers grabbed at Jason's left arm. Instinctively, Jason jerked on the trigger.

The blast was impossibly loud in the close confines of the kennels, the gun kicking hard in his hand, flame lancing into the ceiling.

A blow to the head set the world spinning, sent him reeling back, but he brought the pistol down and shoved the cold metal barrel against an unwashed belly.

The hammer rose and fell. The gun kicked hard against his hand. A warm, salty spray and awful stench splattered Jason's face as the man staggered back, two more rushing to take his place.

Jason shrugged off one attacker and pulled the trigger again, flame lancing out, spearing a slaver in the neck, sending him stumbling back into the bars.

A hairy arm snaked around Jason's throat, but he had already drawn his bowie with his left hand and stabbed backward, slicing into flesh, twisting his knife out when he hit bone. The man's scream deafened Jason's right ear before fading off into a sobbing whimper as he fell away.

"Back *off*," Jason screamed, shooting another one. Three shots; three to go. "*Back off*."

It was all obvious, now; these weren't slaves. They were the trap within a trap—slavers, masquerading as slaves.

Three of them had wrestled Slovotsky up against the bars, and one of them had gotten his knife, setting it against his throat while another clawed at the butt of his pistol. But Slovotsky, his eyes glazed, pressed his belly hard against the bars, trapping the pistol.

"Put it down. Put it down, or he dies," the slaver said, digging the point in for emphasis. "Do it now." Slovotsky's teeth clenched around a groan.

Fuck you, asshole, Jason thought as he brought up his pistol and shot the slaver in the right eye.

Slovotsky elbowed the other slaver away, drew his pistol and shot him, then picked up his sword and quickly speared two of the moving injured.

Jason had holstered his pistol and drew his own sword. He crouched, his bowie in one hand, ready to block, the point of his saber weaving, searching, hunting.

But they were all dead, all lying on the stone floor that was slick with the blood and the piss and the shit, and not only didn't it bother him, he liked it that way.

" 'Put it down or he dies'?" Jason spat on the body of the slaver who had said that.

Durine was in the door. He took it all in with one quick look, then turned to Jason.

"Go get the horses ready," Jason said. "And fire the place. We'll be along."

Walter Slovotsky faced him, his face and beard speckled with blood, not all of it his.

"You could have shot me, Jason," Walter Slovotsky said.

"You complaining?"

"Not at all. Not at all." He pressed a hand tightly against the side of his neck, staggering.

Jason was quickly at his side, supporting the older man. He dug a flask of healing draughts out of his pouch and handed it to Slovotsky, who pulled the cork out with trembling fingers, then drained it quickly.

"Let's get the hell out of here, kid," Walter Slovotsky said, his voice deepening, strengthening. "We can skip the note this time."

"Like hell." Jason was already untying the strings of Slovotsky's pouch; he fumbled out two speedloaders, then quickly loaded both his and Walter's pistols, careful to put the spent brass back in Slovotsky's pouch. He'd leave the bastards only dead bodies and a note to remember him by.

He took the note out of his own pouch, and stuck it in the mouth of a dead man. "Like the man says, the Warrior lives."

He kicked the body in the face. "And we are not nice people," he said. He clapped a hand to Walter Slovotsky's shoulder. "Come on, old man. *Now* we get the hell out of here."

CHAPTER 26

Laughter in the Dark

You know how to win a victory, Hannibal, but you don't know how to use it.

—Maharbal

Jason couldn't sleep. The hold had been dank and musty, and the constant, albeit gentle rocking of the boat had him vaguely nauseated. Again.

Whatever I'm good at, it isn't sailing, he thought. Again.

At least he wasn't alone, and hadn't been all night. He'd taken a turn with the tiller, letting Bothan Ver and Thivar Anjer get some sleep. With the search for the Warrior behind them, and with Salket long vanished over the horizon, tight muscles were beginning to loosen.

They'd made it away, again.

As long as the wind held steady it was easy, and Thivar Anjer had made it easier on Jason by lashing a rod to the starboard rail; he didn't even need to use the compass. From Jason's seat in the cockpit, all he had to do was keep the pole star, high above, over the rod.

*   *   *

Jane Slovotsky had taken the first turn with him, just sitting alongside him on the steersman's bench, his free arm around her, the back of her head resting against his chest. Her hair smelled of soap and sunshine.

"You got any bright ideas about what we do when we get back?" she asked, toying with his fingers.

"Not really."

"You don't want to, like, get married and start making babies and stuff?"

"Nah." He touched his lips to the top of her head. "Maybe later."

She laughed. "Well, that's good, 'cause I don't, either."

"Besides, you've probably got to work your way through most of the young barons-to-be around court."

"Jason *Cullinane*," she said, half-pretending to be shocked. "What kind of girl do you think I am?"

"You're Walter Slovotsky's daughter. And what's the matter—does only one fit?"

They both laughed.

Jane had gone below to sleep, and Durine had come up on deck a bit later, to noisily urinate over the side for longer than Jason would have thought humanly possible.

After he fastened himself up, Durine had started to go below, then shrugged. "Would you mind some company, young sir?"

"Not at all, Durine."

He sat down across from Jason and spent some time with him, not saying much. They just watched the stars and the night sky, and the distant pulsing of the faerie lights, until Durine yawned and got to his feet.

"I don't suppose," he said, "that you and I will be seeing much of each other after this, young Emperor. I just wanted to say that I'm glad to have been with you."

"Getting maudlin in your old age, Durine?" Tennetty's head poked through the curtains covering the hatchway.

Durine shrugged, his massive shoulders working beneath the thin cotton of his tunic. "A bit, perhaps."

She dropped to the deck, squatting tailor-fashion next to Jason. "Walter's been talking a lot about you. He says you did good. Real good."

"Yeah, but he lies a lot."

Tennetty's smile warmed him in the dark. "Pretty pleased with yourself, aren't you?"

Durine started to bristle, but Jason touched him once on the arm; he subsided.

"Yes, I am," Jason said. "I am very pleased with myself."

"You should be," she said. "None of us got killed on this one."

"I noticed." Although that wasn't true. Vator had died, and Vator was Jason's friend, even if Tennetty wouldn't think of him as one of them. But dead was dead, and there was nothing that could be done about it. Next time he'd do better.

He hoped.

She was silent for a long time. "You're not Karl, you know."

"I know."

"But you are a cold-blooded little killer. You'd slice a man open from crotch to his sternum, and then slit his throat for dirtying your boots with his blood and his guts."

He didn't remember drawing it, but his bowie was in his free hand. "Bet your ass, Tennetty," he said. "And not just a man."

She laughed. It wasn't a pleasant laugh, but that was fair enough, because she wasn't a pleasant person.

And he laughed back the same way.

Durine just looked at them as if they were both crazy.

* * *

Bren Adahan hadn't taken a turn, but he had come up on deck to relieve himself, too. He started to go back down, but then shrugged and sat down across from Jason.

"I want to talk to you about your sister."

Jason thought about telling him to go away, but Bren Adahan had been a good hand with the horses, had them at just the right spot down the road. He'd had them wait a few minutes while he walked back down the road and fastened a blackened rope across the road, at about the height of a rider's neck, and he'd even insisted on riding in front, his own sword drawn and held in front and to the side to at least give them a chance to catch any similar trap that had been set for them.

So Jason said: "Good idea."

"I'm a product of my time and place, Jason Cullinane. Don't judge me harshly. In Holtun, a baron has the right to ask. Besides," he added with a smile that was clearly man to man, "Jane is awfully attractive, at that."

"What are you asking me?"

"Don't mention anything to your sister. It wouldn't do any good."

Jason pretended to think it over, then nodded. "Perhaps I won't," he said. *I will,* he thought. Let Aeia decide whether or not she wanted to take official notice of it. "No problem, Bren. Go to sleep."

Betrayal? No. Aeia was family. Family came first.

As dawn broke over the horizon, he felt a familiar presence in his mind.

Jason, are you all right? Ellegon was just a speck on the horizon, but the speck grew.

I'm fine. But this thing about the Warrior—

I know—I've got Ahira and your mother with me.

Jason stood. "Okay, people. Everybody, wake up," he called out. He stood, more tired than a sleepless night accounted for. "It's time to go home."

PART FOUR

AFTER
THE SEARCH

CHAPTER 27

"The Warrior Lives"

A Roman, divorced from his wife, being highly blamed by his friends, who demanded, "Was she not chaste? Was she not fair? Was she not fruitful?" holding out his shoe, asked them whether or not it was new and well made. "Yet," added he, "none of you can tell where it pinches me."

—Plutarch

Jason stood outside the great hall, waiting, until he decided he'd had enough of waiting. It didn't take long for him to have enough.

There were three ceremonial guards at the door tonight: Durine, Kethol and Pirojil.

"Let's do it," Jason said.

Pirojil started to protest that it was too early, but Durine shook his head and Kethol rapped the butt of his halberd on the stone.

"Ladies and gentlemen, the Heir."

Jason walked across the carpet, uncomfortable in his velvet finery. It didn't feel right.

But that didn't matter. Got to keep a sense of proportion about everything. Control what you can, and let the rest go.

He paused for a moment at the foot of the table. Mother's chair. He rested a hand on her shoulder for a moment. She was stronger every day. Just have to keep her away from that damn magic that threatened to drive her crazy. Her fingers gripped his with surprising strength.

Ellegon, tell my mother that I love her— He stopped himself. She knew it.

To her right Walter Slovotsky and Kirah sat; to their right was Doria. A few days' rest had done Slovotsky a world of good; he looked a decade younger, and his I'm-so-clever-to-be-Walter-Slovotsky smile was perhaps a degree wider.

Ahira sat next to Doria, and the dwarf smiled broadly at him. He raised a clenched, hamlike fist to chest level, for just a moment, as though to say, Be strong.

Count on it.

Aeia was next to the dwarf. Jason had already talked to her about Bren Adahan; he didn't know what she'd decided to do about it, but that was her decision.

Flame flared noisily in the courtyard outside. *We all have to make our own decisions.*

That we do.

Thomen is upset that you haven't discussed anything with him.

Tell him to sit still.

"Good evening," Jason said as he walked to his seat at the head of the table. He looked over the assemblage of Holtish and Biemish barons, and their advisers. "Be seated, all. You have a full agenda; I have a short one. I'm going to stand.

"Tennetty—" He tossed her the large brass key to the strongbox. "Get it, will you?"

"Your high—"

"Shut *up*, Thomen," Jason said. "I'm going to speak my piece, then you can talk all you want.

"First item of business," he said. "Thomen, you've got too much to do, what with managing the Empire, sitting in court and all. I'm taking your barony away from you."

It was just as well that Thomen's mother, Beralyn, wasn't there. Of course, that wasn't by accident—Jason had ordered that she absent herself from council. Probably the last time he'd be able to do that.

Thomen Furnael was white-lipped. "And who are you giving it to?"

Tell him to keep his mouth shut, and make him.

As you wish, Jason.

"Me. It's Barony Cullinane, as of now. I've always wanted a barony. I'm going to have Lou and Petros send over a team of engineers to manage it for me. And—oh, thank you, Tennetty," he said, taking the bag containing the crown and tossing it casually to the table. "Garavar, I'm releasing Durine, Kethol and Pirojil from their oaths to you and the crown, and hiring them. I want to have them around me when I'm there.

"Next matter," he said. "The Other Siders." Slovotsky pushed his chair back. "Go ahead, Uncle Walter."

Walter Slovotsky drained his wine glass and stood. "You folks expect a lot of us Other Siders," he said. "Which is fair enough. The ones that Deighton sent over are all pretty special, and I've long since given up on believing that there's any coincidence in that.

"But we can't do everything. I don't build things. Ahira can't work magic—and you'll notice that the Engineer doesn't go around trying to get his ass killed, the way Karl used to. Andy came close to burning herself out by pushing her abilities too far too fast.

"We can't do everything, but you've been expecting that we can. It's one of the reasons that I was able to keep the legend of Karl alive longer than we could keep

Karl alive. The kind of magic that lets somebody do everything doesn't exist." Slovotsky sat down. "It's all yours, kid."

"Which leads us to the last thing on my agenda," Jason said. "I can't do everything, people. And neither could my father. He tried to be everything—prince, emperor, father, husband, warrior—and he fell flat on his face too often.

"His mistake was letting you people put the crown on his head. How many times has one of you said to him, 'An emperor has no business doing this or that?' Garavar, how many times?"

The old general muffled a smile.

He's figured it out.

"But you didn't really believe it, Garavar. It was a joke to you, sometimes. You thought he could get away with whatever he did. You were wrong. He couldn't do everything, and neither can I. The difference is that I'm going to pick what I do. And I will do it very well."

He unwrapped the crown and stood. "Thomen, you've been governing the Empire since my father left to try to save my life. You put the realm first." Jason let his fingers run across the polished silver, resting lightly on the coolness of the central emerald. "About time we stop pretending that it takes a Cullinane to govern." He faced the barons. "Any of you Biemish who thinks this means the Empire's abandoning the plan of raising the Holts to full citizen status had better think again; it was Thomen's idea in the first place. Any of you Holts who think now'd be a real good time to revolt can speak now," he said, letting his hand drop to the butt of his pistol.

Jason waited in the silence. "I didn't think so."

"And what are you going to do?" Tyrnael asked.

"Change the world, Baron," Jason said. There was a friend of his, somewhere out in the Middle Lands, looking for the man that had enslaved him and his family. That was a good place to start.

"I've got some partners to work with, some teachers to learn from," he said, nodding toward Slovotsky and the dwarf, who smiled back as they pushed their chairs away from the table and stood.

Slovotsky shrugged. "I'm going to start by teaching him how to drink," he said.

"Sit still, Thomen," Jason said, placing the crown firmly, not at all gently, on Thomen's head.

Thomen eyed him for a long, long time. "You're not giving me much choice, are you?" he whispered.

"No, I'm not giving you *any* choice." Jason walked to the foot of the table and stood there for a moment, looking from face to face, fully ready and willing to kill anybody who objected. "Don't fuck with him, people. It wouldn't be a good idea."

But there were no objections.

It was time to go; he turned and walked out of the grand hall, Slovotsky and the dwarf beside him.

He paused at the door to shake hands with Durine, Kethol and Pirojil. "See you out at the castle," he said. "And don't get into any fights."

Tennetty was waiting next to Ellegon in the courtyard, leaning against the dragon's bulk, her arms crossed.

Ellegon's wings furled and unfurled. *How does it feel not to be Heir anymore? Just a common baron.*

Jason laughed. "Hey, I'm used to having a title. Can't give it up all at once. —Let's get out of here."

"You're not going without me," Tennetty said.

"Of course not," Ahira said.

"Wouldn't think of it," Jason said.

Slovotsky chuckled. "I wouldn't want to be the one to stop you."

She smiled. "I haven't heard any invitation."

Jason shrugged. "Well, what would you say to coming along with us? We've got to settle Walter's family into Castle Fu—Castle Cullinane, that is, and then we've got some things to do."

I heard something about changing the world.

Bet your scaly ass on it.

She nodded, and hitched at her belt. "What would I say?" There must have been some dust in the air, or something. She rubbed at her eye. "I'd say that the Warrior lives."

ABOUT THE AUTHOR

Joel Rosenberg was born in Winnipeg, Manitoba, Canada, in 1954, and raised in eastern North Dakota and northern Connecticut. He attended the University of Connecticut, where he met and married Felicia Herman.

Joel's occupations, before settling down to writing full-time, have run the usual gamut, including driving a truck, caring for the institutionalized retarded, bookkeeping, gambling, motel desk-clerking, and a two-week stint of passing himself off as a head chef.

Joel's first sale, an op-ed piece favoring nuclear power, was published in *The New York Times*. His stories have appeared in *Isaac Asimov's Science Fiction Magazine*, *Perpetual Light*, *Amazing Science Fiction Stories*, and TSR's *The Dragon*.

Joel's hobbies include backgammon, poker, bridge, and several other sorts of gaming, as well as cooking; his broiled butterfly leg of lamb has to be tasted to be believed.

He now lives in Minneapolis, Minnesota, with one wife, two computers, and three cats.

The Sleeping Dragon, *The Sword and the Chain*, *The Silver Crown*, and *The Heir Apparent*, the first four novels in his *Guardians of the Flame* series, are also available in Signet editions, as are his critically acclaimed science fiction novels, *Ties of Blood and Silver*, *Emile and the Dutchman*, and *Not For Glory*.

Ⓢ SIGNET FANTASY (0451)

BEYOND THE IMAGINATION

☐ **GAMEARTH by Kevin J. Anderson.** It was supposed to be just another Sunday night fantasy game—and that's all it was to David, Tyrone, and Scott. But to Melanie, the game had become so real that all their creations now had existences of their own. And when David demanded they destroy their made-up world in one last battle, Melanie tried every trick she knew to keep the fantasy campaign going, to keep the world of Gamearth alive. (156803—$3.95)

☐ **GAMEPLAY by Kevin J. Anderson.** Gamearth continues, but David had become tired of playing, so he created an evil force to destroy it. But Gamearth would never be destroyed without a fight, as its inhabitants prepare to face off against their deadliest challenge yet. (162366—$3.95)

☐ **THE SLEEPING DRAGON by Joel Rosenberg.** Playing wizards and warriors was good, safe fun until college buddies Karl, Andrea and their gang find themselves transported to an alternate world and into the bodies of their characters. Now, their only "game" is to find the door to the world they left behind . . . a place guarded by the most deadly enemy of them all—the Sleeping Dragon. (162137—$3.95)

☐ **WHERE DRAGONS LIE by R. A. V. Salsitz.** Slumbering in the dragon's graveyard is a power that can rule the world . . . but now primeval powers are stirring from their ageless sleep, preparing for the final confrontation between the forces of Good and the infinite evil embodied in the Black Dragon, Nightwing. (140559—$2.95)

☐ **DAUGHTER OF DESTINY by R.A.V. Salsitz.** Alorie was the last of her line, the one chosen by prophecy as the final defender against the Corrupter's evil, but now the prophecy that brought her to power threatens her chance for happiness. The Corrupter is preparing to strike, as his undead armies crawl forth from the grave to spread their terror through the lands of the living. . . . (156811—$3.50)

Prices slightly higher in Canada.

Buy them at your local bookstore or use this convenient coupon for ordering.

NEW AMERICAN LIBRARY
P.O. Box 999, Bergenfield, New Jersey 07621

Please send me the books I have checked above. I am enclosing $_____ (please add $1.00 to this order to cover postage and handling). Send check or money order—no cash or C.O.D.'s. Prices and numbers are subject to change without notice.

Name_____

Address_____

City _____ State _____ Zip Code _____

Allow 4-6 weeks for delivery.

This offer, prices and numbers are subject to change without notice.

FUN AND FANTASY

☐ **SPHYNXES WILD by Esther M. Friesner.** The sphynx is back—in the guise of a beautiful Greek shipping heiress—and she's got a new set of riddles guaranteed to obliterate mankind. And what better place to start than an Atlantic City casino where trickery and murder will go unnoticed. but the soul-thirsty Sphynx hasn't counted on crossing paths with Sanchi, a casino worker who will lead her straight into battle with the last true sorcerer. (159748—$3.95)

☐ **DRUID'S BLOOD by Esther M. Friesner.** Someone has stolen the Rules Brittania, and Victoria, queen of the realm, is in desperate trouble. Only the world's most renowned sleuth. Brihtric Donne, can possibly help. With the help of Victoria's lover, Weston, Donne begins a hunt that leads to a confrontation with all the darkest magic a would-be monarch's mad ambition can conjure up.... (154088—$3.50)

☐ **ELF DEFENSE by Esther Friesner.** Divorce can be a messy business in any case, but when a mere mortal walks out on the King of Elfland, there's no telling what will happen. Amanda Taylor and her elfin stepson seek refuge in her Connecticut hometown, and the King besieges the town with magical mayhem, with some hilarious results. (152301—$3.50)

☐ **THE ELEPHANT AND THE KANGAROO by T.H. White.** Poor Mr. White is an English writer who has made the mistake of setting up his workshop in an Irish farm cottage. Instead of peace and quiet he finds a crazy landlady and an Archangel with a forecast for rain. Can he save the world from an impending flood by building a modern-day Noah's Ark? Is the world worth saving? Find out in this hilarious romp. "A mad flight of fancy."—*Kirkus Reviews* (160150—$3.95)

☐ **JASON COSMO by Dan McGirt.** Jason Cosmo is prefectly happy as a simple woodcutter until an inept bounty hunger claims he's the Mighty Champion and puts a price on Jason's head—ten million crowns! Against all odds, he must fight the magical forces out to restore the power of the Evil Empire. (162889—$3.95)

Prices slightly higher in Canada.

Buy them at your local

bookstore or use coupon

on next page for ordering.

32390I

Ⓞ SIGNET FANTASY   (0451)

WORLDS OF WONDER

☐ **BARROW A Fantasy Novel by John Deakins.** In a town hidden on the planes of Elsewhen, where mortals are either reborn or driven mad, no one wants to be a pawn of the Gods.   (450043—$3.95)

☐ **CAT HOUSE by Michael Peak.** The felines were protected by their humans, but ancient enemies still stalked their trails to destroy them in a warring animal underworld, where fierce battles crossed the species border.   (163036—$3.95)

☐ **THE GOD BOX by Barry B. Longyear.** From the moment Korvas accepted the gift of the god box and the obligation to fulfill its previous owner's final mission, he'd been plunged into more peril than a poor dishonest rug merchant deserved. Now it looks like Korvas will either lead the world to its destruction—or its salvation....   (159241—$3.50)

☐ **MERMAID'S SONG A Fantasy Novel by Alida Van Gores.** In the world under the sea, the Balance hangs in jeopardy. Only Elan, a beautiful, young mermaid can save it. But first she must overcome the evil Ghrismod's and be chosen as the new Between, tender of the great seadragons. If not, the Balance will be destroyed—and darkness will triumph for all eternity.   (161131—$4.50)

Prices slightly higher in Canada.

Buy them at your local bookstore or use this convenient coupon for ordering.

NEW AMERICAN LIBRARY
P.O. Box 999, Bergenfield, New Jersey 07621

Please send me the books I have checked above. I am enclosing $_____
(please add $1.00 to this order to cover postage and handling). Send check or money order—no cash or C.O.D.'s. Prices and numbers are subject to change without notice.

Name_____

Address_____

City _____ State _____ Zip Code _____

Allow 4-6 weeks for delivery.
This offer, prices and numbers are subject to change without notice.